# A WOMAN SOMEWHERE SCREAMED

It was a short, breathless little scream, cut off before it was more than begun. But I knew somehow that it was Drue.

I knew too that it came from downstairs. But I don't remember moving, although I do have a dim memory of clutching at the banister on the stairs and of the slipperiness of the marble floor in the hall.

The door to Conrad Brent's library was open and there was a light. Drue was there, her face as white as her cap. She had something in her hand and she was bending over Conrad Brent, who lay half on the floor, half on the red leather couch.

He was dead; I saw that. Drue said in a strange, faraway voice, "Sarah—Sarah, I've killed him!"

Then there were footsteps running heavily across the marble floor, toward us and toward the dead man. Drue heard them, too, and turned and the bright thing in her hand caught the light and glittered.

* * *

"A GRAND MASTER OF MYSTERY AND SUSPENSE."
—*Mystery News*

* * *

"THE NOVELS OF MIGNON G. EBERHART EMB̶̶̶
UNUSUAL CLARITY AND D̶E̶C̶̶̶̶̶̶
—*Twentieth Centur̶̶̶̶*

̶̶̶̶

"ONE OF THE MOST POP̶̶̶̶
—*San ̶̶̶̶*

## Also by Mingon G. Eberhart

Published by
WARNER BOOKS

# MIGNON G. EBERHART

## Wolf in Man's Clothing

WARNER BOOKS

A Time Warner Company

*All the persons and events in this book are entirely imaginary.*
*Nothing in it derives from anything which ever happened.*

WARNER BOOKS EDITION

Copyright © 1942 by Mignon G. Eberhart
Copyright © renewed 1970 by Mignon G. Eberhart
All rights reserved.

Cover design by Julia Kushnirsky
Cover illustration by Dan Sneberger

Published by arrangement with Random House, Inc., 201 East 50th Street, New York, N.Y. 10022

Warner Books, Inc.
1271 Avenue of the Americas
New York, N.Y. 10020

 A Time Warner Company

Printed in the United States of America

First Warner Books Printing: November, 1983

Reissued: September, 1993

10 9 8 7 6 5 4

## CAST OF CHARACTERS

**NURSE SARAH KEATE,** *who, so far as the author knows, has been knitting for five years.*

**DRUE CABLE,** *a young nurse, once married to*

**CRAIG BRENT,** *son of*

**CONRAD BRENT,** *now married to*

**ALEXIA SENOUR BRENT,** *whose brother is*

**NICKY SENOUR.**

*Also*

**PETER HUBER,** *staying at the Brent house*

**DR. and MAUD CHIVERY,** *also friends of the Brents*

*and*

*assorted police, state troopers, and domestics, including*

**ANNA HAUB,** *a maid; and*

**BEEVENS,** *a butler.*

*There is a cat, but he did not do the murder.*

# I

Anna Haub opened the door, and at the same time, for me, opened the door upon murder. Naturally, I didn't know that and take to my heels.

Her solid figure was a sharp black and white against the baroque richness and color of the hall behind her. She wore a white cap, as crisp and fresh as her apron. Her face was round and shone; her light straight hair was drawn tightly backward. But what I really saw was the look of frightened recognition in her china-blue eyes. She was not looking at me; she had given me the barest glance. She was looking at Drue, who came with me.

I said, "We are expected," intending to explain that we, Drue Cable and I, were the nurses Dr. Chivery had sent for, but I didn't, for I had to follow the maid's look and I turned to Drue who stood beside me. As I turned, Drue took her hand from her mouth and said on a queer shaken breath, "Anna! Oh, Anna, how is he?"

That—and the look in Anna's eyes—were my first indication that Drue Cable had ever seen or heard of the Brent family in her life. She had been extraordinarily silent and a little pale in the train that February morning; she had been extraordinarily determined that the second nurse (for they had sent for two) should be me, Sarah Keate; but she had not, that morning or ever, so much as mentioned the name of the Brents or the town of Balifold in the Berkshires —and I knew her extremely well.

Neither Drue nor the maid looked at me. Drue's words seemed to give Anna a kind of confirmation that she had, bewilderedly, needed. She dropped an old-fashioned curtsy which billowed her full black skirt around her solid ankles. The look of fright, however, sharpened in her eyes, and she looked over her shoulder, backward into the depths of the house, and said in a low and distressed voice, "Oh, Miss! Oh, Madam, you oughtn't to have come here."

"I know. Anna . . ." Drue put out both her sturdy little hands in their pigskin gloves and caught the maid's hands. "Anna, tell me quickly. Will he live?"

"He—he—I don't know, Ma'am. It only happened last night. Miss—you'd really better go. Before they know."

Drue took a long breath and said, "I hoped you would come to the door, you or Beevens. Anna, I'm coming in. What room is he in?"

"His own room. He, oh, but, Madam," said Anna, on the verge of tears. Drue stepped inside the hall. I followed and closed the door behind me, for Anna was too stricken to move. There was a quick impression of a massive hall and stairway that was all dark wood paneling, and a floor made of squares of black and white marble; of high-backed chairs and long Italian tables; of rich but subdued color in the tapestries and rugs. Anna wrung her clean pink hands together, and Drue said, "It's all right, Anna. I'm a nurse, you remember; they sent me here to take care of him."

She too gave a quick look along the depths of the great hall; there were doors, solid slabs of dark carved wood, but there was a kind of thickness and padded quality in the place that made me feel no one was likely to hear our voices. She went quickly to the stairway and stopped and seemed to listen, looking upward. Her soft, green tweed suit was sleekly tailored to her slender, erect figure; her profile against the dark wood paneling was clear and white, and her crimson mouth was rather set, yet obviously it was held so only by the strongest effort of will.

Just then something happened that threatened it. For there was a tiny scamper of sound somewhere near, a pause and a silence which had a quality of the most intent observation. We all looked at the back of the hall; at the entrance to some passage stood a small creature in a veritable agony of watchfulness. Stood there for only a second or two, then Drue said with a break in her voice, "Sir Francis," and with a tiny rush of feet, a throbbing sound in its throat, the little thing hurled itself across the great hall and toward us.

Toward us? Toward Drue. It leaped into her arms and strove frantically, almost sobbing, to lick her face and her hands. It was a Yorkshire terrier, a tiny thing, his long forelock hanging down over his glistening eyes.

Anna said, "He's never forgotten, Miss."

Drue held the little terrier tight and put her face down

against its little frenzied body for a long moment. Then she looked up the stairway and put her hand to her mouth again. It was no longer the firm resolute line it had been. She took a quick breath, and, still holding the little dog, started up the stairs. The maid made a futile, prohibitive move forward and stopped. Drue did not look back. So again I followed.

And Anna finally followed me. As I turned at the wide landing and looked back, I saw her coming after me, her footsteps soft on the thickly carpeted stairway, round face lifted anxiously and faintly purple as she passed below a band of purple light from the stained glass window above the landing.

When I reached the top of the stairway, Drue was already halfway down a long wide corridor which seemed to run the length of the house and was intersected once by a narrow corridor which seemed to go toward a servants' wing. Along the main corridor toward the north end of the house a man —the workman who had met us at the train—seemed to be sorting my bags from Drue's by examining the initials and tags. Our rooms then were to be where he left our bags. I made a mental note of the door he opened and went along the hall southward, in Drue's wake. Anna followed me.

Halfway along it Drue stopped. The hall was gloomy, for it was a dark day in the early spring with a fine, cold rain falling. But I could see her pause for an instant with her hand on a doorknob; then she opened the door and disappeared. The maid, Anna, who by that time was just behind me, said, "Holy Mother of God! But I could do nothing . . ." And wrung her hands again.

Probably I had some idea of clarifying the situation and my own confused state of mind at the same time. For I stated my position then, in a loud clear voice. "You don't understand. I am a nurse. My name is Sarah Keate. Miss Cable is a nurse, too. Your local doctor, Dr. Chivery, sent for us last night. I was sent here to nurse a Mr. Craig Brent. . . ." I stopped, for the maid didn't hear a word I said. She, too, opened the door and went into the room beyond and naturally, again, I followed.

It was a large bedroom, dusky, so the big, canopied four-poster in the middle of it was outlined bulkily against the gray light from the windows along the opposite wall. There was a fireplace with a couch drawn up before it; and the

9

massive shapes of too much and too heavy furniture. Then I saw Drue, and she was kneeling at the side of the bed with her head down.

Anna gave a wavering little sound, a kind of angry moan. She went to a table and turned on the light in a lamp that stood there. Then I could see more clearly; a man lay on the bed, looking very long under the white blanket cover, and Drue had her face on his hand which lay outside.

Anna stepped toward the kneeling, slender figure and said softly, "Oh, you mustn't. If his father finds you here . . ."

Drue lifted her head. She had flung off her hat, so her light brown hair, brushed upward from her temples and breaking into short curls on the top of her small head, shone softly, like gold, in the light and looked disheveled, like a child's. Her face was very pale; she looked upward beseechingly at Anna and whispered, "Is he going to die?"

"No, no," cried Anna. "No, please God."

There was a moment of complete silence, with only the fine rain whispering against the windowpanes. Then Drue said, "No. I won't let him die. I'm a nurse. I know what to do. . . ." Her fingers were on his pulse. "Where is the chart? The doctor must have left orders. Give them to me . . ."

Anna went back to a table, and Drue rose in a swift motion and followed her. I went closer to the bed and stood there looking down at my patient—Craig Brent. He was asleep.

Obviously it was a drugged sleep. I didn't know, then, what was wrong, and I didn't like the drawn look in his face, young and lean, with good bones, a rather stern, brown profile, and deeply hollowed eyes. I didn't like his pulse either when I put my fingers lightly on his wrist.

Whatever this man, this house and the people in it meant to Drue, to me then, the main thing was my patient. Drue and the maid had withdrawn with the chart to a curtained doorway which seemed to lead to a dressing room. I followed. It was a small room, with windows along one side and cupboards lining the other; at the other end of it was another door leading into a bathroom. Drue was reading the doctor's orders intently, and Anna was close beside her, watching Drue's face and knotting her fingers nervously in her apron. Drue was white, and the upward gleam of the light outlined the clean line of her chin and cheekbones, and cast a soft shadow around her eyes. She looked up directly at me with a poignant appeal in her eyes and her mouth. She thrust the tablet into my hands and said to Anna in a whisper that was as chilled and cold as the rain outside, "Anna, who shot him?"

Well, that gave me a real and most unwelcome start; it was the first I'd known of that. They had said at the registry office (or rather, I remembered suddenly, Drue had said when she persuaded me to take the case with her) only that there'd been an accident. Not that it was a shooting accident. I don't like shootings. I held the tablet in a hand suddenly gone stiff.

Anna shook her head. "They said accident," she whispered. In fact, our whispers and the dreary day, the silence in the great, thick-walled house and the whisper of rain against the windows gave the whole thing a kind of eeriness. Drue's small hands caught Anna's shoulders.

"Anna, you must tell me. What happened?"

"I don't know, Miss Drue. I swear I don't know. They found him in the garden, there by the hedge . . ."

"In the garden? When?"

"Last night. About eleven. They carried him into the house and sent for the doctor."

"But what did they say? How could there have been an accident?"

"They said he was cleaning a gun." Anna's eyes wavered and went back to Drue's.

"At eleven o'clock at night?" said Drue. "In the garden? *Craig!*"

Anna said nothing. The rain swished gently against the window behind her. It was then perhaps three o'clock in the afternoon, but it seemed later because of the dark day. Finally, Drue said, "Who brought him in? Who found him?"

The maid swallowed. "Beevens—you remember him—the butler . . ."

"Beevens! Yes, I remember. Who else?"

"Mr. Nicky and Mr. Peter Huber. You wouldn't know him. He's a friend, an old school friend of Mr. Craig's."

"I don't remember him." Drue was frowning. "Is he here, do you mean? Staying in the house?"

"Yes, Miss Drue. He and Mr. Nicky and Beevens heard the shot; they were in the morning room, and Beevens was locking up for the night. Mr. Craig called for help, and they found him—he'd fainted by that time. The doctor was called at once. Mr. Brent—*oh, you must go!* You can't stay."

Drue paid no attention to the maid's pleading. "Who's been taking care of him? You?"

"Yes, Miss Drue. And Mrs. Chivery. She came right away —as she always does when we need her. She stayed all night. She helped the doctor get the bullet out."

"Bullet . . ." whispered Drue after a moment and seemed to shiver a little, and I looked at the tablet in my hand.

Drue waited while I read it. I knew she was watching me to see what I thought of what I read there and I knew, too, that she was counting on my skill and experience. That was why she had made me come with her.

Well, it was serious enough but not necessarily fatal. The bullet had entered his shoulder; they had got it out, without benefit of x-ray or operating room. It must have been a fairly ticklish task for the local doctor. I frowned, reading and weighing my patient's chances. Drue said whispering, "Will he live?"

"I hope so. I'll take night watch."

"That's the hardest," she said. She put her hands on my arm and, with pleading in her eyes, said, "Let me take it. I'll call you if anything goes wrong."

"All right. I'll sleep with one eye open. There's really nothing we can do now except watch his pulse and his breathing. If he takes a bad turn . . ." I stopped. In that case there would be plenty to do and that quickly. I said to Anna, "Stay with him, please, while I get into my uniform."

Anna nodded and I turned into the bedroom and a woman had quietly entered the room and was standing beside the bed, leaning over the unconscious man, and she had placed one white pointed hand upon his forehead.

Well, of course that particular gesture has much the same effect upon me that red rag is said to have upon a bull. Soothing the fevered brow is a peculiarly revolting idea of nursing. I said in a low but perfectly clear voice, "I'll have to ask you not to disturb my patient," and the woman looked up, coolly, at me. "Oh," she said. "You're the nurse."

She was a young woman of about medium height and beautiful; she had a pointed, delicate face, a slender, fine nose, and a small yet deeply curved mouth with a full under-lip which looked, oddly, both sensitive and cruel. Her hair was a misty, dark cloud, very short, so it molded her small, fine head in a way that made me think of a Greek statue of a boy. Her eyelashes shaded her eyes softly, so you caught only the lights back of them, not a full candid glimpse of her eyes. She reminded me then irresistibly and always after that of a

12

medieval portrait beside a Greek statue, which sounds confusing, but may have been a slight indication of our Alexia's rather remarkable versatility; but there was the same fineness and the same fragile beauty and the same lurking comprehension of cruelty that one catches a faint chilling glimpse of below the beauty and satins and pearls of ancient portraits. Italian, I should say—certainly there was no buxom old-time Flemish or German beauty here. But there was beauty. A watchful, wary beauty. She wore a crimson suit and a white blouse and a string of real pearls. And I didn't like her.

Having looked me up and down, she turned again, deliberately, to the bed and straightened the bed clothing a little and put her hand against Craig Brent's brown cheek for an instant. She did it very possessively, intending, clearly, to put me in my place. Before I could reciprocate (for if it was my case, it was my case), Drue walked out of the dressing room, followed closely by the little terrier and by Anna. The first thing I noticed was that the terrier ducked swiftly back into the dressing room, and Anna made an abortive motion to do so too but misjudged direction and brought up with a bump against the wall.

The woman in the red suit was looking at Drue. Drue stopped. It was rather curious I suppose that they faced each other over Craig. Quite slowly the woman's white, pointed hand went to her long, white throat, and she said in a clear and imperative voice, "Drue Cable! How dare you enter my house?"

# II

Drue whispered, "Alexia . . ."

Well, I didn't know who Alexia was (unless, by the look on her face, a descendant of one of the more expert Borgias), but it looked as if she might leap straight across the bed, tigerlike, for Drue's throat instead of her own, where her lovely hand still clung to her pearls quite as if one of us intended to snatch them.

I disliked her even more strongly. I said abruptly, "Be quiet!"

Neither woman looked at me and neither spoke or moved, although Anna got a good three inches smaller and made an

13

earnest but unsuccessful attempt to shrink into the wall. I went across to the door into the hall, opened it and made a sweeping gesture which must have been rather imperative, for Drue walked toward me, and the woman, Alexia, her eyes still fixed upon Drue, came too. There was an instant when it looked as if they would meet at the door with something of the effect of gasoline and a match in careless juxtaposition, but they didn't, for Drue came quickly into the hall and Alexia followed. I closed the door (it seemed to be my only function so far in the Brent house) and, possibly with some further idea of clarifying things, I said as I had said to Anna, "I am Nurse Sarah Keate. Miss Cable and I were sent here . . ."

The woman in red interrupted, still looking at Drue. "Oh, yes," she said, with a little scorn in her voice, "I'd forgotten you were a nurse. So that's the way you got into the house. These seem to be your tactics. Craig was sick when you got hold of him in the first place, wasn't he? It will be different this time. I'm here and this is my house."

Drue went as white as paper. "But he didn't marry you. I watched the papers. He didn't marry anyone."

There was a gleam of triumph in Alexia's eyes. She said, "You didn't read them thoroughly enough. I'm Mrs. Brent." She added slowly, smiling, watching Drue, "Now you know how I felt the night you came back here with Craig."

"Alexia . . ." Drue said stiffly, and stopped. And Alexia, still smiling, said, "But I'm not Mrs. Craig Brent. I married Conrad, instead. It was a very quiet wedding—Conrad wished it so. But now, you see, this is my house, and I have every right to protect Craig from you now . . ."

"*Conrad!*" cried Drue. "*Craig's father!*" Color came back into her lips.

Alexia said sharply, "Naturally. For your own good I'm telling you you'd better leave. Craig doesn't want you. Conrad won't have you here."

Up to that point the interview had been candid to an embarrassing degree. But just then there was a kind of secret shifting of the emotions which had been hurtling around my defenseless (but I must say heartily listening) ears. Drue said slowly and thoughtfully, "I came here, Alexia, because they said Craig might die. But now that I'm here, if I can, I—I'm going to find out what really happened."

Alexia's eyes sharpened.

"What do you mean?"

"I believe you know what I mean," said Drue rather slowly, watching Alexia.

"I haven't the faintest idea," said Alexia swiftly, too swiftly.

There was a moment's silence. Then Drue said, still very quietly, "Perhaps not. But I'm going to talk to Craig."

"He's—he's too sick," said Alexia quickly. "You can't. Besides, Conrad won't let you."

"Conrad can't stop me," said Drue.

"Oh, *can't* he!" cried Alexia. "You'll see."

Again Drue seemed to consider for a moment. Then she said with something very honest and appealing in her voice and face, "Alexia, you are Conrad's wife. It's nothing to you —what happened in the past. I don't suppose we can be friends . . ."

"Friends!" said Alexia with a sharp little laugh.

Drue went on steadily, ". . . but there is no reason why you should object to my nursing Craig, and to my having an understanding with him."

"You've had your understanding," said Alexia, "via the divorce courts."

"But that," began Drue, very white now and firm, "was because he wanted it and . . ."

"Certainly, he wanted it," cut in Alexia. "Did he ever come back to you later? You don't need to answer that. I know he didn't. It's no good arguing with me, Drue. Besides, even if I used my influence with Conrad in your favor—and I have influence, don't mistake that—he would still not listen. You wrecked all his plans for Craig. He won't have you in the house. And Craig doesn't want you. There's no mystery about the thing; if you've come here with that in your mind, you may as well leave voluntarily. You left Craig; you went to Reno; you sued for divorce. You were offered a settlement which you, rather unwisely, I thought, refused. The divorce went through without a hitch. That's all there was to it." Alexia paused, caught her breath and added quickly, "If that's why you've come back—to get some money, I mean— Conrad won't give it to you. He would have given it to you at the time of the divorce. He offered what must have seemed to you, in your circumstances"—her glance swept Drue up and down quite as if Drue's skirt were threadbare and her shoes patched (as a matter of fact, Drue has all the American woman's clothes sense and always looks soignée and smart, and did that day)—"what must have seemed a fortune to you," said Alexia, and smiled. At that Drue went dead white

15

and so rigid that only her eyes were alive, and they were blazing. Alexia stopped smiling and became perfectly still, too, and tense. So I knew it was time to do something. I've dealt with too many hysterical patients and even occasionally a hysterical student nurse not to know that when a woman stops talking and looks like that one must act—but quickly.

I put my arm through Drue's and said with some haste and firmness, "I'm going to change my uniform. Come with me, Drue."

I drew her along with me toward the rooms at the end of the hall where our bags had been taken. Alexia called after us, lifting her voice, "There is a six-thirty train. The station wagon will be at the door at six." She stood there, I was sure, watching our progress down the hall. The little terrier had quietly emerged from the bedroom close to Drue. I wasn't aware of him until we reached my room and I saw that Drue went inside first and the terrier came, too.

Again I closed the door. I said, "Well . . ." a little forcefully and put down my handbag and gloves, and took off my hat.

It was a pleasant room, plainly furnished, but bright with chintz and plenty of windows. It was obviously intended for just such use—a trained nurse, an extra guest. Along one wall was a door into a bathroom which connected on the other side with the room Drue was to have, and her bags were stacked there, for I went and looked.

When I came back, Drue was standing by the window, holding the dog tight in her arms, looking down through the streaming rain. I took out my keys, knelt to open the suitcase that held a supply of uniforms and said, "All right. What's all this about?"

She turned from the window. "I had to do it this way, Sarah. I had to come and I had to have you with me. I didn't dare tell you he'd been shot. I was afraid you wouldn't come."

"You knew good and well I wouldn't have come."

"They telephoned to me, you see, from the Registry office. As soon as I heard it was—was Craig, it was like—well, fate. As if . . ." Her voice stopped and, after a moment, she said in a kind of choked way, "As if that was why I had learned to be a nurse. So I could nurse him. They said he might not live, and"—she finished in an unsteady whisper—"there is so much I haven't said to him."

The room was very quiet for a moment. That's the gnawing heartache of death, of course; the thought of the things

16

you didn't say and now cannot ever say. The permanent severance of communication.

It did no good to think of that. I rustled out a starchy uniform and said briskly, "Well, you're here now and so am I." I got up from my knees—not too easily, for I'm well past the age of springing lightly from cliff to cliff like a gazelle, or perhaps I mean a mountain goat—well, at any rate I got up and put the uniform on the bed. "He looks pretty tough. That's why you telephoned to me yourself?"

"I made the girl at the Registry office let me telephone to you and make the arrangements. I was afraid if she talked to you she'd tell you the truth . . ."

I said tritely, "Honest confession is good for the soul," and got out my nursing watch with the second hand on it and strapped it to my wrist.

"Oh, Sarah, you are a darling."

"Fiddlesticks. You mean, I'm a good nurse." But I let myself look at her then and she smiled faintly.

"You'd better take off your jacket and get on with the story," I said practically. Obediently she slipped off her suit coat. She looked very young in her plain white blouse and short green skirt; she pushed her shining curls upward with one hand, absently, and said bleakly, "You heard Alexia. They'll try to make me leave. But I'm not going."

Well, certainly the interview with Alexia had left little to the imagination in that respect. But I didn't think Drue had stolen the family silver or murdered Grandpa during what must have been a fairly brief sojourn under the Brent roof. For I had known her when she was in training, a thin, hard-working child of eighteen or thereabouts, with a gay smile and intelligent eyes. I had then been a Supervisor (which I understand the student nurses spell with an n and two o's) but had liked her nursing and remembered her later when we met again, both doing private duty. We knew each other well, in spite of the constant coming and going—the interruptions, the weeks and sometimes months of dropping out of sight while on a long or troublesome case—that make up a private nurse's life. Yet she had never mentioned nor hinted at this particular interstice, so to speak. Unless the sudden dropping away of a very smitten and attentive young interne, a few months ago, was such a hint.

I got out studs. "I've got to hurry. You and this Craig Brent met and married. It must have been very quiet—I usually know about these things. Well, then you were divorced. Conrad must be Craig's father and he must have money. Alexła, who does not appear to be exactly a friend . . ."

"She was, well, expecting to marry Craig, when we met, Craig and I," Drue said in a dry voice and stopped.

"It must have been charming for her," I said.

"Sarah." She whirled around. "It wasn't—I didn't mean—oh, . . ." She bit her lip and looked at me with eyes that were bright with tears.

"Charming for all of you," I said. "At any rate, last night Craig was shot and you inveigled me (under false pretenses) to come here with you on the case. That's all I know."

"It's all there is to know," she said, bleakly. "It was all wrong, you see, from the beginning. I'd better tell you. We oughtn't to have married. He—we were so young. That was over a year ago."

A year ago! So now she felt aged and adult and looked back on herself a year ago as being very young. She couldn't have been, allowing even for the years of her training, more than twenty-four at the very most.

She went on quickly, "Craig—you see, he was sick; he was home on leave and he was in an auto accident and broke his arm. It was a compound fracture and he was in the hospital five weeks. Five weeks," she said, "and three days. I was one of his nurses. And the day he came out we were married."

"On leave?"

"Yes. That—that was one of the troubles later. His father, you see, wanted him to be in the diplomatic service. All his life he'd been destined for that and he'd got, a year or so before, his first appointment. It was a consular appointment, not much, but a beginning. It was in South America, and it was when he was at home on his first leave that we met. Like that."

I put in a stud and said, "And married."

"Yes. He—oh, it's one of those stories. So simple really and so wrong. We oughtn't to have married then. We didn't know each other, really. There wasn't time. We'd tried to tell each other things; things about our lives and the things that had happened to us before, but none of it seemed to matter then. We . . ." She stroked the little dog's head, her face bent above him. "We had a little time together; not much, because his leave had been extended but still it was nearly up. So we had to come home. That is, we came here. To see his

18

father." She stopped again. I fastened in the last stud and said, "I take it Papa was surprised."

"He hadn't been told." Her face was still lowered over the dog but had a kind of fixity and whiteness. "You see that was wrong, too. He had other plans for Craig." She stopped again, stroking the dog's head.

"Alexia," I said.

She glanced at me once, quickly. "Yes. They weren't really engaged, she and Craig. If they had been, Craig would have told her, before we married, in another way. But it was a kind of understanding; it had been for a long time. I didn't know that, then. Until we came here and Alexia was here. It was a clear, cold night in January over a year ago and we came into the hall downstairs. It was after dinner and they were having coffee in the library and his father came out of the library with a cup in his hand and then Alexia came. She was so beautiful—she wore a crimson, trailing dinner gown and she went straight to Craig and put up her face to be kissed and he said, 'Alexia, this is my wife.' "

"Dear me," I said, keeping to myself the strong impression that young Craig might have well deserved the shooting he had got. Certainly Alexia couldn't be expected to greet Drue now or ever with anything like joy.

"Yes. Oh, I told you it was all wrong. Everything. But in a queer way, Sarah, we couldn't help it. It was as if we had been caught in something we couldn't stop. It wasn't Craig's fault, any of it, any more than it was mine." I thought there were tears in her eyes again, but she lowered her face over the dog so I couldn't see and began to smooth out his long forelock with fingers that trembled.

"So there were fireworks," I said.

"It meant Craig's career, really. I didn't realize that when we were married. Perhaps it's why Craig hadn't told his father until after we were married. His father told me our marriage was impossible. He said it was a terrible mistake. He said Craig's career demanded money; he simply had to have money to get anywhere. I hadn't any money, of course. But that wasn't the main thing: he made it clear that he had intended to help Craig himself with money. But he said that now, in view of our marriage, he wouldn't. He said Craig's career was washed up because of our marriage and that for that reason alone he would have refused him the money that was necessary, even if he had approved of his wife—me—as

19

a person. He didn't like me; but that wasn't all. I—I was a nurse, you see." She lifted her shining head a little proudly. "My family were good and old, too. But I couldn't help him, socially. Not directly, you know, with wires at my hand to pull. He explained all that to me."

I sniffed. You couldn't look at Drue Cable and not know she had good breeding; it was in every line of her face and every motion of her body as it is in a thoroughbred. I am no snob. I've nursed too long to have anything but a kind of respectful recognition of certain qualities like courage and truth and gentleness which, Heaven knows, can exist anywhere. But I've nursed long enough to have seen something of heredity; natural laws are natural laws, and you can't get around them.

"So Pa Brent resorted to the good old-fashioned disinheriting threat. Or what amounted to it. What did Craig say to all this?"

"Craig laughed at first. Then he wouldn't even talk of it. He told me to forget it; he said it wasn't important, to pay no attention to what his father said. But I couldn't help paying attention. Because Mr. Brent told me that the only thing to do was for us to end our marriage as—as abruptly as it began." She was quoting. I could tell it from the bitterness that then, for the first time, came into her voice.

I got out of my wool dress and reached for my uniform and I remember that I stood there for an instant staring at her. For the way she spoke gave me a hint as to what was going to come next, and I really couldn't believe it. "You surely don't mean to say you agreed to that," I cried, astonished.

She started to braid the dog's long forelock, her fingers very gentle but still unsteady. "Not just then. I couldn't. We stayed on a little. Craig's leave had been given another month's extension. Then Alexia came back and—and Nicky," she said, bending over the dog. "Her twin brother."

There was a rather long pause while she braided and re-braided the soft forelock. "Then," she went on finally, "Craig had to go to Washington. His father wanted me to stay here; he said we must get to know each other better. That pleased Craig; he hoped it meant his father was coming around. So he asked me to stay, and I did. I went to the train with him and he kissed me and said he'd be back in a week. It was there at the station—where we got off the train . . ." She bent closely over the dog again. "I never saw Craig again until today."

"*Never*—why not?"

"He had to stay longer in Washington, two weeks, three weeks. It—it wasn't . . ." She broke off and, after a moment said, "His father didn't want to know me better. Alexia was here all the time, too. It wasn't very pleasant." Her voice hardened a little and she said, "Besides, there was Nicky. Craig didn't come back, and I couldn't stay here. I went away." She stopped, as if that was all the story.

"Do you mean to tell me you let them influence you like that? So you walked out and never returned?"

"That wasn't all," she said and seemed to think for a moment, arranging facts in the order which would make them clearest to me. She frowned and said: "You see, Sarah, I couldn't stay here. So I left. But that wasn't all, because Craig gave up his job. That was why he stayed so long in Washington. He had decided to get training as a pilot. It was before the war began. I mean before we got into it, naturally . . ."

I nodded. Naturally. It had been then only a matter of weeks since Pearl Harbor.

"He wanted to get into the air force. He hadn't talked to me about it before he went, and I understood why. It was because he knew that I would feel that he was giving up his chosen career because of me. I wouldn't have let him do it, at least, I would have tried to stop him. But, you see, he didn't know that at that time, and if he got the training he wanted he had to be unmarried. Then, and for that particular course of training, they wouldn't take a married man. He didn't know that until he applied for it. I didn't know it until Mr. Brent wrote to me and told me."

I am not a profane woman. At the moment it was really a pity, for it left me simply nothing adequate to say. She nodded slowly, as if I'd asked her a question. "Yes," she said. "That's what I did. I believed him—Mr. Brent. How could I help it? He was obviously sincere about the whole thing. He wrote a letter that I wish I'd kept. I didn't. I burned it. He said that I had wrecked Craig's chosen career. He said that Craig now wanted to take training as a pilot and that I was—again—the obstacle. He said that he regretted everything he had said to me; he said that he was ready to accept our marriage—that is, our eventual marriage." She stopped and took a long breath and I saw the picture complete.

It was incredible, of course. Except that women like Drue can be just that incredible.

"So you believed him. You agreed to let bygones be bygones. And you promised to divorce Craig, let him complete his training, and then remarry."

"That," said Drue, "was the idea."

"Good heavens, Drue!"

"I know. But then it seemed right. We had married so quickly, you see. Craig was giving up his job; and his father convinced me that the one thing he wanted was to get into the air force. Mr. Brent was—I can't tell you how convincing he was. He asked me to forgive him for everything he'd said in anger. He said that he believed at last that Craig and I really loved each other. He said that Craig had set his heart upon becoming a pilot and getting into the army or the navy air force. He said Craig was deeply patriotic—and he is. I knew that. He said that what it—the divorce, I mean—really amounted to was merely a long engagement, and not very long at that. He made it seem so reasonable and so right. He said that Craig would never ask me for it himself and if I loved Craig I would get the divorce. And that as soon as the year of training was up we could remarry."

It was clear enough; still incredible, if one didn't know Drue, but clear. What was also pretty clear was dirty work at the crossroads.

"So you got the divorce?"

"Yes. It took six weeks."

"And Craig got his training?"

"Yes."

"What happened then?"

"I don't know."

"You don't . . ."

She shook her head and looked away from me. "He didn't come back."

"But didn't he understand why you did it? Didn't you see each other and write and . . ."

She shook her head again. "No. That is, I did write a few times. But he didn't answer. The divorce went through very quietly and—and so quickly. And that was all."

After a moment, I said, "And you never tried to see him?"

"No." Her mouth moved a little wryly. "You see, I had my pride."

And it had cost her enough. Well, I didn't say it. I pulled my uniform over my head and struggled through it and glanced at my watch. For all she'd said so much it had been only a few minutes.

"But now," she said unexpectedly, "it's different. Pride doesn't seem to matter so much. I'm older; I'm an adult now and a woman. I know what I want. I was—such a child then."

She was still a child. I didn't say it, but took my cap and went to the mirror so as to adjust it to hide the white lock in my rather abundant auburn hair. "And now you've come back."

She sat for a moment in silence. In the mirror I watched a look of determination come slowly into her face. Finally, she said, "Yes, now I've come back. I had to."

Watching her instead of what I was doing, I jabbed a pin into my thumb and muttered. So she'd made up her mind to fight, and she'd given up long ago her best and strongest weapon.

"I can understand your getting too much of Alexia," I said briefly. "I can understand your leaving the house. I can even understand your—well, believing Pa Brent. And letting Craig go without any effort to keep him. But I cannot understand Craig."

"Well, neither can I. Now," she said, in a kind of abject voice which was not at all like her. Except for her flair of defiance with Alexia, she had been in a rather crushed state of mind ever since we started to Balifold, I realized then. This was not, however, her natural and customary reaction to life. She was a perfectly sensible and altogether charming young woman with considerable backbone—which up to then had certainly, however, been held in abeyance to a marked degree. But then love does do very odd things, and obviously she was still heartbreakingly in love with the man whom, nevertheless, she had divorced.

She patted the little dog. "Sarah, it was all so clear then. It's only now, after I've had time to think and time to regret that I see it was all wrong. I believed it then, though. I never suspected."

"Suspected what?" I said with a rather nervous glance at my watch again. "Suspected whom?"

"Anything. Anybody," she said.

"And now you do?"

"Now I do. Now I"—she stopped and said in a kind of whisper staring at the rug—"now I've got to know what happened."

That at least was a step in the right direction and one

23

clearly indicated by the foregoing little tale. I said briskly and, I remember, almost gaily, "Good for you. It's high time. I'm proud of you."

"It's not easy," she said, and gave me a quick and rather diffident glance. "I mean—well, suppose Alexia is right. Suppose Craig *doesn't* want to see me. I mean—well, I've no reason to think that he does, you see. He had every chance."

"Look here," I said, still briskly and full of energy and approval. "Obviously you had two people against you in this house—Pop and Alexia. I don't know Pop, but I can't say I took to Alexia. Maybe Craig repented his quick marriage and asked his father to get him out of it. But maybe not. As I see it, you'll have to brace yourself for whatever comes. I mean, have an understanding with Craig."

"That's why I came," she said in a whisper.

I went on, "You may have to take it on the chin, you know. Craig is free, white and twenty-one; he could have come to you."

"I know," she whispered again.

"On the other hand, all sorts of things could have happened. It's a little difficult and melodramatic to suspect people of that particular kind of finagling—I mean, oh, destroying letters, lying, that kind of thing. Still it could have happened."

"I've got to have it clear," she said.

"Right. It comes under the heading of unfinished business. It . . ." I stopped abruptly, for someone knocked. I thought it was Anna and went to the door. But it wasn't Anna; it was a man, young and slender, whose pointed, rather delicate face was instantly familiar to me, although I couldn't possibly have seen him before. He was very sleek and very elegant with a wonderful brown and maroon color scheme (brown slacks, checked coat, maroon handkerchief and tie) and he seemed surprised to see me.

"Oh, I beg your pardon! I thought—Alexia said Drue was here."

There was a quick kind of rustle behind me. I glanced over my shoulder and Drue wasn't there. Dog, coat and all had vanished.

The word Alexia gave me the clue; he was amazingly like her. This must be the twin brother, Nicky. Hadn't Drue told me?

He said, "Where is Drue?" and tried to look over my shoulder into the room.

It didn't look as if Drue wanted to see him. I took my fountain pen and my thermometer. "Sorry," I said, "I'm just going to my patient."

He moved aside to permit me to step into the hall. As I turned along it toward the big bedroom where the sick man lay, he dodged along with me as gracefully as a panther and about as welcome. I'm bound to say that I instantly added Nicky Senour to my rapidly growing list of dislikes in the Brent house. He was watching me with a gleam of bright curiosity in his face. "I say, you know," he said, "Drue can't stay here. She's got to leave. You must make her leave."

I had reached the door to my patient's room. I opened it and turned to Nicky Senour and hissed (literally, because I didn't want my patient to be roused), "If I stay, she stays," and closed the door on his handsome but startled face.

There was no change in Craig Brent's pulse or breathing. I didn't want to rouse him, then, to take his temperature. He had an intelligent and a sensitive face and, from the nose and chin, a will of his own; his behaviour had shown anything but that. I thought of the gaps in Drue's story. It was brief; it was necessarily elliptical. Obviously there were only two alternatives by way of explanation; either Craig had repented his hasty marriage and ended it in that way (in which case she was well rid of him, but that wouldn't help Drue just then), or there was actually dirty work at some crossroads. In that case, a few words between Drue and the man before me would clear up a mere lovers' misunderstanding.

But nothing in her brief and very deleted account of her almost equally brief marriage even touched upon a question that was beginning to assert itself more and more ominously in my mind. Definitely there was something fishy about the story of the shooting. So Craig Brent had been shot, intentionally, with murderous design, then why? And, furthermore, who?

Anna rose from the armchair across the room, within the curtained niche where old-fashioned bay windows made a semi-circular little room of their own. She had been crying and was wiping her eyes. I went to her and said a little sharply, "You can go. I'll stay now."

When she had gone, I pulled a chair up near the bed where I could watch for the faintest shadow of a change in Craig Brent's face. The brown was sunburn; under the tan his face was a kind of gray. I was sitting like that with my fingers on his lean brown wrist when the door opened and two men walked quietly into the room and closed the door behind them. One was the doctor. I had never seen Dr. Chivery before, but a kind of antiseptic spruceness about him identified him at once. He was a short, gray man with no chin, slender, except for a little watermelon in front, and pouches under his eyes. He looked nervous.

The other man was a state trooper in beautiful brownish gray uniform with bars on his sleeve. I must say, though, that the uniform was not a welcome sight; it was like a confirmation of general fishiness.

I got to my feet. The doctor and the policeman (a lieutenant, I thought, by the bars) came straight to the bed. The doctor glanced at me once absently, and they both looked down at my patient for a long moment. Then the doctor said, whispering emphatically, "Nobody shot him. Nobody could have shot him. It was an accident, I tell you."

And the policeman said, "I'll have to see the bullet. And the gun."

# III

Dr. Chivery's hands started toward each other and then thrust themselves in his pockets; they were pink hands, a little shiny and wrinkled and none too steady. He said, "Well, that's what I'm afraid you can't do."

The state trooper turned abruptly to look down at the doctor. He didn't ask why, and the doctor fidgeted a little and said, "You see, the bullet was thrown out—accidentally; and the gun is gone. Nobody knows what happened to it."

Again the state trooper said nothing but simply waited, watching the doctor and looking very tall and formidable in his trim uniform. Dr. Chivery said, "In the excitement somebody must have picked up the gun without remembering. It will turn up. But it hasn't yet.

He waited for an answer again and this time the state trooper obliged. He said, "Ah."

It was just then, by the way, that I discovered an odd thing about Dr. Chivery, and that was his habit of looking at the edges of things. For he glanced at the left corner of my cap, at a post of the bed, at my patient's brown hair (so inordinately neat and wetly plastered that I surmised Anna's fine firm hand) and at the trooper's coat buttons. He said,

"You know me, Lieutenant. Or perhaps you don't. But the fact is, if I had had reason to think it wasn't an accident (which is simply absurd on the face of it) perhaps I wouldn't have been quite so frank and prompt about reporting it. Ha," said the doctor, still whispering vehemently. "Ha."

It was intended to be a laugh and his mouth twitched upward nervously to accompany it. The trooper's face was as grave and untouched as a stone image. He said, "Now let me be sure I have the facts straight. It happened last night at eleven?"

Dr. Chivery, eyeing the bedpost, nodded.

"The butler, Beevens, Mrs. Brent's brother, Nicky Senour, and a guest, Peter Huber . . ."

"You talked to them yourself," interrupted Dr. Chivery.

". . . Yes, were in the library when it happened; the butler was locking up and looking at the window catches and Mr. Huber and Mr. Senour were reading the papers. They heard the shot and then heard his"—he nodded once toward the man in the bed—"call for help. They went to the garden, found him and—and no one else. They brought him to this room. . . ."

"And telephoned for me," said Chivery nodding.

"At the time of the shot, so far as you know, Craig Brent was alone in the garden?"

"He was alone," said Dr. Chivery. "I was at home, reading in my library. My wife was upstairs, writing letters. I mention us because we are—ha, ha," he interpolated painstakingly again, "almost members of the family here. Mr. Conrad Brent —Craig's father had gone to bed. Mrs. Brent was likewise in her own room; she had said good night to the others and gone upstairs only a moment or two before it happened. The servants . . ."

"I'll question them. Thank you. You don't know of any family disagreements . . ."

Dr. Chivery interrupted indignantly. "My dear fellow— really—this is not an inquiry into murder."

The trooper looked at Craig. "Well, no—not yet," he said somewhat pointedly.

"But, really," began Dr. Chivery again, rubbing his pink hands together. His voice had risen shrilly and unexpectedly, so in spite of my intense interest I felt obliged to rustle and put my hand on Craig Brent's wrist and look hard at the doctor.

Dr. Chivery glanced at my right eyebrow. Preoccupation

27

sat like a gray mask on his face; yet it seemed to me that behind that mask there was a kind of flicker of disapproval directed at me. The trooper had looked at me too. It was the trooper who moved quietly to the door and, incredibly laconic to the last, nodded and disappeared. The doctor hesitated, looked at the pin on my collar and said, "Miss . . ."

"Keate," I said.

"You found my orders?"

"Yes, Doctor. And I wanted to ask you . . ."

One pink hand fluttered. "I'll return later and we'll go over the situation. Just now, has our patient said anything?"

"No, Doctor."

"Oh. Umm. Well," he said, "he may be a little delirious, rambling; pay no attention to it. But—er—Nurse . . ." He glanced nervously over his shoulder toward the door and lowered his voice. "I trust I don't need to remind you that anything said in a sick room . . ."

I drew myself up and almost, but not quite, forced him to look into my eyes. "I am not a gossip," I said with some energy.

Again I saw the flicker of disapproval behind that curtain of preoccupation. I could almost hear him think, I'll get rid of this nurse as soon as I get around to it. He said suavely, "Not at all. Not at all. I'll be back presently." With that, and a slanting look at my Oxford ties, he went away.

It left me alone again in that big gloomy bedroom with the rain whispering against the window and a sick man, a man who'd been shot, on the bed.

I was a little shaken. Shootings, guns and bullets. Police and a doctor who wouldn't look at me.

To complicate it, Drue with her loveliness and her honesty linked so strongly with that dreary, secretive house and everybody in it. Especially the man who had been shot.

The dark panels of the door reflected a dreary light from the windows opposite. My patient gave a kind of weak chuckle and said quite clearly, "Nice going."

It gave me rather a start. I hurried to the bed. His eyelids fluttered and opened; there was a gleam of laughter in his eyes and the corners of his mouth twitched. Otherwise he hadn't moved. He made a great effort and said, "Nurse . . ."

"Yes. You'd better not talk."

But there was something he had to say. I watched him struggle for the words, his bright eyes seeking into mine.

"Thought—there was a girl. Here . . ." he said laboriously, and waited for me to reply. I hesitated. His hand still lay outside the cover and it moved a little and he said, watching me intently, "Somebody I know . . ."

"There is another nurse," I said then. "You must sleep now."

"Another—nurse . , ." he said and, as a wave of drugged sleep caught and engulfed him again, his voice drifted away. I waited. He'd gone back to sleep, I thought; but as I started to move away he spoke again. And he said quickly, in a jumbled rush of words, something that ended with the words "—yellow gloves." That was all I could understand, for the rest was only a blurred mumble and he was overtaken by sleep like an avalanche while I stood there watching him and wondering what yellow gloves had to do with anything at all.

Well, in the end I decided he was rambling and it meant nothing. Although his recognition of Drue had been sensible enough, unless it was merely deeply instinctive.

That, when I thought of it, was queer—that he'd known she was there.

As I have indicated, my encounter with the doctor and the state trooper was not exactly conducive to a quiet state of mind; there was also the matter of the missing gun, and the bullet that had been thrown out. I am a sensible woman. It is my nature, and I see no reason to hide my light under a bushel, to enjoy a certain poise. Master of my fate and captain of my destiny, under even the most untoward circumstances. But I won't say I didn't feel uneasy, for I did. And the story Drue had told me, naturally, added to my uneasiness.

For when I had considered everything I had heard and observed (not much, perhaps, but enough), it all summed up to just one conclusion. I'm not sentimental or unduly sympathetic; quite the contrary. But I liked Drue Cable and even if I hadn't it was obvious that she had no friends in that household. It was as obvious that she was determined to stay.

And I didn't like the look of things.

So I had to stay with her. There simply wasn't anything else for me to do. And if they sent her away I still had to stay. No question of that.

While I was very reluctantly reaching that conclusion, Craig Brent continued to sleep heavily, without stirring or saying anything more. After a while, finding it difficult to sit still, I drifted to the deeply recessed bay windows and looked out through the streaming rain. That was how it happened that I saw Drue go to the garden and return.

It was by that time fairly late in the afternoon. The room and the whole great house seemed perfectly still, except for the rain. Once somewhere away off in the distance a radio was turned on—apparently for a news bulletin. I wondered what fresh turn the war had taken, and wished, as I'd wished so many times, that they would take me. I nursed all through the other war. I am twenty years older and thirty pounds heavier but, as they say of an old work horse, I'm sound in wind and limb. And I want to go to war. In a swift poignant wave of memory I could see the mud of France, feel the rain and cold, and smell the sweet, sickly odors of ether (until it ran out) and of antiseptics—all of it in the past these twenty years. I thought of that—and of Bataan and Corregidor, and the nurses who were there and what they did.

My heart gave a kind of bow of homage. But it was heavy with longing, too. So I tried to put the war out of my mind and looked out at what I could see of the landscape from the window.

The Brent house stood on the very edge of a little town called Balifold; it was not quite country and not quite suburb. It was, I believe, among the outlying hills of the Berkshires, not far from Lenox and Stockbridge, although we had changed trains, I think, at Springfield. It had once been, and indeed still was, a rather elegant neighborhood. The Brent house itself was enormous, solid and ugly, except where ivy had crept over the chimneys and around the stone balustrades, softening their rather grim outlines.

The grounds were extensive and were enclosed with a very high and solid stone wall. There were tall, grilled iron gates, formal lawns, thick, clipped shrubs, old trees and, directly below me, a wide slope of lawn, bordered by a tall thick hedge. This hedge was broken at one end by steps and another gate which led, I guessed (and correctly) to the garden, where my patient was said to have been cleaning a gun—at eleven o'clock of a dark February night.

I was looking down at the lawn and steps when there was a flutter of a blue cape and Drue came hurriedly from somewhere out of my range of vision and crossed the lawn. She was running, so the red lining of her long blue nurse's cape fluttered, and I could see the hem of her starched white skirt. Her hood was pulled up over her head but still I was perfectly sure it was Drue. She disappeared down the steps and behind the hedge and was there for a long time, for I watched.

Indeed when she did finally emerge it was perceptibly darker with the fall of an early, dreary twilight. She came directly toward the house and she was carrying something under her cape. I was sure of it because of the way she held the edges of the cape toegther, the crook of her elbow beneath the heavy folds, and the oddly surreptitious way she hurried toward some side door.

However, it wasn't more than ten minutes after that that she came, all fresh and crisp in her white uniform and cap, with only the color in her lips and in her cheeks to prove that she'd been, not a quarter of an hour ago, running across the lawn in what I could only describe as a surreptitious way. She came in quietly, closed the door behind her and went at once to stand beside the bed. Her eyelids were lowered, so I couldn't see her eyes, but I could see her mouth and the passion of anxiety in the lines of her slender figure.

Young Brent moved a little and spoke again. He said, "But that's murder. Murder. Tell Claud. There'll be murder done."

He said it clearly; he said it imperatively; he said it with a complete, forceful conviction. He was drugged and unconscious and did not know what he was saying, at least, I sincerely hoped he didn't know.

But Drue cried, "Craig!" in a sharp whisper. *"Craig— what do you mean?"*

She waited and I waited, and he didn't move, or speak.

"Delirium," I said finally, my voice sounding unnaturally high.

"Delirium?" She seemed to weigh it, still watching him fixedly, and to arrive at some secret rejection. "Why would he say that? If it's delirium."

"Why wouldn't he?" My voice was still a little high. "They say anything in delirium. Who's Claud?"

"That's Dr. Chivery," she said. "The Chiverys are very close friends."

It didn't help much; if there was any remote and fantastic grain of truth in Craig Brent's words, which Heaven forbid, Dr. Chivery wasn't the man to do anything decisive and prohibitive about it. My one encounter with that gentleman was sufficient to convince me of that

Drue was leaning over the bed again. "Craig." Her voice was low, but clear and urgent. "What do you mean? What murder?" After a long pause, she said, *"Who?"*

There was no answer, and I had had time to pull myself together.

"He spoke in delirium," I said again but more positively. "If there was going to be a murder, I don't think the murderer would take anybody into his confidence beforehand. It isn't done."

She turned that over in her mind and smiled a little and looked at me. "No. You're right, of course. It was silly of me to think of anything else. There isn't any change, is there?"

I shook my head and just then the door opened again. A man, the butler, I thought, stood there. He was a big man, enormously dignified in his black coat, with intelligent, light-blue eyes. He didn't come into the room but made a kind of gesture toward me, which was a nice blend of respect and authority. Drue said, "He wants you. I'll stay."

She was right. For when I had crossed to him the butler (William Fanshawe Beevens, age fifty-four, in the Brent employ for twenty-one years; so the record, later, ran) beckoned me into the hall.

"Mr. Brent," said he, "wishes to speak to you. It will be only a moment." Well, of course I could leave. Drue could stay with our patient. The butler added, "Will you come this way, please?" and started off down the hall.

We went downstairs, making almost no sound on the padded steps. The great hall with its black and white marble floor was empty, except for the butler and me. I thought fleetingly of the state trooper; if he had been about I believe now that I would have told him of my patient's words, delirious though I thought—at least, I preferred to think—they were. But in any case the trooper was not about and, when I inquired (very casually), the butler said briefly that he had concluded his inquiry and gone.

"It was merely a matter of routine; customary when there is an accident with a gun," said the butler. He gave me a fleeting look from those intelligent, light-blue eyes and led me to a door with carved, dark wood panels which looked extremely thick. Just as we reached it, it opened and a woman came out.

She was rather an extraordinary woman; very small and dark with dead black hair, done in a high pompadour after the fashion of thirty years ago; she wore a white starched blouse (the kind that used to be called a shirtwaist and had a starched stock collar) and a very full black skirt which all but touched the floor. She had a tiny waist with a big belt and extravagantly curved hips. On one 'shoulder a watch was pinned and she smelled of violet sachet. She wore pince-nez, rimless, with a gold chain fastened to a gold button on her other shoulder. She must have been fifty or more; it was difficult to tell. Altogether she was a page out of the past and a page that I may as well admit I am fully equipped to remember.

But the thing I noticed mainly was the bright, inquisitive way her dark eyes peered out of her small, sallow face. She gave a short kind of nod and went on and, as I am a truthful woman, petticoats rustled as she crossed the marble floor. Otherwise, however, Maud Chivery moved with an utter and complete silence which never ceased to astonish me. You had to have your eyes fixed rigidly upon her to be aware of her activities; you would be sitting in the very room with her and, if you didn't watch and let your thoughts drift away and then turned to speak to her, she would be gone, vanished altogether from the room without a sound, unless there was that faint taffeta rustle and you couldn't always hear that. An unnerving woman, really, but one I learned reluctantly to respect.

Naturally, I didn't then know that it was Maud Chivery, Dr. Chivery's wife and an intimate, indeed almost a member of the household—for she had been all but its mistress (ordering the household, hiring and training servants, getting Craig off to school and seeing that he went to the dentist, acting, even, as a hostess for Conrad Brent on occasion) during the long years of Conrad's widowerhood. I checked her down then as another member of the Brent household and, candidly, one not likely to raise its level in point of general attractiveness. Then Beevens had opened the door and was ushering me into the presence. It was exactly that.

My first feeling was a wave of sheer self-amazement that I had had the enormous temerity to call him, flippantly to Drue, Papa Brent. My second was another kind of shock; for I found myself instantly, yes and seriously, on guard. Against what I didn't know, unless it was some quality of incalculability in the man who stood there on the hearth-rug watching me.

I did know then, too, that Drue Cable's position (or rather lack of position) in that household was not in any possible

33

sense due to a mere misunderstanding between lovers that a word or two might have cleared up. It was nothing so trivial. When I saw Conrad Brent I sensed that. I also thought (queerly, unexpectedly) that there was danger somewhere in that house.

Naturally, one may say that where guns go off and shoot people there must be danger, and it doesn't take any sixth sense to realize it. But it was more than that. It was something else entirely; something that had nothing to do with reason. In fact, it didn't seem to have anything to do with me; it was just an intangible thing that hovered in the very air of that room. The queer part of it, of course, was that it should be intelligible to me. I am never prescient; I have a good stomach, no nerves and little imagination.

Beevens closed the door behind me, and Conrad Brent said, "My wife tells me that the nurse who accompanied you here is a woman who was once my son's wife. I am sending her away at once. I expect you to care for my son yourself until I can make other arrangements." He paused then, and added, "Mrs. Chivery will help you if you need her."

# IV

It is easy now to understand Conrad Brent; his strength and his weakness; his vanity and his consequent self-deception; his procrastination; his pride and his blind and obstinate prejudices; and, above all, his reluctance to admit a mistake. But then I only sensed that there was something wrong about him; something too hard and too bold which seemed to cover an inner uncertainty.

It was an odd impression. Certainly his outward behavior had no faint hint of uncertainty or secret uneasiness. Certainly, if my impression was a true one then, there was little hope of softening or changing his hatred for Drue; if his bold and arrogant front really concealed weakness then he would cling to a decision, once he made it, merely to keep up that front. I've seen it happen before; there is nothing like the obsessed obstinacy of a basically weak and uncertain nature.

He stood on the hearth-rug, waiting for me to say, "yes, sir" (and, unless I was wrong, a little afraid I wouldn't). He was not a tall man, but he was rather muscular and thick; he had a brown face, a sharply aquiline nose and a bearded and

34

thus equivocal chin. His eyes were heavily lidded and rather bright in color. He was a little bald; he wore, besides the somewhat stringy beard, a short gray mustache with two sharply waxed points at either side.

Just above him on the breast of the mantel was a coat of arms, carved and painted in somber, rich colors; it was an animal, an obese and unidentifiable creature which may have been a unicorn, standing sportively on one leg on a bit of green. The coat of arms was not quartered, which was unusual and showed me how old the direct line must be. It might have showed me too, but I didn't think of it then, the deliberate casting away of all the hundreds of intermingling and intervening blood streams in order to cling with absurd stubbornness and self-deception to one chosen ancestral line.

I didn't consciously think of anything however but Drue. I said, so emphatically that my voice rang out against the dark woods and books and red leather of that study, rather more loudly than I intended, "I'm afraid Miss Cable will have to stay."

"I beg your pardon," he said, although he couldn't have helped hearing me.

I made it clearer but lower in tone. "You can't send Miss Cable away. She is here as a nurse. We are both needed."

"We can get another nurse up from New York by morning. Tell her to be ready to leave in half an hour."

I suppose he was not often defied, so, whether his arrogance was assumed or real, obviously it worked. He just didn't believe my own opposition. So I took a long breath and walked up nearer him. "Look here," I said, "do you want your son to die?"

That touched him. Something flinched and moved back of his bright eyes and one hand reached out toward the tall back of a chair near him. He said, "He's not going to die," and looked at me as if daring me to deny it, but it had frightened him all the same.

"Twenty-four hours—thirty-six at the most will tell the tale. If things go well, there's not much for us to do, only routine. If things go wrong, that's different. I'd advise you to let her stay. Besides, he knows she's here." That told on him too; I saw it again in the flash away back in his eyes.

"I thought he was unconscious. Chivery told me he would be unconscious for some time."

"He roused a little, said a few words and then went back to sleep."

"Said . . ." he began quickly, checked himself, and then resumed in a more deliberate way. "What did he say?"

"Sorry," I said. "I'm a nurse. Dr. Chivery reminded me just now of my oath. Florence Nightingale, you know," I said gently, and watched the purple come up into his cheeks and lips. Too much purple, in fact, in his lips. I couldn't help making a brief professional note of it.

"Florence Nightingale blazes," he said. "I'm paying you. I'm his father. What did he say?"

He glared at me and I looked back at him and said, "Sorry. Is that all?" and made a motion toward the door.

"Wait a minute," he said abruptly when I touched the doorknob. There was a short pause. Somewhere a clock was ticking in a measured way. It was almost dark by then and heavy red curtains had been drawn over the windows and one or two table lamps had been lighted. A cannel coal fire was burning in the hearth below the queerly contemptuous coat of arms; a lump cracked open and sputtered; blue sparks shot upward and Conrad Brent said, "Did he say anything about the accident?" and lifted his light eyes to watch me.

Well, there he had me. In spite of the antagonism Conrad Brent had instantly roused in me, it was clearly my duty to tell someone in authority of the thing Craig had said. So I did.

"He said, well, as a matter of fact, he said this: 'But that's murder. Tell Claud.' And then he said, 'There'll be murder done.' "

I watched Conrad Brent, and he looked back at me without the slightest change of expression and that was rather odd because he ought to have been, to say the least, a little startled. He ought to have questioned me too; but he didn't. After a long moment he only shrugged and said, "Delirium. Obviously."

I said nothing. And Conrad Brent added, "And he did recognize the—the woman?"

I discovered a streak of sadism in my nature and said archly, "Oh, but definitely!"

That affected him as the other hadn't. He didn't have a stroke, but it was touch and go for an instant. Then abruptly he crossed to the long, polished desk which stood in the window embrasure. He put his thumb hard upon a bell there and, when after another silence, Beevens opened the door, he sent for Drue.

"Tell Anna to stay with Mr. Craig," he said. "And bring the other nurse here."

Beevens said, "Very good, sir," and vanished.

"I've got to go back to my patient. . . ."

He interrupted. "You stay here."

"But . . ."

"Anna took care of him till you got here. She can do it for another five minutes."

He didn't ask me to sit down, and he didn't sit down himself. But after a moment of staring down at the desk, he turned and lifted a crystal decanter that stood, with small glasses, on a silver tray. There was brandy in the decanter; it had a rich, golden-brown gleam when the light fell on it and when he had offered me some and I shook my head, he poured some for himself, a generous amount which he drank quickly. I rather felt that he was fortifying himself against the coming interview, which bore out my curious, but thus far unsubstantiated, impression of him.

The library was a warm room, with rich panels which alternated with bookshelves that went to the high ceiling. There were several great, high-backed chairs, upholstered in needlepoint, a long, rather shabby red leather divan, and a rug that, Peter Huber told me later, had been willed to a museum and yet was put down for people to walk upon, which seemed to upset Peter but which struck me as perfectly logical, in that, after all, it was a rug. But he said it ought to have hung on the wall.

Then Drue came. Beevens muttered and closed the door behind her so she was silhouetted sharply against its dark wood, white and slim with her chin held high. Her face was white, too, and her gray eyes quite bright and dark. Conrad Brent put down the glass he still held.

"Why did you come here?" he said heavily.

Drue took a sharp breath. "I was sent here as a nurse."

Conrad Brent frowned. "No. I'll tell you why you came. You came because it was my son. You wanted to see him. Well, he does not want to see you. That ought to be clear by now."

Drue's face went, if anything, whiter. She said. "I came here to nurse him. He's sick and he needs me. . . ."

"Not you," cut in Conrad Brent. "Anybody but you. I tell you he doesn't want you."

Drue hesitated. Then she lifted her little chin higher. "I don't believe that," she said.

Conrad Brent with a sharp and yet small and controlled gesture of anger lifted the decanter and set it hard and abruptly down again. He said, "Look here, Miss Cable."

Drue interrupted and said quietly, "Mrs. Brent."

"Mrs. . . ."

"I did not actually resume my maiden name. I am legally Mrs. Brent."

A small purplish flush crept up into Conrad Brent's cheeks. "But you are not my son's wife," he said, biting off the words. "And I must tell you, painful though it is to me, that my son doesn't want you. He asked me to arrange the break with you. I didn't want to tell you that at the time. I didn't want to hurt you needlessly; I am a kind man. And Craig wanted to spare you as much as possible. He thought it was kinder to break off his marriage to you as it was done. Gradually. And in a way that saved your pride and feelings. I'm sorry to have to say this. Nothing but your defiant and suspicious attitude would have induced me to say it. But you must understand that Craig doesn't want you to be his wife and didn't. He realized that his marriage was ill-considered and too hasty."

All this time Drue was standing, outlined sharply in her crisp white uniform, against the door. Her face was almost as white as her uniform, but her eyes didn't flinch.

Conrad Brent touched the decanter again, absently, and said, "As I say, I'm sorry. But you must have known the truth when he didn't come back to you after he finished his training."

Drue took a step forward at that. She said, "He did finish then?"

A queer, a completely indecipherable expression flitted across Conrad Brent's face; it was something curiously secretive and yet shrinkingly secretive, somehow; as if he didn't want to think of whatever it was that was in his mind. He said, however, stiffly, "Yes. He leaves soon. I don't know his destination."

"Why is he at home?" said Drue.

"I don't really know that you have a right to ask," said Conrad Brent. "However—" he lifted his shoulders and replied briefly—"he is home on leave. Now, of course, his leave will have to be extended. As I say, I don't know where he is to be sent. He doesn't know. He is"—again that queerly shrinking and secretive look came into his face—"he is to be a bomber pilot."

38

"Bomber . . ." asid Drue in a kind of numb and expressionless voice.

"Yes," said Conrad Brent. There was a strange little silence in which, I thought, for the first time probably Conrad Brent shared an emotion with the girl he hated. He seemed then to realize it, for he drew himself up, gave her a hooded, hating look and said, "That is not the point. The point is you are no longer his wife. And he doesn't want to see you." He waited, and Drue didn't move, and he said suddenly in a kind of burst, "Do you doubt my word?"

Drue said quietly and simply, her eyes straight and unwavering, "Yes."

Conrad Brent turned so purple and swelled so visibly that I gave a preparatory glance at the decanter of brandy and the sofa; but nothing happened in the way of a seizure, and Drue added simply, "You see, Craig loved me."

"That was a boyish infatuation!" said Conrad Brent, with a kind of controlled violence. "He was soon cured. Your marriage to my son is past and ended completely. I only wanted to make sure you understood that before permitting you to stay on in this house. I see you prefer not to, so you can leave at once . . ." He turned to the bell and had his hand outstretched when I said, "She'd better stay."

His head jerked toward me, startled. I said, "All this is beside the point. The only thing that matters just now is whether your son is going to live or die." I said it quite coolly and looked at the fat and frolicsome animal above the mantel in a detached fashion.

There was a little silence while he digested that. Then he turned to Drue again. "You might be needed tonight. But, understand, I'll have no attempts to talk to my son. If you stay at all you stay on my terms."

Well, it was clear enough; shut up or out you go. After a moment, Drue said, whispering, "I'll stay. I've got to stay. . . ."

"Very well," said Conrad Brent. "You take the noon train tomorrow. That's all."

She waited an instant or two, looking at him; then she went to the door. But with her hand on the doorknob she turned to him again. Her clear gray eyes had a thoughtful, queerly measuring look. She said very quietly, "You are his father. I suppose you love him. But I could kill you for what you've done to me." With which remarkably quiet and unexpected remark she walked out of the room and closed the door behind her.

Well, I must say I was a little disconcerted. I turned to Conrad Brent and he had got out a handkerchief and was touching his bluish lips with it. "Look here," I said abruptly. "I know that girl. She'd made anybody a good wife."

"And a charming daughter-in-law," said Conrad Brent, "threatening to murder me."

"She didn't mean that; you know it. She . . ."

He interrupted me. "My dear Nurse. I have no doubt she would make an admirable wife for, as you aptly put it, anybody. But not"—he drew himself up and glanced up at the coat of arms and said in a different voice—"but not for *my* son. That's all, Nurse." Without giving me another chance to speak he went to the door and opened it for me, and I was obliged to precede him into the hall.

The aspect of the great, solemn hall had changed. A fire had been lighted and there was a little group of people having tea there, with chairs and tables drawn up near the fire and Beevens hovering in the background. Alexia, sitting behind a lace-draped table, was pouring from an old silver service that was polished till it looked as soft as satin.

Conrad Brent asked me to have tea with them. The fact itself astonished me so I looked at him incredulously. But it was as if the opening of the library door had been the rising of a curtain and Conrad Brent had a scene to play. He was a different man—poised, urbane, gracious in a lordly way.

Well, naturally, I refused. I'd been too long away from my patient as it was. But he insisted upon introducing me to Maud Chivery, who nodded briefly and watched me brightly, to Nicky Senour whom I had already encountered and who remembered it for he was barely civil, and to another young man, tall and blond and nice-looking who arose at once from the bench before the fireplace and bowed, and answered to the name of Peter Huber. This then was Craig's friend and the man who had helped Nicky and the butler carry him to his room after the shooting.

Maud Chivery stirred her tea with a shriveled, brown little hand and said in a soft-as-silk voice, "I'll be glad to stay with you tonight, Nurse. When the other nurse leaves."

Alexia's beautiful, pointed face turned seekingly toward her husband's. Conrad didn't look at her. "The other nurse will stay until morning," he said.

Maud Chivery's eyes glistened with interest. Alexia's face

40

stiffened, and she made a small quick motion as if to rise from her chair, but Conrad walked over to her and put his heavy hand on her shoulder. Alexia put one soft white hand caressingly over his own and instantly his face changed and softened. It was obvious that whatever had happened in the past Conrad Brent was almost fatuously in love with his young wife. The young wife who had been once, and not so long ago, his son's fiancée. "She goes tomorrow," he said.

Alexia did not relax; her eyelids drooped a little but it seemed to me that under the soft shadow of her eyelashes she shot a demanding glance toward her brother Nicky. Nicky looked into his cup for an instant and said, "I wonder what Drue wants."

Maud Chivery made a little shushing motion with one brown claw but glanced eagerly at Conrad. "That is not a name I or Alexia wish to hear uttered in this house," said Conrad with really astonishing command and dignity. It argued sincerity on his part and a determination to control circumstances which seemed to me remarkable in this day when there are no medieval castles nor medieval rulers and no matter how much you hate anybody you really can't help hearing his name now and then. Nicky's pointed, elegant face and small crimson mouth looked fleetingly a little ugly; but he lifted his cup again without replying.

Rather abruptly I said that I had to get back to my patient and Peter Huber straightened suddenly, put down his cup and said something polite to Alexia who nodded. She hadn't said a word, yet she had made her will fully marked by her quick inquiring look at Conrad to know if Drue was to be sent away, no less than by her covert but imperative glance toward her brother which seemed to enlist his aid against Drue. Decidedly, Alexia held the reins of power in her pointed, soft, white hands. She didn't look at Peter Huber as she nodded to his polite murmur, and he walked across the hall beside me and started up the great stairway when I did.

At the curve I glanced down. Alexia was sitting perfectly still in her great chair, her crimson suit a spot of rich, soft color, her pearls reflecting a rosy glow from the fire. Her head was bent a little thoughtfully, and there was in her face again, despite its indubitable beauty, a hint of underlying cruelty. Perhaps it lay subtly in the shape of her mouth, small yet so crimson and so eager, or in her delicately pointed chin. Nothing she could help, certainly. I told myself that and then looked at Nicky and saw exactly the same thing, a subtle, indefinable twist of his red mouth, a brooding quality in the soft repose of his face, something you couldn't analyze and describe, and something cruel.

Maud Chivery's dark little face twisted over her white stock to watch us go up the stairway. Then we went above the landing and could no longer see the silent group below.

Peter Huber was still with me when I turned along the corridor toward my patient's room. Once we had passed beyond earshot of those in the hall below, he said, "Wait a minute, Miss—Nurse. I'd like to talk to you. It won't take a moment. Here's a chair."

Well, I suppose it could have been called that, although it had almost certainly been culled from one of the bigger and better medieval torture chambers. A bulbous-legged cupid leered at me from a dark tapestry across the opposite wall, and Peter Huber said, "Is he going to die?"

"I hope not. I don't think so."

He was a nice-looking fellow, as I've said; very blond and very big but not so boyish as my first impression led me to believe. He was tanned as Craig Brent was tanned. There were fine lines around his large blue eyes and around his squarish mouth; his features were large and rather blunt, his blond hair curly and strong-looking. He had rather good hands, long and muscular and was dressed in very British tweeds but was not British, although there was a slight flavor of something European about him; perhaps it was his enormous politeness. Anyway, he looked at me then, earnestly and worriedly, and said, "Has he told you who shot him? I'm sure he knows."

# V

Telling Peter Huber the things Craig had said was not like telling Conrad Brent. Conrad was Craig's father, his own flesh and blood; besides, he was in a position of authority. If there was the smallest grain of reality in Craig's muttered words, Conrad was the man to deal with it, no one else.

"It was an accident," I replied discreetly. "He was cleaning a gun."

Peter Huber looked straight at me. "In the garden?" he said after a moment. "At night—no, Nurse. What really happened?"

I got up. "You should know more about it than I," I said briskly. "I've got to get back to him now."

"But—oh, all right." He walked to the door and put his hand on the doorknob. "I won't bother you," he said, smiling a little, "but if I can do anything . . ."

"Thank you." He glanced in the room over my shoulder, and then, without attempting to enter, closed the door behind me.

Drue was standing beside the window.

It is strange, really, that women deck themselves in silks and jewels and furs. There is nothing that sets off beauty like the simplicity and whiteness of a nurse's uniform. The white, starched dress outlined the slender curves of Drue's figure. Her white cap rested lightly on her hair with its gold highlights, and framed her face like a coronet, stately and yet with a kind of piquance. Her eyes were very clear and intent below it, her lips scarlet. The whiteness brought out (in the way a reflecting light and its corollary shadows do bring out lines) the delicate hollows below her cheekbones, the white, generous temples. There was strength there and decision, and yet tenderness, too.

I went to my patient and there was no change. Drue said, watching the rain, "Thanks for what you said to Conrad Brent."

"Perhaps in the morning . . ."

"No. He won't change his mind again. I've only tonight."

Only tonight. And Craig Brent unconscious and drugged, and for that night hovering in the nebulous, incalculable margin between life and death.

There was nothing I could do or say. Presently, she said, "I'm going now. I'll try to sleep. I'll take over at twelve," and went away.

It was then nearly six o'clock with rain coming now in gusty squalls against the windowpanes, and the house was very quiet.

I had plenty to think of as moments dragged along, and I must say I didn't at all fancy the sum total of my thoughts. For, any way I looked at it, Drue was fighting a losing battle and yet she was determined to fight it.

The trouble was, of course, Craig Brent had done nothing at all to find her again. In these days, I told myself, fathers don't deal out autocratic commands to their sons. The sons won't let them. They say, in effect, Okay, Pa, I'll go and dig ditches if I have to, but I'll marry my own wife and support her, too.

Craig Brent had done nothing like that. I was thinking that, watching him, when he moved a little, sighed, and tucked the hand Drue had kissed under his cheek. He did it without opening his eyes, without really waking. He sighed again like a contented child and dropped back into sleep. It only goes to show my feeling about Craig Brent when I say it exasperated me beyond words. I got up and went to the fire, and stared down at the dying coals.

But, if I didn't like Craig Brent, still less did I like the fact that he had been shot and I didn't think it was accident.

Well, time went on and I wished I had my knitting. Nobody came near me until Beevens silently brought my dinner tray and, half an hour later, returned as silently to carry it away again. Somehow, I half expected Alexia or Maud Chivery or even the doctor, but as far as I knew no one so much as approached the door. The night had turned stormy and colder, with gusts of wind and rain, and it wasn't very pleasant sitting there in the gloomy bedroom with the wind blowing wisps of smoke back down the chimney now and then, and a shutter somewhere flapping. I began to watch the clock a little nervously. Once, overcome by a distinct impression that everybody else had gone away, vanished mysteriously into the night, leaving me and my patient alone in the great and somehow forbidding house, I got up and looked into the corridor.

My first glimpse of the long, night-lighted corridor all but confirmed my fantastic notion, it was so completely empty. But, as I watched, Nicky came out of a door down toward the stairs and on the right, glanced along the corridor, saw me or my white cap, paused for a fractional second and slipped back into the room from which he had just emerged and closed the door. He wasn't wearing a dinner jacket; he was still in a checked coat and brown trousers; I was sure it was Nicky.

It was just then, by the way, that Delphine entered my life—and the bedroom. I felt something soft brush against my ankles and on suppressing a sharp cry and looking downward I discovered an enormous Maltese tomcat, with blazing green eyes and battle-scarred ears who stalked to the hearth-rug, turned around twice, sat down and looked at me.

He had apparently drifted silently along the shadows of the hall under chairs and tables and near the wall, so I hadn't

44

seen what was a habitually stealthy approach. And I couldn't get rid of him. I held the door open invitingly and whispered, "Kitty, kitty," and he merely looked disdainful. I went to him and swished with my skirt and he was only slightly entertained. I started to take him up in my hands and he simply lifted one solid gray paw and planted it upon my hand and firmly put out his claws. He didn't scratch or dig them in, but he gave me to understand then and there that he had little if any scruples.

So in the end I let him stay. He took a complete bath, paused to stalk something that was not under the couch and went to sleep in a tight gray ball. I moved to a chair, to the sofa, to the bed, to stare down at Craig, and then back to a chair. The trouble was, of course, I knew too much and still too little. It was an uneasy kind of night, wakeful, somehow, and troubled. But nothing happened. Nothing happened really, I mean, although once in a lull in the wind and rain I thought I heard quiet footsteps in the hall. The house seemed to sleep, yet there was a listening, sentient quality about it, too.

The cat didn't move. My patient slept heavily. The wind creaked the shutter outside and sighed down the chimney. Twelve o'clock came and Drue didn't come with it.

Twelve o'clock and twelve-ten, and still she was not there.

At twelve-fifteen two things happened. Delphine opened his eyes, opened them all at once without blinking, sat up and stared fixedly at the blank panels of the door to the hall. Just stared at it, for a long time. Then something bumped, hard and sharp, against the door.

A long silence followed. I must have got up, for I remember standing very still, listening. There was no other sound, no retreating footsteps, no movement, no voice.

Because of this, or because of something less easily accountable, a moment (perhaps two or three) elapsed before I went to the door and opened it. No one was in the hall; it stretched emptily away on either hand with the chairs here and there making heavy shadows. But no one was there.

I believe—indeed I know—that several moments passed, while I stood there. Long enough, at least, for me to discover the rather queer thing I did discover and that was a kind of dent, small and not deep but still a dent, in the waxed gleaming surface of one of the panels of the door I still held open.

It was as if someone had been carrying something (a ladder, fireplace tongs, perhaps a hammer) along the hall and had accidentally bumped it against the door. But people don't carry hammers, or ladders, through sleeping houses after midnight.

But I was looking at that little dent, touching it with my finger, when a woman somewhere screamed. It was a short, breathless little scream, cut off before it was more than begun. But I knew somehow that it was Drue.

I knew too that it came from downstairs. But I don't remember moving, although I do have a dim memory of clutching at the bannister on the stairs and of the slipperiness of the marble floor in the hall.

The door to Conrad Brent's library was open and there was a light. Drue was there, her face as white as her cap. She had something in her hand and she was bending over Conrad Brent, who lay half on the floor, half on the red leather couch.

He was dead; I saw that. Drue said in a strange, faraway voice, *"Sarah—Sarah, I've killed him!"*

Then there were footsteps running heavily across the marble floor, toward us and toward the dead man. Drue heard them, too, and turned and the bright thing in her hand caught the light and glittered.

# VI

In a time of shattering emergency and haste one's action is altogether instinctive. It's only afterward that you question that action and then it's too late because it is already accomplished—for good or bad but certainly forever. I reached out and took the shining thing from Drue's hand. It was a hypodermic syringe; the barrel was empty and a needle was in place.

Drue was staring down at Conrad Brent, her eyes wide and dark in her white face. She said, in that queer, faraway voice, "I didn't mean to kill him. I was trying to help him. But he—he died. . . ."

I couldn't put my hand over her mouth, for it would have been seen; the sound of the footsteps had abruptly stopped at the door. I thrust the hypodermic syringe into my pocket and said loudly, to cover whatever Drue was trying to say, "Don't be frightened; we'll get the doctor . . ." and turned around. It was Peter Huber who stood there; at least, it wasn't Alexia who might have heard what Drue said, or Nicky which would be the same thing.

Drue shrank into silence; I hoped it was prudence but was afraid it was not. Peter Huber uttered an exclamation and came quickly into the room.

"Sick?" he cried. "Good heavens! He looks horrible. . . ." He stopped beside me, clutching his red dressing gown over vividly striped pajamas. "He's dead—isn't he?"

Well, I've been a nurse for a long time; I know death when I see it. But I made sure while he watched me.

"Yes, he's dead," I said at last.

"What was it? Heart?"

"I don't know. Yes, I suppose so." All three of us stood there for an indecisive moment, staring down at Conrad Brent's body—sprawled there awkwardly, with his face sunk over one shoulder and his mouth a little open. I remember feeling that I ought to get a towel and tie that square, but no longer formidable, jaw before rigor mortis set in. And then instantly I thought the police wouldn't like it; I must touch nothing. *Police*? But Drue's wild words hadn't meant that she had murdered him. I'd thought of murder and police only because Craig had said, there'll be murder done.

*Craig!* I'd forgotten him.

"I've got to go back to my patient! I believe Mr. Brent is dead, but call Dr. Chivery!" I reached the door and thought of Drue. I couldn't leave her there in that room beside Conrad Brent, to be questioned by this young Huber or by anyone else. Not just then. I went quickly back to her. "You go up to Craig," I said. "Stay there with him."

"But I . . ." she began. I interrupted, *"Hurry!"*

I hoped Peter Huber would not notice how urgent it sounded. However, Drue gave the sagging thing on the couch another long look, blank with shock, and went. I made sure she was on the way upstairs then said again, sharply, to Peter Huber, "Get the doctor. I'll stay here."

"Wouldn't you rather I would stay with him? I don't mind. You can call the doctor."

"No," I said. "I don't know the number. . . ."

"But the telephone operator . . ."

I said again, *"Hurry,"* and must have sounded as if I meant it, for he gave me a startled look and went away. I closed the door behind him and went to Conrad Brent.

"I've killed him," Drue had said, clutching a hypodermic

47

syringe. Presently I found the mark. It was a tiny red spot on his left arm—so very small—yet, if they found it, what would they say? Everyone in that house knew that the man who lay there, dead, had come between Drue and her young husband, and now that she had come back he was still determined to give her no quarter. "I've only tonight," she'd said.

Well, perhaps Claud Chivery wouldn't see that tiny red mark. I rolled down the cuff, fastened it and adjusted the brown velvet sleeve of his lounge coat; then I looked around the room.

Nothing much was changed since my interview in that room during the late afternoon. The desk lamp was still lighted; the fire had burned down to gray ashes with crimson undertones; the decanter of brandy still stood on the desk—not, however, on the tray but on the edge of the desk. The room was warm and so still that everything in it seemed to have a quiet, intensely observant life of its own, as if the chairs and books, the coat of arms over the mantel, the objects on the desk, things intimately associated with the life of Conrad Brent, were all watching me—me and that forever silent figure, gray-faced and inert on the couch.

Craig *had* said murder and now Conrad Brent was dead.

It was not a comfortable thought. Even so, I was a little taken aback to find my hand had gone out toward the brandy decanter. I was, indeed, in the very act of lifting it and reaching for a glass when I stopped. Having been a practicing teetotaler all my life. I withdrew my hand quickly, although, as to that, there was not enough brandy in the decanter to make a very black mark on my record. I had, however, already touched the decanter—but I thought nothing of it, then, and looked again about the room. I don't say I was looking for clues; still, there weren't any. Not even a cigarette or cigar ashes. A cuff link would have come in handy just then, I thought, or burned papers in the fireplace. But there was nothing.

Nothing but Conrad Brent, and the only thing I could be fairly sure of was that however he had died, it was due in the end to an acute heart block. His face was ashy gray, with a tinge of blue in the lips—what is called cyanosis. He still wore dinner clothes, except he had taken off his dinner jacket and replaced it with a short, brown velvet lounge coat; his black tie hung in strings, and his collar was open. I was looking at that when without any warning at all the entire Japanese army began to drop bombs on the house.

At least, it sounded like it. For all at once somewhere in the house there was a thud, a series of loud thumps and then a clatter as of shattering glass. I ran to the door of the library and flung it open. The noise stopped as suddenly as it began, except it seemed to me there were echoes all through the house. No one was in the hall, and I had started toward the stairs when Peter Huber came running from the end of the hall, beyond the stairs, gave a wild look around the great empty hall, saw me and shouted, "What was that?"

He didn't wait for an answer but ran up the stairs taking the steps three at a time and I ran after him. The noise seemed to come from the second floor and Drue was up there alone with Craig. Craig—who had been the victim of one attempt at murder the previous night.

Anyway, there was certainly nothing that I, or anyone, could do now for the man who lay in the study.

Well, I'm not too fleet on my feet, although I took the stairs at what amounted to a gallop. When I reached the hall above Peter Huber had disappeared. The main, wide part of the corridor stretched dimly away ahead of me and behind me; there were two or three night lights along it; they were not bright and the shapes of occasional chairs ranged against the walls loomed up like clumsy dark creatures waiting there for prey, but did not move. In fact nothing moved.

A narrow corridor crossed the main one just on the other side of the stairwell and appeared to lead toward the servants' wing and backstairs; Peter Huber must have turned into that or into some room. I didn't stop to look for him. As I ran along that dim, wide corridor, my starched, white skirt rustling and whispering against the shadowy walls, the house began to stir. Someone rang a bell somewhere, so its distant peal was audible even there. Someone flung open a door. Then I reached my patient's room.

It was lighted as I had left it. But the bed was empty. The room was empty. Craig Brent was gone and so was Drue.

I must have gone into the room and searched it a little frenziedly; I remember looking under the bed and pulling out the heavy red curtains and looking behind them, though not even a cat could have hidden successfully there. The cat—but the cat was gone, too. No one was in the bathroom, no one in the little dressing room. As I came out of it, hurrying, Maud Chivery, in a voluminous, flowered dressing gown came sweeping into the bedroom and aimed a flashlight directly into my eyes. "What was that noise? What happened?" she cried. Then she saw the bed and squealed, "What have you done with Craig?"

What had *I* done with Craig!

"Conrad Brent is dead. He's in the library. You'd better call the doctor." I snatched the flashlight from her hand. Her face turned waxy and her bright eyes became two sharp points of light; I thought she was going to faint, for she said, "O-o-o-oh," in a kind of whistle from utterly blanched lips. So I gave her a push toward a chair and turned to the door.

Alexia was standing there in the door; a crimson dressing gown clung to her lovely, curved body and fell, trailing, around her feet; her small, pointed face loomed from a cloud of fine black hair.

"*Conrad . . .*" she said in a kind of whisper. "*Conrad.*" And then, as I made to pass her, she clutched at me. "*Where is Craig? What has happened to him . . . ?*"

"It's what I'm trying to find out." I unloosed her pointed, vehement fingers and went hurriedly into the hall. Craig couldn't be far away. So I tried the bedroom nearest me; the door opened upon chill, orderly emptiness and a "Stag at Eve" gazed mournfully at me from above the mantel. No sign of Craig or Drue. I started toward the door opposite and, as I turned, I bumped into a man hurrying along. We collided with a shock that whirled us around toward each other and it was Nicky. He all but pushed me out of the way and I dropped Maud's flashlight. It struck his foot, I believe. At any rate, he swore in a sharp, startled way and cried, dancing on one foot and clasping the other in his hand, "Did you see Conrad? Where is he?"

"In the library. Why don't you look where you're going?" I caught my balance and my cap and wondered if I'd damaged the flashlight.

"Is he dead? Are you sure? Is he dead?" His eyes were bright as jewels in his elegant, small face.

"Go and look for yourself," I snapped, and retrieved the flashlight as he hurried limping toward Maud and Alexia who were at the door of Craig's room. I heard Alexia say, "I'm going down. Come with me, Maud. . . ."

Then I opened the next door and found Craig. The room was a kind of linen closet, narrow and long, lined with cupboards and smelling of lavender, and Craig lay at full length on the floor with Drue bending over him apparently trying to drown him, for she was holding a towel dripping with water to his head.

"Drue!"

"Sarah, he's been hurt! Look . . ."

His face was drained-looking and white; she lifted the towel from one temple and it was broken and cut and bleeding.

"What happened?"

"I don't know. He wasn't in his room when I came upstairs. I looked for him and found him here. Like this . . ."

He wore a dressing gown and slippers and a blanket had been put around him. "Blanket and all?" I asked, kneeling to look closer at the cut.

"No. I brought the blanket. He must have heard us downstairs, and tried to come, and fell against something."

"What was he doing in here?" His pulse wasn't bad; I took a gingerly look at the dressings on his shoulder and the wound hadn't opened again for there seemed to be no fresh bleeding.

"I don't know. But he was here, not in the hall. Sarah, is he hurt?" There was a sharp anxiety in her tone.

"Oh, the cut isn't bad. Painful maybe, later. We'll put something on it. The thing to do is get him back to bed before he gets pneumonia."

I sat back on my heels and took a long breath. At any rate he wasn't dead. And she had thought of that too; for she said then, jerkily, "When I saw him like that I thought he was dead. There'd been no sound of a shot. But I thought . . ." She stopped and leaned over him and pressed the towel to his temple again. "I've got some surgical dressing in my bag."

My knees were still shaking. "What was the noise?" I asked.

"What noise?"

"*What* . . ." I stared at her face, bent over Craig. "*That* noise! Surely you heard it."

"I didn't hear anything," she said, intent on Craig. "Perhaps I was in the bathroom. Sarah, do you think we can carry him?"

I gave up. "No," I said. "I'll get somebody to help."

I got up, and, as I moved, Craig Brent's eyelids fluttered and opened. His eyes were hazy, the pupils were small and sharply black so I knew he was still heavily drugged. But his eyes fastened upon Drue's face leaning close above him, fastened and then changed as if a flame leaped into them. His lips moved a little and he said in a faint whisper, "Drue . . ."

She didn't speak; she only leaned over him, her white cap haloish in the light, her face inexpressibly tender and brooding. I cleared my throat abruptly and said, "How did you get here? What happened?"

He didn't look at me; I don't think he heard me. He just kept on looking up at Drue with something alive, something urgent and important and so vital it had almost a being of its own, in their meeting look and in their stillness.

Yet Conrad Brent lay dead in the study; a hypodermic syringe was in my white pocket; and Craig had said, there'll be murder done.

It was curious and extremely unpleasant how the word murder—somewhere in that house, somewhere in that night—kept thrusting itself at me with a grisly persistence.

But I was cross by that time too; fright affects me like that. I said something which emerged as only an exasperated mutter and went to the door. No one was in the hall; Alexia, Maud and Nicky had vanished. I hurried to the stairs and just at the landing was Beevens (in a long white bath-robe, vaguely Ku-Klux in character) ascending and puffing. I said, "Come and help me. Hurry!"

He didn't question. Not even when we arrived in the linen closet and there was, so to speak, the young master stretched full length on the floor. Full length, that is, except that Drue had lifted him a little so she held his head against her breast and the towel pressed against the ugly bleeding bruise on his temple. Beevens said something that really did sound like "Tush-tush . . ." and stooped over. "Take his feet, Nurse, please," he said efficiently.

So we got Craig back to bed. By the time we had him covered warmly and hot water bottles around him to ward off pneumonia, he was completely unconscious again. Beevens, still without a question, helped us. It took time—all of it had taken time.

At last everything we could do was done, and Beevens looked at me. "They want you in the study, Miss Keate," he said.

Drue looked at me quickly, so her little white cap jerked toward me.

Something seemed to jerk and tighten within me. I won't say that my mind began to work, for I have since then doubted its existence, but I did take a kind of hold on myself.

"Very well." I straightened my cap. I said to Drue, "I won't be long."

I didn't give her a chance to say anything but hurried away, following Beevens. I had reached the landing of the stairs just below the stained glass window when I remembered that Drue's hypodermic syringe was still in my pocket.

Well, they weren't likely to search me, those people waiting in the library, but I hid the syringe.

There was a kind of ledge at the bottom of the long, arched window and a funereal but very thick fern stood there. Beevens turned around the landing and started ponderously down the remaining flight of steps and I thrust the syringe under the thick ferns. I hadn't time to do more. Beevens was already aware of my pause and starting to turn majestically around. Feeling as if I'd hidden the body, I moved hurriedly away from the fern and went on down the steps. We crossed the hall and I was vaguely aware of two or three people huddled together at the entrance to a passage beyond the stairs that went to the rear of the house—two women servants, I thought, and the stocky, thickset man who had met us at the train.

The library door was open; Alexia was pacing up and down at the other side of the great desk, taking a few steps, whirling, returning. Anna stood beside the door; she was huddled into a blue, faded bathrobe and her blue eyes were staring from a colorless face.

The others were grouped around Conrad Brent's body on the couch and Dr. Chivery had arrived. He knelt beside the body, his back toward me. Maud was on the other side of the sofa, her face a rigid, yellowish mask with two bright eyes that watched Chivery. Peter was there too, looking thoughtfully downward and, as I entered, Nicky turned away from the sofa abruptly, walked around the long desk and flung himself into Conrad's armchair.

Alexia saw me first. She paused as she turned to kick her short crimson train out of the way, looked at me and said, "Here's the nurse. Did you find Craig? Where was he? What happened?"

"He's all right. He's in bed again. Miss Cable is with him."

Maud glanced at me swiftly. Dr. Chivery got up a little awkwardly, dusted his knees absently and looked around in a bewildered way. "I—I wasn't expecting Conrad's death just now," he said. "Well, I'm afraid it's all over." He glanced irresolutely at Maud. Nicky said, "It must have been quick. None of us knew he was having an attack."

Claud Chivery passed an unsteady hand across his small chin. "He had some medicine," he said. "He always took it for these attacks. I suppose this time . . ." He leaned over the body and seemed to be searching about it and the sofa. "Well, it isn't here. The box of pills, I mean. It must have taken him so quickly he didn't have time to get the medicine. He's had this heart condition, you know, for years."

"We knew," said Alexia.

Dr. Chivery glanced at me. "You found him?"

"Yes. He was dead. I could do nothing for him."

He looked at my wrist watch and seemed to wait a little tentatively for me to elaborate on my statement. As I didn't on the principle of least said soonest mended, he nodded. "Ah—yes. I was afraid he would go like this."

Maud said stiffly, "His medicine was digitalis, wasn't it, Claud?"

Again Claud Chivery glanced uncertainly at his wife. "Why, yes, of course. Everyone knew it. He kept it in the drawer of his desk, over there."

It was natural for all of us to glance at the desk. It was natural too, I suppose, for Alexia to reach out and pull open a drawer—the top right-hand drawer—as she did.

"It isn't here," she said. "He must have it somewhere about him."

"But I . . ." Dr. Chivery shrugged. "Perhaps I overlooked it."

He turned back to Conrad Brent's body. There was a silence that had a quality of question that was still, unspoken and undefined. We all watched while he searched swiftly and with a kind of gentleness, so I remembered that Conrad Brent and his physician had been friends and neighbors for many years.

"No, it isn't here." He straightened up at last. Perplexity struggled with a queer kind of new uneasiness on his ever uneasy face. Maud said, "That was digitalis. Everyone knew where he kept it. Claud—Alexia—if anyone removed that box of pills it would have been murder. Murder . . ."

So there it was again, I thought almost angrily to myself —murder. Doggedly persistent.

But that's all I thought just then, for Beevens uttered a

kind of stifled exclamation and vanished from the door with an effect of consternation. We all heard his footsteps cross the hall and the heavy sound of the front door opening. We heard the voices, too, loud and authoritative.

"We got here as soon as we could. Where's the murdered man?"

"*Murdered*—but we—but he . . ." Beevens seemed to master himself by a great effort. "You are mistaken, sir. There's no murder here. No one sent for the police."

There was a kind of jumble of several voices and the sound of motion; then quick, hard footsteps crossed the hall toward the open library door and the state trooper of the previous day stopped in the doorway.

He took one quick look around the room. Then he addressed Dr. Chivery. "There was a telephone call to headquarters about fifteen minutes ago from this house. Whoever it was said Conrad Brent had been murdered and asked us to come at once. Who killed him?"

# VII

No one spoke. Even Beevens goggled in the doorway like a stricken fish. Nicky's small head and graceful body seemed to freeze into wariness like a young animal, sensing a trap.

Then Maud said, "Tell them, Claud. There's a mistake." And Dr. Chivery blinked rapidly, looked at his wife's dark hair and the Lieutenant's left shoulder and said that they were mistaken. "Mr. Brent was my patient. He died of a heart attack. No one called you and he was not murdered."

The Lieutenant came into the room slowly; he was tall and spare as a whip and not unlike one, in suggesting a kind of coiled and wiry strength. A couple of policemen (troopers, by their uniform, so I reasoned that the Brent place was well outside any borough limits and thus in the jurisdiction of the state) followed him. He said, "I see. But who telephoned to us?"

Which was what developed the trouble. For no one had telephoned, or at least no one would admit it. Chivery looked uneasy but blank, Maud angry but equally blank—Nicky, Alexia, Peter and even Anna, when questioned directly denied it with various degrees of indignation, but with a kind of concerted and astonished ignorance of such a telephone call which sounded sincere. Beevens from the door was fervent in his denial. Perhaps I was, too. I remember saying I hadn't thought of the police, in a voice that rang out positively in clarion tones against the book-lined walls.

Alexia drew herself up to her full height and assumed a wonderful lady-of-the-manor command. "You see, Lieutenant," she said, "you must be mistaken. My husband died of a heart attack. The nurse"—the Lieutenant's eyes flicked toward me and back to Alexia—"the nurse found him like this. She called us, and we telephoned for his doctor. My husband was not murdered."

Nicky said eagerly, "You've got the name wrong. You'd better hurry along, too, hadn't you, Lieutenant? I mean if someone in the neighborhood has been murdered or—or anything like that—and they want you . . ." The officer looked at Nicky, and Nicky stopped rather suddenly. The Lieutenant had narrow, gray-green eyes, narrow high cheekbones and an expression of complete taciturnity. He said, "I took the message myself. It was a woman's voice. There's no mistake."

"A woman!" cried Nicky. "But . . ." He stopped and flapped his small hands helplessly. *"But he wasn't murdered!"*

Claud Chivery stepped forward. "I agree to that, Lieutenant. I'm going to give the death certificate, and I have no question at all in my mind. Remember, he was my patient." There was a sharp silence except, from the hall, Beevens could be heard evicting the servants clustered there from their observation post. "You'll be called if necessary," he said. "Now get along. . . ." Beevens himself remained, however, hovering in the hall and in all probability straining his ears out of all nature.

The Lieutenant said quietly, "If you'll permit . . ." stepped to the sofa, and looked down at Conrad Brent.

I don't mind saying I was nervous. In the course of a not uncheckered career (far, now, in the past) I have chanced to see a little of the scope and persistence of a police investigation.

They had been summoned by telephone, so whoever had summoned them must have had reason to believe it was murder.

Everybody was watching the Lieutenant when he turned at last to Alexia and said, "I'm sorry, Madam. We shall spare your feelings in every possible way; we'll do our best to protect you from public comment or annoyance. If Mr. Brent wasn't murdered, we can soon satisfy ourselves and you in that respect. If he was . . ."

"But he couldn't have been!" cried Alexia angrily. Then all at once her rigid, masklike face softened. She went quickly and gracefully to the Lieutenant and put her white hands on his arm; leaning very close to him and lifting her beautiful face beseechingly, she said softly and musically, "Lieutenant, no one would have murdered my husband. It is impossible. . . ."

The officer detached himself without effort and without compunction. "Will you please leave the room to us now?" he said politely. "It will be better that way. All of you, please, except Dr. Chivery."

"But I . . ." Alexia's voice was no longer musical. Her small face was set and the gleam in her eyes was not a pleasant one. Maud was watching every move and every look and had said nothing. The Lieutenant interrupted Alexia coolly. "We'll have to have an autopsy, Dr. Chivery," he said. "I'll send to Nettleton for the appointed medical examiner; he should be here in an hour. He'll assist you in making the autopsy."

Dr. Chivery looked at the buttons on the police officer's coat. "Conrad had a bad heart. He'd had it for years. He had digitalis which he took for these attacks, and we'll probably find some. But not a fatal amount and . . ."

Maud interrupted, "But that was the point! What about the medicine? Where is it? If it was removed—if he removed it himself, that is—he died from the lack of it. It's as I—as I was saying when the police arrived."

Well, it wasn't quite what she was saying. She was saying that if it had been intentionally removed, that was tantamount to murder.

"What's this about digitalis?" demanded the Lieutenant, falling upon it like a dog upon a bone and Claud Chivery, helplessly, explained. The medicine had been kept in the top drawer of the desk; it wasn't about the body of Conrad Brent, and he might have died for lack of it.

But that didn't prove that anyone had removed it with that result in mind. The Lieutenant didn't say that, he only asked if anyone had removed it or knew of Conrad Brent himself removing it.

"It was in the drawer just after dinner tonight," said Alexia suddenly. "I saw it."

"Did you give it to Mr. Brent?" asked the Lieutenant.

"No. He was not ill then; he didn't want it. We were having coffee here. He wanted a clipping, something about the war that he'd cut from the papers. It was in that drawer and I got it for him; and I saw the medicine, then."

"I remember," said Peter Huber. "He read it to us."

Maud's black eyebrows were pinched together. "I remember, too," she said. "It was about the arrest of some enemy aliens, some former Bund members."

"It doesn't matter," said Alexia. "But I saw the medicine then. It was in that drawer."

No one had seen it since, however, or if so did not admit it. I got to thinking of the autopsy and wondering if whatever Drue had given him (some kind of stimulant certainly) by way of the hypodermic would show up in the blood stream.

While I knew something of autopsies, I didn't know enough, and I stopped thinking along that line when the Lieutenant abruptly and very definitely told us we could go. "Get some rest if you can," he said. "The things we have to do will take time. I'll have to question you later."

I started quickly toward the door. I had to see Drue as soon as I possibly could. But Nicky got there first and then turned back toward Alexia. "Come, darling," he said in a voice of sudden sympathy, which reminded everyone that Alexia was a recently—indeed, a very recently—bereaved widow. Even Alexia looked a little startled and then instantly drooped against the arm he put around her. "If they insist upon this investigation, we'll have to make the best of it."

Alexia looked at the still figure on the couch. I thought she was going to approach it, to say a kind of farewell perhaps, but she didn't. Her shadowing lashes fell softly over her eyes and she turned toward the door, leaning on Nicky's arm. She said softly, musically, "I am stunned, I think—the shock. Yes, I'll go now. Nicky . . ." She leaned on his arm as far as the stairway, for I watched them go. I would have followed instantly, quickly, eager to get to Drue, but the Lieutenant stopped me.

"You were here when he died, Nurse?"

"He was dead when I reached him." Maud was leaving too, and Peter Huber, looking uncertain of his status in that house of death and tragedy—a stranger plunged into a dreadful intimacy—followed her. Anna had disappeared, I didn't know when. There were left only the police, the Lieutenant, Dr. Chivery and me in that room. And Conrad Brent.

"Wait a minute, please, Nurse," said the Lieutenant sharply as I made another move toward the door. "I want to talk to you. Did you telephone for the police?"

He had asked that before; presumably he was asking it again because, the family being now out of earshot, I might be willing to admit suspicion and the reason for it.

"Certainly not," I said. "If I had, I'd have told you so. This is nothing to me, any of it. I'm a nurse here. I arrived today—that is, yesterday afternoon. I . . ."

"Yes, I know," he said. "You and Miss Drue Cable, who was formerly married to Craig Brent."

I caught my breath so hard that I nearly choked myself trying to conceal it. "Yes. Some time ago. That has naturally nothing to do with . . ."

"They were divorced last year. You were the first to find Mr. Brent, is that right?"

Dr. Chivery passed his hand over his forehead and thin hair and I said cautiously, "It's as I told you. He was dead when I reached him."

"Yes, I know," said the Lieutenant. "But how did you happen to find him? You were upstairs in your patient's room, weren't you?"

I had seen it coming but was still unprepared and it put me on what I believe is called the spot. If Peter Huber hadn't seen Drue with me, leaning over Conrad Brent—but he had. I said very carefully, "I thought I heard a kind of call of help. Miss Cable must have heard something, too. But we could do nothing for him. Then—then Peter Huber came running down the stairs, too. He had heard the same thing, I imagine. I sent him to telephone for the doctor . . ."

"Why?"

"For the death certificate, naturally. Miss Cable went back upstairs to our patient" (I was rather pleased with the implication of that) "and I stayed here. But there was nothing I could do. And then all at once there was a loud noise." Suddenly, I remembered that no one had inquired about that, yet almost certainly it was the thing that had roused Maud and Nicky and Alexia.

"Noise? What was it?"

"I don't know. It sounded as if the house was coming down." I was anxiously making a clean breast of everything I could and hoping desperately to divert his inquiry from Drue. "Peter Huber ran upstairs to see what it was. I ran after him, but when I got upstairs he had disappeared and

I was afraid that—that something had happened to my patient . . ."

"Something had happened to him? What do you mean?"

"N-nothing. Naturally he was on my mind. And I was right, because when I got to his room he wasn't there. Miss Cable had found him, though; he had apparently got up and put on a dressing gown and started downstairs and fallen. We got him back to bed."

"Where was he when you found him?"

I told him briefly.

"But I thought he was drugged."

"He was," said Dr. Chivery suddenly. "He is. But nothing is so variable as a drug plus a bit of temperature with a man like Craig. He probably got some fuzzy notion of something going on and fainted on the way downstairs."

The Lieutenant (Nugent his name was, I learned later; just Nugent; if he had a Christian name he kept it a secret) looked at Claud Chivery. "He had had a quarrel with his father, hadn't he, Doctor?"

Dr. Chivery looked up quickly and uneasily; he looked terribly tired, his eyes swollen and the nervous lines deep and gray in his troubled face with its receding chin. "Why—why, no," he said. "That is, in the past perhaps, yes. But not . . ."

"You'd better know, Dr. Chivery, just where we stand," said Nugent, suddenly. "You—and everyone here told me a story about that shooting business the other night that frankly, Doctor, was phony."

"Lieutenant Nugent . . ." began Claud Chivery, rising indignantly.

"Well, it seemed so to me. But, as things were, my hands were tied. If Craig Brent died I intended to start an investigation into murder . . ."

"Murder . . ." said Dr. Chivery in a high protesting voice, his little hands tremulous.

". . . if he didn't die I intended to insist upon his preferring charges. But yesterday, while he was so heavily drugged as to be entirely unconscious, there was nothing I could do. I couldn't even question him. Now, you see, I'm going to."

"But—but it wasn't Craig that died. It's Conrad. . . ."

"Exactly," said Lieutenant Nugent, cutting off Chivery's fluttering expostulation. "Could Craig Brent have walked down here to the library, poisoned his father and walked back upstairs and collapsed there in the storeroom . . ."

"Linen room," I said.

". . . where he was found?"

*"Poisoned!"* cried Chivery shrilly, his uneasy face turning gray. "That's horrible! I tell you Conrad died a perfectly natural death. I'll do an autopsy. And your medical examiner can help me. But mark my words we'll find he died of a heart attack—and anyway . . ." his nervous eyes darted about the library, toward the desk, toward the sofa, anywhere but at the Lieutenant. "Anyway, Craig shot himself! Accidentally. Why—even you cannot believe that there are two murderers here in this house . . ."

"Unless Craig shot himself for that very reason," said Lieutenant Nugent watching Chivery's frightened, uneasy face.

"Shot himself—oh, I see! To make it look as if somebody else tried to kill him and then succeeded in killing his father? To establish a kind of alibi before the deed? Why, that's preposterous, Lieutenant! That's absurd! Ha, ha, ha," again it was meant to be a laugh and sounded like anything else in the world.

And I said, "But he does have an alibi. Craig, I mean. I am it." Both men looked at me. "I was in the room. I would have known if he had moved. He didn't."

There was a moment of silence. Chivery hadn't looked quite at me, just at my left ear. Nugent jerked his head toward one of the two waiting—and intently listening—policemen. "Telephone Dr. Marrow," he said. "Get him over here at once." One of the troopers vanished.

Claud Chivery said slowly, "Conrad must have just got back from his walk. He went for a walk every night. About eleven. Said it made him sleep. Walked very slowly . . ."

Nugent said abruptly, "That's all now, Nurse." He was bending over Conrad again when I left—trying not to run.

No one was in the hall. Claud Chivery, I think, closed the door behind me. At the stair landing I stopped, looked quickly around, saw no one and plunged my hand under the ferns. The syringe was not there.

I looked and looked and still it wasn't there. The only possible conclusion was that someone had seen me hide it and had taken it away.

There's no use in trying to describe my feelings. Naturally, it wasn't myself I cared about; it was Drue, whom I had delivered into the hands of her enemies—if, that is, Alexia or Nicky had taken the syringe. Or even Maud; there was a look

61

in her dark eyes that suggested depths and no way to tell what kind of depths—true or false, as the radio programs put it.

All three of them—Alexia, Nicky and Maud—had passed that fern on their way upstairs; Peter Huber also could have taken it. Or Beevens, presupposing eyes in the back of his head, for he certainly had not turned while I hid it.

The library door was visible from the landing, and it had been open when I came downstairs; but I had seen no one, for I had looked.

Eventually, hearing steps coming from the end of the hall beyond the stairs (where there proved to be a tiny telephone room, and a hall going to the back stairs and kitchen regions) and guessing correctly that it was a trooper, I had to give up. I trudged up the remaining stairs with a heavy and a troubled heart. Murder is no pleasant thing, and I kept seeing Drue's face—so young and so lovely, with the childish, honest curve of her young mouth, and the look in her eyes when she'd lifted them to mine and said, "I've only tonight."

And I had to tell her what I had done.

She was sitting by the bed when I entered Craig's room; her eyes leaped to mine. Craig was unconscious, asleep, I thought; his pulse was all right; the wound hadn't opened and she had sterilized and dressed the bloody bruise on his temple so a neat patch of surgical dressing and adhesive adorned it. I beckoned Drue into the dressing room and told her everything, except that the syringe was gone—quickly whispering, hating to see the color drain out of her lips when I told her the police were there.

Her hands went out to grip mine, hard.

"Sarah, do they know I . . ."

"No. I hid the hypodermic. I didn't tell them that you were there before me. I—oh, my dear child, don't look like that. You didn't mean it . . ."

"I gave him digitalis. Sarah, I had to. He was sick. His medicine was gone. I thought he was dying. I hurried to my room and I had some digitalis. I had it left over from old Mrs. Jamieson—remember, we nursed her together . . ."

I nodded. A nurse either destroys or hoards for an emergency drugs that are left over from a case and I had nursed old Mrs. Jamieson with her. Every nurse, I imagine (at least I always had done so) accumulates slowly a kind of first-aid, emergency kit of her own. I had then in my bag enough sedatives to bring upon me the highly unfavorable attention of any policeman who happened to discover it.

"So you gave it to him?"

"Yes." There was horror in her eyes. "You see, I'd been talking to him. Then he . . . I saw he was really sick. He said to get his medicine; he gasped horribly. He told me where it was, but I remembered. He's always kept it there in the right-hand drawer of his desk. But I looked and it wasn't there so I . . ."

"You opened the drawer?"

"Yes, of course." (I thought, then, of fingerprints; yet Drue's fingerprints on the drawer couldn't be made to prove anything. Or could they?) She went on quickly: "But there was no box of pills. Then he begged me for something; said even if I hated him I'd have to help him, and I—I got my syringe from the bag in my room. I sterilized it quickly with alcohol and prepared the hypodermic and hurried back to the library. He rolled up his sleeve himself and told me to hurry. So I did. I gave him what I thought was the right amount . . ."

"How much?"

She told me. I nodded. Conrad hadn't taken any of the pills he had ready for emergency during the few moments that he was alone while Drue was preparing the hypodermic. That was obvious, for if he had done so he wouldn't have permitted her to give him the additional medicine. "Go on," I said.

"That's all, Sarah. He . . ." She took her hands from my wrists and put them to her throat. "He died. Then. Just—just died and I couldn't stop it."

She was shivering; I took her hands again and held them tightly. And thought hard.

"You're not to tell about the hypodermic. Not tell anyone. Lie if you have to."

Her hands clung to mine. Her eyes, dark with horror, searched my face. "They'll say I murdered him," she whispered. "Is that what you're afraid of?"

I had to tell her, then. "Listen, Drue. I lost the syringe. That is, I didn't lose it. I hid it and someone found it and took it away."

There was a little sharp silence. In the next room Craig slept heavily. Outside, rain and sleet whispered against the windows. Drue whispered stiffly, *"Who . . . ?"*

"I don't know. I hid it in the fern; I guessed what you had done; I didn't want them to know. It's gone now, so someone must have seen me hide it. I don't know who. But it's gone, and your fingerprints are on it. They can easily prove it was yours; there will be traces of digitalis in it."

# VIII

After a long moment she said with a kind of incredulous horror, "He wasn't murdered, Sarah! I saw him die. If I killed him, it was some terrible, unforgivable mistake on my part, but I didn't murder him. I didn't . . ."

"You didn't kill him. Listen, Drue; you can't tell them what you did. You *must* not. I've seen something of police investigation; circumstantial evidence has hanged many a man. No, no, I didn't mean to say that! I only meant you must promise me not to tell. Not yet. Not until—well, until we see what's going to happen."

"But if I'm wrong, if it *should* be murder I've got to tell them, don't you see? If the police are right, if he was murdered, they ought to know what I gave him and how much." She stopped, caught her breath and said again, fighting it, "But he *couldn't* have been murdered!"

"No. Yet who called the police then and why? Who shot Craig? And why? What did Craig mean when he said there would be murder done?"

"But he didn't mean—he couldn't have meant—*this!*" She stared at me with a kind of terror for a moment, then shook her head. "No. I'd better tell them exactly what I did."

It frightened me, but more than anything it exasperated me. "All right," I snapped. "Go ahead and tell them you murdered him! That's exactly what it will amount to. Or shall I tell them? Craig may come to see you in jail but I doubt it."

"Sarah . . ."

"There's a time for nobility, Drue Cable, but this isn't the time. However, if you're bent on making a martyr of yourself I won't stop you. Heaven knows it's nothing to me. You make me come here; I didn't know I was walking into anything like this. I hate shooting and I hate murder and I hate the police. I'm going home. Unless they stop me. You can do exactly as you please. Just go ahead and tell them you killed him and I don't care, for I won't be here."

"Sarah . . ." She caught my arms. "Sarah, I'm not that kind of fool."

"Oh, yes, you are. I can see it. . . ."

"No. No." Her hands dropped away from my arms. She stared down at the dressing table with its rosy little lamp and crystal bottles. "I won't tell them. I cannot believe that he was murdered. I saw him. Yet if—oh, you're right, of course."

"Certainly, I'm right." I paused thoughtfully. There was only one thing we could do and it had its dangers. Yet they had already mentioned digitalis; and it was a piece of material evidence really leading to Drue.

"Did you use all the supply of digitalis you had, Drue?"

"No. Only enough . . ."

"We ought to get rid of the rest of it."

"But Sarah, when—if I eventually tell them about it, as I may have to do . . ."

"I know. It might look guilty. But I think it's better to get rid of the rest of the digitalis now in the hope it needn't ever come out—about the hypodermic, I mean. Some blundering fool" (which was exactly the opposite of what I meant) "of a policeman might get his hands on the digitalis; Chivery may see the hypodermic mark. No, no, Drue, it's better to dispose of the rest of the digitalis now. I'll do it . . ."

"No," she said quickly and sharply and then caught herself as quickly. "I'd better do it myself," she said. "I know exactly where it is. I'll go. Now."

So she went, leaving me oddly perplexed by the look of sudden and sharp anxiety in her face. It was as if she had remembered something she didn't want me to know about— which was nonsense, of coure. What could there be in her room, in the little nursing bag, anywhere in the house, which she wanted to keep a secret? When presently she came back, slipping quietly into the room while I was sitting beside Craig, I had decided it was nothing.

"Did you get it?" I whispered.

Her face looked very white and her breath was coming quickly; her hand was in her pocket. She shook her head. "They were already there. They . . . Sarah—they've got your little black bag—you know; and mine. I saw a policeman go downstairs with them. Oh, Sarah . . ."

We stared at each other across Craig's bed, and rain whispered against the windows. Finally, I said—I had to say, "Never mind. It doesn't prove anything. Don't worry."

After that there was really nothing we could do. We didn't even talk much. The rain beat and murmured against the windows and all we could do was wait.

Digitalis. And they had thought of us, nurses, and had taken the little instrument and medicine bags to search even before they could possibly have got results from the autopsy. I didn't like that, but I didn't tell Drue (although she knew it, naturally), and Craig slept and the rain beat down and there was no way of knowing what the police were doing. What Alexia was doing and Nicky, or Maud. Waiting, too, I imagined, as we were waiting.

I couldn't then, even, try to discover the syringe. If the person who had found it in the fern (who must have seen me place it there) had taken it to the police then we were already lost. But if not there might be some chance.

If it was murder, then who? Who had shot Craig? Who had killed his father?

I had ensconced myself on the couch in front of the fire by that time, feeling that since we could accomplish nothing by further talk, Drue and I, I might as well try to get some sleep. I remember their names kept going around and around in my head like a nightmarish kind of merry-go-round— Alexia, Nicky, Maud, Peter Huber, Dr. Chivery (for he was not in the house, but he was fairly near presumably, and could have returned somehow without anyone's knowledge), Beevens, Anna—the other servants.

Just as I was about to catch the tail of a nap I began to think again of the telephone call to the police. Who had called them? And more important—tremendously important— *why?* In that answer, I thought suddenly, with that queerly elusive clarity one discovers on the edge of sleep, might lie the answer to the whole ugly problem.

After that I was wide awake for what was left of the night. Craig slept heavily and seemed none the worse for his mysterious peregrinations; Drue sat in an armchair near the bed with her starched cap off and her hair a little rumpled from pressing her head back against the cushions of the chair—her face pale, her eyes very dark, watching Craig's sleeping face broodingly. It rained all that night, rain and sleet and rain again. We could hear nothing of what was going on in the house. Twice I got up and tiptoed into the hall, once going down the stairs, pausing again at the fern. But the syringe was really gone.

The hall below was deserted, but Nicky Senour and Peter Huber were sitting in the morning room in front of the fire, smoking. There were state troopers in the library; I went down into the hall and as far as the library door. No one stopped me and I wanted to see what they were doing. I was little wiser for my pains but convinced, if I had not been before, that they were in earnest about an investigation. For they had been taking fingerprints from smooth surfaces in the room; they had been using a tiny hand vacuum on furniture and rugs; the decanter of brandy had been removed; there were chalked crosses on the sofa and on the rug indicating, I thought, the position of Conrad Brent's body. Pictures had been taken, then. But the body of Conrad Brent had been removed.

Two troopers were still there, one of them writing shorthand notes rapidly in a little tablet; the other blowing a small cloud of yellowish powder from a contrivance that looked like a tiny bellows upon one of the wooden panels across the room on the right side of the fireplace—a panel that I saw then, was actually a swinging door leading into a tiny washroom, for I could see walls tiled in shining, pale green beyond. He turned to look at me and the trooper with the tablet stopped writing to look at me, too, and there being, to say the least, no welcome in either look but rather the contrary, I retreated; anyway I had seen all I wanted to see. Nicky looked up as I passed through the hall but did not stop me. Peter however came out.

"Have you told Craig?" he asked me.

"No."

"Better not for a while."

"What was that noise, Mr. Huber? You remember—while you were calling the doctor. Did you find out about it?"

He frowned; his face looked tired and worried. "I didn't find anybody," he said. "I guess I'm not much of a detective. From the sound I thought a window had been broken somewhere, but I was wrong. I looked all along the hall leading toward the back of the house. But I found just nothing to account for it."

"Could there have been some—some intruder? A thief, perhaps?"

Peter Huber shrugged. "I don't know. I'll tell the police about it. I take it Craig is all right?"

"Oh, yes."

"They took him away—Conrad Brent, I mean. I suppose they are doing an autopsy now."

Nicky watched, bright eyes intensely curious, as I took my way upstairs again. That must have been about four or five o'clock—a cold, still, gusty February dawn. By six o'clock Craig hadn't wakened. At about seven Beevens, clothed in his right mind as well as trousers and dark sack coat, brought Drue and me some coffee and toast. Breakfast would be along soon, he said; in the meantime he thought we might enjoy the coffee. He spoke to me and looked at Drue with a kind of sympathy and kindliness; naturally all the servants knew of her position in that household. Perhaps the romance of it appealed to them, but I think they liked her, too.

Beevens could tell us nothing, though, of what the police were doing and, looking very haggard himself with great puffs under his eyes, went away. After we drank the coffee and Drue nibbled at some toast because I made her, I sent her to her room. Sometime that day she would have to face the police and she'd had no sleep at all that night. So I made her rest; and thus I was alone with Craig when he awoke.

He awoke rather suddenly; in full possession of his senses. He looked white and tired, but his pulse was good. He had no temperature and the wound in his shoulder, while stiff and sore, seemed to be healing with normal rapidity.

He said almost at once, "Where is Drue?"

"In her room, resting."

He looked at me, frowning a little. He was very sober, and there was a kind of authority about him. All at once I seemed to see a very faint likeness to his father—his nose, perhaps, and brown, decided chin. His eyes, however, were darker and had spirit and luminousness. His father's eyes had been very cold and chill. He said, "You're the other nurse. Yes, I remember you."

"I'm Sarah Keate. I'll ring for some breakfast. I think you can manage something light. . . ."

He interrupted me. "Listen, Nurse, something happened last night—something—I can't remember. . . ."

I did not hesitate. "Nothing happened, except that you got out of bed once when I was out of the room and got a bump . . ."

He put his hand to his bandaged temple. "Why, yes," he said. "I remember that! But something had happened down-

68

stairs. Somebody screamed. You left and I—I got up to see what it was. I put on slippers and a robe and . . ." he stopped. There was a sudden and clear recollection in his eyes.

I said, "And you fell . . ." and he said, shaking his head, "No. Somebody hit me."

"*Somebody* . . ." I stopped with a kind of gulp.

He gave me a look of annoyance. "Don't gargle," he said briefly.

"B-but you said . . ."

"Certainly I said somebody hit me. Somebody did. I was just at the top of the stairs. I heard someone behind me and I turned and that's all. Just as I turned it hit and I went out like a light. I remember that."

Suddenly and completely I believed him. His look and his voice were perfectly clear and rational. I said, after a moment, "*Who?*"

"I don't know. I tell you that's all I remember except later —a long time later—Drue was here." His voice when he said her name changed subtly, so it was grave and yet somehow warm and tender, as if it spoke a loved name. But he had left her and had let her shift for herself, without ever a word from him. A nurse's life is not an easy one. I hardened my heart against him.

All at once he caught my wrist in a quick, impatient grip. "But what happened? Who screamed?"

So I told him. I would have evaded but I couldn't. I knew an attempt would only make a bad matter worse and excite him unnecessarily. I did it as gently and as kindly as I could, and I reminded him that his father had had a bad heart condition apparently for years. I also said it had been quick.

I didn't mention the police or Drue or the digitalis.

When I had told him I went to the window and stood there, my back to the room, looking out at the gray daylight. After a long time he called me.

"Yes?"

"Thanks . . ."

"It—it wasn't unexpected," I said again. "And it was mercifully quick."

"Yes; yes—I'll see the doctor when he comes, Nurse."

"Certainly." He hadn't asked again about Drue's scream, and I was thankful for it. He let me wash his face and ring to order breakfast. Anna answered the bell. "I'm sorry, Mr. Craig," she said, her eyes filling with tears.

"I—yes, Anna. Don't cry." He patted her hand a little, kindly, and she went quickly away. Almost at once Alexia came.

I was straightening the bed and thought it was Anna. Alexia was in the room before I realized it was not. She had dressed and wore a sleek black dress with white lace at her throat and small wrists. She came quickly to the bed and knelt there.

"Craig, they've told you . . ."

He looked at her for a moment without replying. There was a queer look on his face—a kind of grimness all at once that, again, made me think of his father yet was totally unlike, too, for it held sensibility, or concealed it, where his father's look was only obstinate and a little cruel.

Alexia put one arm across him so her hand on the bed supported her and leaned very close to him. Her mouth was lightly lipsticked that morning and looked very tender and tremulous in spite of that full, cruel underlip; her misty, short, dark hair was a soft frame for her creamy, small face with its delicate features. She said, "I'm sorry, Craig. He was your father."

Craig's eyes narrowed. "He was your husband, Alexia."

Her face didn't change, unless her eyelids lowered a little; but I could see the curving lines of her body stiffen slightly. She said rather slowly, very musically, looking into Craig's eyes, "I never needed to be reminded of that. You know that, Craig, better than anyone."

There was a short silence. I prepared to remove the top blanket and thus oust Alexia, but as I moved to do so she said, "It's horrible—the police and all, I mean! They found the revolver in Drue's room."

"*Drue! What do you mean? What about the police? What revolver?*"

"Really, Mrs. Brent, I'll have to ask you to leave! My patient isn't . . ." I was hurrying forward, my starchy uniform rattling.

Alexia silenced both of us. "Don't try to think, my darling," she said, putting her face against Craig's. "Oh, Craig, you knew—you always knew I never loved Conrad. And now all that is ended for us both, my darling."

Over her shoulder Craig's eyes plunged into mine. "For God's sake, what does she mean? What revolver?" he cried urgently.

# IX

Well, I couldn't have told him even if I'd known, I was so livid and gibbering with rage. I put my hand on Alexia's shoulder and may have taken a tighter grip even than I intended, for she wrenched herself away from me with a rather startled look and got quickly to her feet, clasping her shoulder with her other hand. "Nurse, you forget yourself! How dare you touch . . ."

"What revolver, Alexia?" demanded Craig again. *"What revolver?"*

Her eyes had retreated behind those soft, satiny eyelids. She said breathlessly, "Conrad's revolver. It was in Drue's room. The police found it."

Craig was as white as the pillow, and I intended to put Alexia out of the room by sheer physical force if nothing else sufficed. He said, "But he wasn't shot!"

"No! He wasn't shot," I said quickly. "He died of a heart attack, just as I told you. Now then, Mrs. Brent . . ."

"But the police," said Craig. "Why are they here?"

"Someone called them." Alexia answered him. "No one knows who. But someone got on the telephone just after Conrad died and told the police your father had been murdered. So they came, and they are going to investigate his death. . . ."

*"Murder!"* said Craig. *"But that's impossible!"* He made a motion to get up, winced as he moved his shoulder and turned even whiter. Peter Huber knocked, entered quickly, stopped as quickly as he seemed to sense something electric in the atmosphere and then said, "It's only—well, they want you downstairs, Alexia. Right away. They are waiting. You too, Nurse Keate." His eyes went past us to Craig, and he said, "You've told him?"

Behind him on the threshold Anna appeared with the tray. "I'm not going," I said. "I'm on duty."

"Is it the police, Peter?" asked Craig.

Peter Huber nodded. "Craig, I'm sorry about your father. . . ."

Craig closed his eyes as if to shut out talk of that. "Yes, Pete," he said. There was a little silence while Anna went to the bed with the tray and I followed her. Craig looked up

71

at me. "Go on down," he said. "Anna will stay with me. Don't you see, I've got to know. . . ."

"I'll tell you, Craig. I'll tell you everything the police do." Alexia started toward the bed, stopped as I straightened up rather abruptly from adjusting the pillows and looked hard at her, said softly to Craig, "Don't think, darling. Don't try to think now. I'll be back," and went out the door. Peter came to the bed and Craig said again to me, "Please go downstairs, Miss Keate. I want you to tell me everything they do. . . ."

So in the end I went; not because of the police, but merely to keep Craig's temperature down. Anna stayed with him and Peter Huber, too, for a while, although they sent for him also before that morning's long inquiry was over.

It lasted nearly three hours. Three hours of steady questions and answers—statements, repetitions, explanations, and probably a few lies, spoken or implied. But there was no way of identifying those.

It was already under way when I entered the little morning room, with its ivory woodwork, green and rose chintz, and blazing wood fire.

Everyone except Craig, and for the moment, Peter, was there: Lieutenant Nugent and two troopers, very lean, and silent as their chief; a man in gray, fat and rosy-cheeked with winking eyeglasses who proved to be the District Attorney (so I knew, then, that they were sure it was murder); Nicky; and Alexia who was, subtly, a broken reed. Their two faces were so much alike, so secretive, so delicate and beautiful that it was as if one was the mirror of the other; as if some deep affinity joined their very thoughts. Which, as a matter of fact, was very far from the truth.

Maud was there, too, little and indomitable in sweeping black with her pompadour rising high above her narrow, sallow, little forehead, her collar of boned white net lifting her little dark chin in the air, and her eyes brooding and angry, watching the police, watching Nicky and Alexia—watching even me, fixedly. I don't think a move or a look or a quickened pulse escaped her eager, antlike eyes. Claud Chivery wasn't there.

Then I saw Drue; she was sitting in a tall armchair, her hands around the arm of it, her white cap like a crown upon her shining hair. She was very pale; her dark gray eyes had a kind of terrified stillness. I thought she tried to communicate with me, mutely, with her look, and I tried, mutely, to remind her of danger, and in the same fractional glance that I was on her side. So it was a rather complicated glance, I daresay; certainly it didn't seem to accomplish anything in the way of improving the situation.

Then I felt that somebody was watching us and turned. It was Lieutenant Nugent, his eyes narrow and thoughtful, more green than gray—which was, as a matter of fact, a bad sign. All through that interview he was as laconic as ever and when he was forced to say more than a few words did so with an air of positively grudging distaste and terseness.

He said then, "Sit down, please, Nurse Keate. The District Attorney, Mr. Soper, wants to question you."

I sat down, and that long bout of questioning began for me. It began badly and ended badly.

The first thing Soper said was a flat, bald statement to the effect that they had found enough digitalis in Conrad Brent's blood stream to kill him, and they believed it was murder.

From there they went on to that inevitable conclusion.

They did it slowly, detail by detail, taking so much time at bypaths and crossroads, so to speak, that it wasn't till the very end that I could look back and see that Soper, at any rate, had planned and charted his whole road to arrive at exactly that destination. As I have said, it took a long time; they questioned me and I told them again exactly what I had already told Lieutenant Nugent, no more and no less. They questioned Maud and Nicky and Alexia; they sent for and questioned Peter Huber; they questioned everybody. Gradually the story built itself up—much of it by confirmation, for it was obvious that they had already done considerable, less public, questioning.

Conrad Brent had spent the previous day about as other days were spent, except for his anxiety about his son, two or three morning visits to Craig's room (before Drue and I arrived) and a talk with Dr. Chivery. This (according to Maud) was entirely about Craig's condition. The Lieutenant already knew that Conrad had had an interview in his study with me and then with Drue after our arrival. I was questioned again about that almost immediately. It was about his son, I told them firmly, and that was all. There was a speculative look in Nicky's eyes as he turned to look at me then, and Maud said abruptly, "That isn't all, Lieutenant. Don't forget that Conrad was furious because Drue Cable came here, and told her she had to leave. She was to go this morning. She . . ."

73

"Yes, you told me that," said Nugent. Drue's lips parted a little and she leaned forward as if to speak, but Nugent did not permit her to do so. "Now, then," he said briskly, "there were no callers yesterday except Dr. Chivery and myself. What about dinner?"

I couldn't tell whether or not they had yet questioned Drue. It seemed logical that they had, but somehow I thought they had not and it seemed wrong—an ominous omission.

They were replying, one and then another. The whole inquiry began to seem more and more like a formal assembling of already established facts. Except for the impression I continued to have to the effect that Drue herself had not been questioned directly and alone. Consequently, it began to look more and more as if the already established facts had been established, so to speak, around her. When they did question her they would have a solid framework of evidence on which to base their inquiry.

I listened anxiously.

Dinner had been at the usual hour, they were saying; Nicky, Peter, Alexia, and Maud and of course Conrad had been at dinner. Drue was there, too, said Maud, but the other nurse (her eager black eyes went to me) was on duty so a tray was sent up to her. But nothing happened at dinner; no one talked much; all of them ate the same food. So he couldn't have been poisoned then.

"Digitalis," said Nugent, "has a very rapid effect. Almost instantaneous." And went on. The evening had been passed, again, much as usual. They had played bridge, Conrad, Maud, Alexia and Peter—Nicky had read and watched. During the game there had been the usual talk of current news, the war, affairs at home; sometime during the game (no one remembered the time) Conrad had sent Alexia to get the clipping; the box of medicine had been in the desk drawer then. All efforts to discover more exactly when it had disappeared were without result.

~At about eleven they had stopped playing. Conrad had gone for his walk, the others had gone to bed. Dr. Chivery had stopped shortly after eleven (Maud told this, too; she was altogether more eagerly informative than anyone else); he had gone to the room she always occupied when she stayed as she so often did at the Brent house, but he had not remained for long. He had walked to the Chivery cottage.

"There's a path, a short-cut," said Maud, and Nugent nodded.

"He said he didn't see Brent?" said Soper to Nugent who nodded again. So I knew they had already questioned Dr. Chivery.

Usually Conrad returned from his walk in about forty-five minutes; he walked very slowly, so probably he had not taken a really long walk. His coat, stick, and hat were in their usual place in the closet off the hall. His dinner-jacket hung there, too, and he had put on a lounge coat and, apparently, gone directly into the library.

"He liked to rest a little before going upstairs," said Beevens. "He had a nightcap or smoked a cigarette or two as a rule and then went to bed. He never wanted me to wait up for him; he locked the front door himself."

Nightcap. Brandy? Well, they had taken away the decanter; they would know if there was poison in it.

Nicky then created a small sensation by saying abruptly that he had seen Conrad return. "I was here in this room," he said easily. "I saw Conrad come in, lock the door, remove his coat and hat and put on his lounge coat."

"*Nicky!*" cried Alexia twisting around to look up at him.

Soper said, "But look here, Mr. Senour, why didn't you tell us?"

"I didn't think it was important," said Nicky silkily. "That's all there is to it, you see. He didn't see me. I was sitting over there by the fire, reading. He went into the library and after a while I went upstairs. That's all."

Drue was looking at him steadily. I don't know how I knew that she was holding her breath, perhaps because I was.

"Are you sure that's all?" said Nugent. "Did anyone—you, for instance,—go into the library?" There was a silence. Nicky smiled and examined the fingernails on one slender hand. "That's all," he said with a kind of silky stubbornness. Soper said, "Well, well; let's get on," and began to question about motives and about possible enemies. Nugent looked thoughtfully at Nicky. Soper did the questioning, his little eyes suspicious, except when they rested upon Alexia, of whom he obviously approved and who did look, I must say, very lovely and helpless, except when she lifted her shadowy eyelashes and one caught a glimpse of the very cool and self-possessed look in her eyes. Nicky leaned against the back of her chair in an ostentatiously protecting way, still with the shadow of a smile on his lips, and Alexia sat perfectly still for the most part, answering only when she had to and that briefly, one leg crossed over the other and the toe of her pump making impatient little circles.

After a while they sent for Peter Huber, who came into the room and sat down not far from me. He had told Craig, I imagined, as much as could be told. He sighed a little, unconsciously, as he sat down and then lighted a cigarette and listened. As we all listened.

Presently they questioned him—or rather recapitulated some earlier bout of questioning. When he came downstairs he had found both nurses in the library, was that right? Yes, that was right; he nodded. Why had he come downstairs at all?

"I told you that," he said. "I'd dropped off to sleep, reading. I hadn't put up the windows or turned off the light and, when I awoke, the room was too warm. I put up the windows and turned off the light and then I opened the door to the hall, thinking I'd get air into the room more quickly that way."

As he did it he heard a kind of scream from somewhere downstairs. He'd listened for a moment and as he was closing the door again I had run along the corridor and down the stairs. So he thought something was wrong, went back to get a dressing gown and slippers and had come down after me.

"Mr. Huber," said the District Attorney, "I want you to think back carefully; this is very important. When you came into the room, were the nurses—either or both of them—doing anything for Mr. Brent? I mean, definitely, did either of them have a hypodermic syringe in her hand? Think back. . . ."

My heart came up in my throat. I didn't dare look at Drue.

Then Peter said, positively, "No."

"Are you sure?"

"Absolutely. They were just standing there. We looked at him but he was dead. So Miss Keate sent Miss Cable back upstairs to Craig and me to telephone. I didn't succeed in getting the doctor then. I couldn't find the number; I was upset. Anyway, all at once there was this sound of something falling. . . ."

"Yes, yes, you told us about that," said the District Attorney testily. "Something falling and the sound of a window breaking and we can't find anything that fell and there is no window broken." He turned to me. "Miss Keate, was there anything else? Anything that happened last night before the death of Mr. Brent that struck you as being—well, out of the way? Unusual."

From the way he said it, I had a quick impression that he had asked everyone that. Maud looked rather scornful, and Alexia all but yawned. It was one of fate's dangerous little jokes that I would have answered in the negative (as I imagine everyone else had done) had not Delphine at that point slunk across the hall, with a wary green eye toward the trooper in the doorway. The fleeting glimpse I had of him reminded me of a very trivial thing I had forgotten up to then. "Why, yes," I said. "As a matter of fact there was something."

Alexia stopped yawning so suddenly her jaws snapped together and Maud's scorn changed to alert interest. I went on, "There was a kind of bump against the closed door to my patient's room."

"Bump!" said the District Attorney.

"Yes. Something in the hall struck against the door."

"*Something!* What?" cried the District Attorney. He looked a little astonished at having, so to speak, got a bite. "Well—well, go on," he said impatiently as I hesitated. "What was it? Didn't you go to the door and open it and look?"

"Yes. Yes, I did open the door and I saw . . ." I stopped again on the verge of saying I had seen Nicky coming from a room down the hall. But that was wrong. I had seen Nicky, but that was before something—whatever it was—had struck against the door, and struck so sharply it roused me and the cat. No; that was wrong, too; the cat had already aroused, as if he heard someone in the hall. The bump against the door had come later. And when I had got to the door and opened it no one was in the hall.

The District Attorney said, "Well, who did you see? Who did you see?"

Nugent was very still and very observant—as, I suddenly realized, everyone in the room was watching, too, and listening. There was indeed a strained and queer silence. I said slowly, confused not so much by the silence as by the singularly intent quality in it, "I didn't see anyone. I don't know who it was. I saw nothing."

"*But you . . .*" began Soper explosively, and Nugent said, "All right, Miss Keate. We believe you." His eyes looked very narrow and green. He went on quickly, "You were in the library when you heard the sound of something falling. What did you do?"

"I ran upstairs." I told him of it again, briefly. And brought forward what seemed to be, up to then, a bit of new evidence, or at least a new fact. That was the matter of Craig's being found in the linen closet, unconscious and bleeding from a bruise on his temple.

"He says somebody was in the hall and struck him," I explained.

The District Attorney interrupted. "Who?"

"He said he doesn't know. But if someone did that it proves there was an intruder, a—a thief . . . ."

"But he said he was in the hall when he was struck," said Soper, looking a little impressed with his own astuteness, and very pompous. "You say you found him in the linen room."

"I did. Or rather Miss Cable found him there first." Again glances went to Drue; again no one questioned her. "Someone must have dragged him into the linen closet and left him there. A man, I mean."

"A woman could have done it," began Soper, and Nugent cut in rather quickly. "I'll question Craig Brent later," he said, his eyes still very green and thoughtful, however. Soper, brought up short, frowned, tapped his stomach and began again briskly. "Now then, about Conrad Brent's business affairs . . ."

That did not take a very long time; everyone I think was convinced that Conrad's business affairs were in good order and in any case it would be an easy matter for them to find out through his bankers and his lawyer. There seemed to be, however, little question on that point. He had been a rich man, living well within an income which was, certainly, on the more or less lavish side. Only later inquiry could confirm it, but just then there seemed to be no reasonable doubt but that his affairs were perfectly balanced and sound.

Nothing however was said of his will—which seemed to me another omission. After that they went into the matter of alibis—very cautiously, very suavely, so one didn't at first realize the exact trend of all their detailed questions of time. In the end, however, so far as I could see, no one really had an alibi except Craig. Nicky, at least, had admitted his presence in the morning room when Conrad returned. Had he seen Drue? Was he going to tell of her interview with Conrad?

There was no way to know and no way to read Nicky's enigmatic face. At length the District Attorney observed, rather pettishly, that there was no alibi, really, for murder by poison, looked impatiently at Nugent and fidgeted. Nugent looked back at him and shook his head, only a little, almost imperceptibly, but as if he'd said, "Wait—not yet."

I saw that. And I thought I prepared myself for it. I didn't really; no one does against catastrophe. But I knew that it was coming; they had asked about a hypodermic, so they had seen that tiny red mark on Conrad Brent's arm. They had searched Drue's room and mine and had taken away the little bag in which she carried instruments and the few drugs she had, so they knew she had a supply of digitalis and knew she didn't have a hypodermic—as I had and as any nurse normally would have. They had established the fact that Conrad's medicine was gone, box and all, so he couldn't have taken it himself. They wouldn't have far to look for a motive, or a witness of sorts, either, for Nicky must have seen Drue going to the library even if, for any purpose of his own, he did not then admit it. Above all, the look Soper and Nugent exchanged admitted a previously agreed-upon purpose.

So they had not yet questioned Drue. My feeling about that was right. Obviously they thought that it would weaken her to have to sit there before them and hear the case built up —possibilities eliminated, circumstances set forth so they were indisputable.

I felt cold and queerly stiff, as if all my muscles had tightened hard. I felt that I had to look at Drue and I wouldn't.

It came sooner than I expected and it was worse. Maud at last brought the thing to its ugly climax. She said, suddenly and impatiently, interrupting a question as to any possibility of the medicine box having been empty and thrown away by Conrad himself, previous to his attack, *"Nonsense!"*

Everyone looked at her. She said again, "That's utter nonsense! Conrad never would have done that. He always kept a supply of digitalis on hand. Besides, as Claud has already told you, his prescription had been refilled only three days ago. He hadn't had an attack since, so it was a full, new supply. And I don't see why you don't get to the point. He was given a hypodermic, you know that; Claud saw what he felt sure was the mark and told me. Nobody but a nurse would have given him a hypodermic—a nurse or a doctor, and Claud wasn't here. And you know who had a motive."

I saw quickly, "A hypodermic mark?"

Nugent glanced at me and Maud stopped, shooting a light black look at me. Nugent said, "Do you want to say something, Nurse Keate?"

"Yes. I don't see how anyone, even a doctor, can make a positive statement about the mark made by a hypodermic needle. It is very small; frequently so small that it can't be seen at all. The skin is elastic and instantly closes after the needle is withdrawn."

Maud's eyes snapped. "It frequently shows, too."

I shrugged. "I don't question Dr. Chivery's statement to the effect that he found some sort of small mark that might have been made by a hypodermic needle. I do question anyone being able to say with any degree of certainty that a—well, a bare pinprick is the mark of a needle."

"Miss Keate," said Maud. "You are not here to question the veracity of the doctor you are working for!"

"It's the plain truth," I said. "Ask anyone."

Maud whirled around toward Nugent. "Dr. Chivery's word has never been questioned. As I was about to say, it is obvious that only one person in the house had a motive. That was Drue Cable."

"Mrs. Chivery . . ." began Nugent, but she went on so vehemently that her tight little body jerked; her black eyes plunged in little bursts from one to the other of us.

"She must have come down to the library to see him; to try to persuade him not to make her go. He had told her she must leave today. She threatened him, yesterday afternoon. I heard her and so did you, Nicky. You heard her say, 'I could kill you for this.' I know exactly what happened. She came to the library and she accused him of breaking up her marriage. Conrad had an attack and asked her for medicine; she went to the desk and—and took the medicine away, pretended it was gone. So Conrad, dying, begged her to help him. She was a nurse. How could he know what she would do . . . ?"

"Stop! We'll get a lawyer. You can't accuse . . ." I rose and Nugent was at my side, his hand tight on my arm. Drue looked like a ghost, white, rigid, with great dark eyes fastened on Maud. There was a shadow of a smile on Alexia's lips. Maud swept on vigorously, black eyes snapping. "So she gave him a hypodermic of digitalis and she gave him too much. It killed him. As she planned. She thought it would never be traced. That's how it happened . . ."

"That's enough, Mrs. Chivery," said Nugent. But Soper's

voice rose over Nugent's. "She's perfectly right," he said loudly. "I've thought so from the very first. She's perfectly right, Nugent; there's no other real explanation. I've been patient, I've covered every possible line of inquiry. But that's enough . . ." He got up and looked at Drue, his little eyes bright and accusing. "She did it. The girl did it. She intended to kill him with the revolver. Then he had a heart attack and this way was easier for her, a nurse, and she jumped at it. She hid the medicine; she pretended to him that it was gone; she told him she'd save him. And then she killed him. Arrest Drue Cable now, Lieutenant. It's a clear case; I'll take the responsibility for it, and I'll bring the charge. We'll get a grand jury indictment at once. It'll be murder in the first degree."

Nicky looked at his fingernails. "Well," he said softly into the sudden silence, "I may as well tell you, then. Drue *was* with Conrad in the library. I saw her. And I heard her say, 'I've got your revolver.' They had a terrific row."

# X

Drue rose automatically, as if she didn't know what she was doing, but she didn't speak. I was close beside her and I would have known. Alexia smiled a little and said something low to Nicky. Maud looked openly triumphant; Peter quickly started for the door as if to tell Craig and then as quickly came back into the room again. Soper said loudly that he was right, he'd known it from the first, but Nicky ought to have told it earlier. I believe I said loudly, too, a number of times that Drue wouldn't talk without a lawyer. I couldn't think of anything else to say. Then Nugent's voice cracked like a whip, so viciously that it brought us all up short.

"Do you mean she had the revolver with her? In her hand?" he asked Nicky.

"Oh, no," said Nicky. "I would have seen it."

"Then she wasn't actually threatening him with it?"

"I can't say about that," said Nicky airily.

"And what did you do then?"

"After I saw her go into the library?" Nicky's tone was very nonchalant. "I thought from the sound of Conrad's voice that she—well, might need somebody to back her up. But she seemed able to take care of herself, so I went upstairs.

I'd just got to sleep when something fell—I don't know what—and they said Conrad was dead."

"What else did you hear?" demanded Soper quickly. "What did Brent say when she told him she had his revolver? Did he call for help? You must have heard what else they said!"

Nicky paused, looked at his fingernails, thought for a moment and said, "N-no. No, I'm afraid not."

"But if you heard their voices . . ." began Soper, and Nugent said abruptly, "You'll swear to all this, Mr. Senour?"

And Nicky said he wouldn't.

It was an inexplicable and sudden *volte face* to which he clung with silky stubbornness. "I can't swear to anything," he said. "I won't. I've only said that Drue came downstairs while Conrad was in the library."

Soper was furious. "You said they had a row. You said you saw her in the library with him just before he died. You said she threatened him with his own revolver!"

"I won't swear to anything," said Nicky, ignoring Alexia's frown and Maud's angry eyes and clutching little hand upon his arm.

"You don't have to," shouted Soper angrily. "Every word you've said has been taken down in shorthand. Perfectly openly; you were all aware of it." One of the troopers in the corner, scribbled that too, rapidly, in his shorthand tablet. But Nicky shook his head.

"You'll never get me to sign it or to admit anything of the kind on the witness stand. I won't be the one to bring evidence like that against anybody—in court."

Alexia was biting her full underlip with sharp white teeth, her eyes ominously fixed on Nicky. Maud made an angry little exclamation and must have vanished about then, silently, for when next I looked for her she was gone. Soper said angrily that Nicky would be a witness; he couldn't help himself; he, Soper, would see to that. Nugent said suddenly, "We'll question Miss Cable alone. Right, Soper?"

"But . . ." said Alexia, and Nugent said again, "Alone. If you please . . ."

So the others—Alexia, Nicky, Peter and Beevens—were obliged to leave, and did so rather reluctantly, I thought, as if they wanted to stay. But Nugent closed the door after them briskly, and Soper looked at me.

"Well?" he said sharply, "are you staying here?"

"I am," I said simply but firmly.

"You're not! You heard what . . ."

"Oh, let her stay," said Nugent. Soper shrugged and Drue, standing very slim and erect beside the tall armchair, her gray eyes level and clear, said; "I didn't murder him." Said it like a simple statement, clearly and distinctly, like a child reciting a lesson. I suppose it seemed unreal to her. Yet it was real enough, too.

"You were with him," said Soper. "You had a motive. . . ." He began his attack with bluster, but Nugent's voice cut sharply into the bluster, "Miss Cable," he said, "will you make a statement of exactly what you did do? Just tell it to us in your own words."

"I think she ought to have a lawyer," I said again. "You can refuse to talk, Drue." I wasn't sure that she could refuse to answer their questions, but in any case she lifted her firm little chin and looked at Nugent.

"I'll tell you," she said. "I'll tell you as much as I can." I held my breath again and tried to think of ways to stop her if she said too much.

"I was in the library as Nicky says," she began.

"All right, Miss Cable, go on."

"I did want to talk to Mr. Brent. So I waited until he returned from his walk, then I came to the library. We talked for some time. He had a heart attack then and . . ." She faltered, and I was sure she was going to tell about the hypodermic. I rustled warningly. A faint flush came into her face and her hand went up to her throat, almost as if to stop the words on her lips. "And—he died," she said. "If such a large amount of digitalis was found, I don't know how he got it."

Well, that was true enough and so far safe. But I wished I could be sure that she saw, as I saw, that the one thing they were after was an admission that she had given Conrad digitalis. It was the important material evidence; it was the clinching fact, it was the missing link in the chain they had forged. There was no possible way for her to prove, ever (to them, or to a jury), how much she had given him, and that it was not a lethal amount. Her instinct was for telling them the truth, I knew that; and the truth would have been, literally, the most horrible and fatal trap, as things stood then. Soper burst into question again.

"But this revolver, Miss Cable. You had a revolver. Why?"

She turned to face him. "I found that revolver in the garden," she said steadily, "yesterday-afternoon."

"G—garden," said the District Attorney.

"Where my—that is, where Craig was shot that night. It was hidden and I found it. In the burlap wrapping around one of the rose shrubs."

Nugent's eyes had an odd expression. "Why did you look for it, Miss Cable?" he said. "Why did you bring it to your room?"

She turned back to him; there was less defiance in her manner when she spoke to Nugent, more confidence—which might be her undoing. She seemed to trust him and to want to tell him the whole story and Soper was ready and eager to pounce upon any unguarded admission. She said, "Because I didn't believe the story of an accident. I went to the garden just to have a look at the place where my"—again she corrected herself quickly—"where Craig had been hurt. I searched it and I found the gun. That's all. I brought it to my room because I intended to show it to Craig when he was better."

"Why?" said Nugent rather softly.

"Because it proved someone shot at him," she said.

"He says it was accident," said Nugent, watching her closely. "He ought to know."

"I wanted him to have that revolver," she said with a kind of obliquity.

"You're saying that his accident was actually an attempted murder?" cried Soper.

Again she whirled around to face him, her chin high, her voice steady. "He wouldn't have shot himself like that! He wouldn't have been cleaning a gun in the garden at eleven o'clock at night!"

"Did you know that the revolver belonged to Conrad Brent?"

"I wasn't sure. I knew that he'd had a revolver."

"Did he admit it belonged to him? When you took it to the library, I mean?"

"Yes. That is, by implication. He recognized it and asked where I'd found it."

"See here, Miss Cable," said Soper with a crafty look, "did you accuse him of trying to kill his son?"

"No. Certainly not."

"Why did you give him the revolver?"

"Because I wanted him to know of it, of course. I wanted him to know that I had found it in the garden, hidden. I wanted him to know."

"Why?" said Soper again.

"Naturally because something ought to be done about it.

It proved that Craig didn't shoot himself. He wouldn't have hidden it."

"Exactly what did he say?"

Drue flushed. "He said I couldn't have found the revolver just there. He said I was—was trying to make trouble."

"And you . . ."

"I saw then that he was ill. I told him he'd better lie down. I started to leave but he—he asked me to stay with him. And then he got worse. All at once. And—and died."

After a moment Nugent said, "Who do you think shot Craig?"

Again the defiance went out of her. She shook her head. "I don't know. I don't know . . ."

"*Don't know!* Of course, you don't know! It's an obvious attempt to divert your inquiry, Lieutenant. I'm surprised that you can't see through this girl's story." Soper came close to Drue, his face red and threatening, shaking a pudgy but forceful forefinger under her nose. "Now, you see here, Miss. We want the truth. You did quarrel with Conrad Brent, didn't you?"

"I didn't quarrel with him. I asked him to permit me to stay and take care of Craig."

"You quarreled with him! You were heard yesterday afternoon when he tried to send you away. You blamed him for breaking up your marriage. You came here in the hope of getting young Brent back again. But his father wouldn't let you, so you killed him."

Drue's face wasn't white any more; two scarlet flames were in her cheeks, her eyes flashed. "I came here to nurse Craig," she said. "And he was my husband until his father . . ."

"Drue, Drue!" I cried, my hand on her arm.

And Soper said, "Arrest her, Nugent. I insist upon it. I'll make you responsible if she gets away. It's a murder charge, there's no use in prolonging this thing. Take her away. . . ."

"I don't think there's enough evidence—material evidence —to convict," said Nugent softly but very coolly.

"Enough evidence!" snorted the District Attorney. "What more do you want? There's the hypodermic. . . ."

"We haven't made sure that she had one."

"You will, you will! No use asking her, she'd only lie. Yes, and you"—he pounced on me, his eyes angry, bright slits in his red face—"you are putting her up to it. Well, we'll take care of you, too. Besides, there's the witness. . . ."

"Nicky Senour," said Nugent again softly. "And he says he won't swear to it. Besides, he didn't see her kill him. He said only that she was in the library with Brent. . . ."

"He said they were having a row. That kind of thing goes a long way with a jury. Don't be a fool, Nugent. You'll get the evidence. But put the girl under arrest; make sure you've got her. All the evidence in the world won't do you any good later if you've let the girl who did it get away. Arrest her. . . ."

"I'll take her into custody," said the Lieutenant slowly.

"Custody! What do you mean by that?"

"I'll keep her here, in her room. Under guard," said Nugent.

And in the end, incredibly, that was exactly what he did. But first they questioned her again, and made me leave before they began. I would have stayed; but when a District Attorney, a Police Lieutenant and two remarkably stalwart and able-bodied troopers are lined up against one, there's nothing much to do. I retired as ungracefully as it lay in my power to do and sat on the bench in the hall watching the door. Never before in my whole nursing experience have I let anything come between me and my patient but frankly, while I sat there, eyes glued to the door of that room, trying and failing to hear anything but a rapid murmur of voices, I didn't care whether Craig Brent lived or died, except I hated him so, just then, for being the cause of Drue's presence in that ill-omened house that I'd a little rather he'd have died, preferably in boiling oil. If I could have made him come alive again. My own impulses to murder, while vehement in their way, are not very lasting.

Once I did go upstairs. The door to Craig's room was open and I peeked in cautiously. Peter Huber was sitting in a chair beside him, smoking. Anna was standing at the window, her back toward the room and her head bent with a handkerchief to her eyes, and Craig and Peter were talking in low voices. Craig looked all right, certainly the police were not hounding *him* from trap to trap, from admission to admission, from refuge to refuge. I went quickly back to the bench downstairs and they were still in the little morning room.

I was there when they emerged. Drue was white and drawn-looking; even her lips were chalky. She looked at me with great, haunted, dark eyes and I could read nothing in them, although I thought she was thankful I was there, waiting for her. And they took her straight upstairs, and put her in her room, under guard! I followed. Soper, giving me a suspicious look, had turned into the library.

Well. Nugent, if he had eyes in his head as he certainly did, couldn't have failed to see that my room connected with Drue's. But the trooper already on guard didn't stop me when I entered my own room. And of course I went straight through the bathroom to Drue.

She was standing in the middle of the room, facing the door, head up, hands clenched at her sides as if at bay. When she heard me she whirled and suddenly crumpled down on the bed. "Oh, Sarah, Sarah, what shall I do?"

I sat down on the bed beside her and took her hands. "What have you told them? What did they make you say? Quick, Drue. Tell me."

In the end it wasn't too bad; which is to say it could have been worse but not much worse. They had questioned her at length about her interview with Conrad, about her reasons for coming to Balifold, about the hypodermic syringe they had not found among her other nursing tools, about the supply of digitalis they had found. Somehow (as if she saw now, clearly, her own danger) she had evaded them; she had not admitted that she had given Conrad a hypodermic, she had not admitted that he asked her for the medicine and that, when she went to look for it, it was not in the drawer.

She had indeed fought and evaded—especially about the box of medicine—in a way that was not like Drue; she was, as most of us are, naturally and innately truthful. If she had been fighting thus to protect somebody else (somebody she loved) it would have seemed to me more comprehensible and more like Drue. She had that kind of courage; I've seen her fight to save a patient with the courage and fury of a tigress. But I didn't stop then to think of that; I was only thankful that she had kept them from grinding any really convicting admission out of her.

"I kept saying I didn't know, I didn't know. I remembered what you said, and told them I wanted a lawyer. Sarah, when they asked me a direct question: did I give him a hypodermic of digitalis? Did he ask me for his medicine?—I—I squirmed and evaded and wriggled out of it." She pressed her hands over her face. "Funny," she said unevenly, "how hard it is to tell an outright lie, even when you've made up your mind to do it. Instead of lying, you—you evade, you weasel out of making a direct statement, you—oh, it's fantastic, really. You employ all the spirit of lying and yet you can't make yourself conquer the fact. Well," she took her hands from her face and stared at the rug, "they don't know I gave him the hypodermic—not certainly. But—oh, Sarah, what *can* I *do!*"

Well, I said what I could, which was little enough. I told her we'd get a lawyer. I told her they had nothing but circumstantial evidence.

"But they convict people on circumstantial evidence. Don't they, Sarah?"

"Never," I told her stoutly and falsely. "It isn't legal." And made her lie down flat on the bed and fixed her some aromatic spirits of ammonia which she didn't drink. But before we could really talk or outline any kind of sensible course of action there was a knock on the door, and it was the trooper Wilkins, the man on guard. And they wanted us to come to Craig's room.

"Right away, please," said the trooper.

Drue went to the mirror before we went, however. It gave me a kind of lift to see her put cold water on her eyes and powder her face and touch her lips with crimson. It was like a little, unconscious declaration of war.

But if Craig saw it, or was aware of anything but the bare fact of Drue's presence, there was no hint of it in his attitude when we entered his room. He gave us both a remote and impersonal look; Drue might have been the barest acquaintance, certainly anything but a woman who was once his wife.

Soper was there, suspicious the instant his eyes fell upon Drue again. Nugent was there and the ubiquitous trooper with the shorthand tablet. Anna was hovering in a corner but Peter had gone. After a closer glance at Craig I sent Anna away and took up my post at his side with my fingers on his pulse. I did feel a wave of compunction. There was a flare of color in his cheeks and his eyes were too bright.

"I sent for you, Miss Keate," he said to me, "and for Drue. I thought this concerned both of you."

"I'm afraid you'll have to be quick," I said to Nugent. "Ten minutes . . ."

The District Attorney swelled up as if about to protest and at a look from Nugent went down again. Drue went quietly over to stand in the shadow of the window curtains; the light fell upon her white skirt and her face was in the shadow. But I think all of us, all the time, were poignantly aware of that slender, listening figure.

"We weren't going to question you, Brent, if we could help

it, until you were better," said Nugent. "However, we both wanted very much to see you. . . ."

"All right," said Craig. "But first, exactly what is your case against Miss Cable? Facts, I mean. That you can substantiate."

"I'll tell you," said Lieutenant Nugent, and did, wasting no words and outlining their case against Drue in black and white. She had quarreled with Conrad Brent; she had held him responsible for her separation from her husband; ("that is," said Nugent looking carefully past Drue's white figure and out the window, "from you, Mr. Brent . . .") she had had digitalis; the medicine was missing from its customary place and there was the mark which might be that of a hypodermic needle on the body of Conrad Brent. He explained, still briefly but pungently, that since no one else knew anything of the missing box of pills there was only one construction that could be placed upon their absence, plus the hypodermic and the fatal amount of digitalis found in Conrad Brent's body. And that was that Drue had removed the medicine as a pretext to administer a fatal dose of digitalis.

"Am I to understand then that your whole theory is based upon a presumption that Miss Cable came here with the purpose of effecting a reconciliation with—with me, and that her purpose was so overwhelmingly strong that she murdered my father because he opposed her?" There was an edge in Craig's voice. He went on. "Because that's out of the question. As a motive that is preposterous. Neither Miss Cable nor I have any desire to remarry. Miss Cable did not come here with any such purpose."

"Why did she come here?" said Soper.

A flicker of a smile came into Craig's eyes and vanished. "She is a nurse. It was sheer coincidence that she was called when I was injured. She needed the money and, as our divorce was entirely amicable, there was no earthly reason why she shouldn't come."

"Then why," said Soper acutely, "did she quarrel with your father?"

Craig lifted his eyebrows. "I'm not sure she did quarrel with my father—but if so I suggest that that was no difficult achievement."

"Really, Mr. Brent," said Soper looking shocked. "Your father . . ."

"I know, I know," said Craig. "But you are making this an inquiry into murder; there's a duty paid the living, too. However, it is likely that my father asked her to leave and she, professionally, resented being kicked out of the house. In any case, that is neither here nor there. For in the first place, your evidence against her is altogether circumstantial. You can't prove any of it. . . ."

"There I beg to differ with you," interrupted Soper. "If we find her hypodermic outfit and it has contained digitalis  . . ." Nugent was looking very glum.

Craig said quickly, "But you haven't. So you have no proof whatever. And even so, you see, she wasn't here the night an attempt was made to murder me. And it isn't likely that there are two murderers floating around in—in this house." He said it rather lightly and looked gray and terribly grim around the mouth.

"Two—but you told everybody it was accident . . ." began Soper explosively and Nugent broke in again, driving neatly through implications and repetitions, "Who shot you?"

Craig closed his eyes wearily. "I could have told you all I knew of it yesterday if Chivery hadn't doped me so thoroughly. I understand you were here making an inquiry."

"The girl had the revolver, too!" cried Soper. "You didn't say anything about that, Nugent."

"Mr. Brent wasn't shot," said Nugent.

"You mean Conrad. Craig here was shot and . . ." .

"Miss Cable was not here when I was shot," said Craig.

Soper paid no attention to that. He said, "How do we know she's telling the truth about the revolver? Sounds much more likely to me that she took Conrad's revolver and threatened him with it. And then changed her mind as she thought of an easier way to get rid of him. Then she thought up this story of finding the revolver in the garden in order to explain why she had it . . ."

"Why did she have it, in that case?" said Craig.  ,

"Why, to—to clean off her fingerprints! Or perhaps she was excited and forgot the revolver. Left it in her room when she went to get the digitalis and forgot it. We found it; she had to explain it. And also she saw a chance to throw dust in our eyes; to suggest that Craig's accident was attempted murder and thus, that the person who shot Craig and the person who killed Conrad were the same, which would let her out inasmuch as she was not here that night."

"No, no," cried Drue from the window. "I didn't. I . . ."

"I can corroborate Miss Cable's story of the revolver," I broke in hastily. "Or at least part of it." But when I had told them as convincingly as I could of seeing her return to the house from the direction of the garden they were not very much impressed.

"Could you see what she was carrying?" asked Nugent.

"No. She was wearing her cape."

"So you didn't see that it was a revolver?"

"Not exactly. It had to be something small."

"But in fact you are not sure she carried anything."

"It was my impression . . ."

"Impressions!" snorted Soper.

Nugent shook his head. Drue turned suddenly back toward the window; suddenly, I thought, to conceal tears.

"Let's get back to your accident," said Nugent abruptly, addressing Craig. "Did somebody shoot you? If so, *who?*"

"All right," said Craig. "This is what happened. I was walking in the garden; no reason for it—just walking. It was dark; there's no moon. There was a rustle in some shrubs. I turned around, thinking it was the dog. I stepped a little nearer the shrubs; anyway, I could see a hand. Barely see it, the rest was in the shadow; I think there were outlines of a figure. And then something hit my shoulder, as if somebody had given me a kind of hard slap. Then I realized I'd been shot. I think I started for the shrub; I must have called for help. I remember stumbling and then that was all until they were carrying me upstairs. Beevens and Pete. Then Chivery came. But I didn't see anybody clearly in the shrub; I just knew somebody was there. I didn't even really see the revolver," he said. "But I imagine that Miss Cable found it and that that is the revolver she had in her room. I asked her to try to find it; I had a kind of lucid moment, the way you do when you're drugged. She was here and I asked her to look for it. Naturally I wanted to know who shot me; I wanted the evidence."

Soper's cold little eyes practically lost themselves in suspicious wrinkles. "That's not Miss Cable's story. She didn't say you sent her to look for the revolver."

Craig shot a glance at Drue. "Didn't she?" he said imperturbably. "Well, that's the way it was."

Nugent said, "The revolver belonged to your father. Mrs. Brent and Mr. Senour have identified it."

"He kept it," said Craig, accepting the fact of the revolver's ownership without question, "in the desk in the library. He never locked the desk; anything valuable he put in the safe. The safe is behind one of those panels in the library."

"You mean anybody might have taken the revolver," said Soper.

"Obviously."

Nugent was looking thoughtful. He said, "Was the hand you saw wearing a glove?"

Craig's pulse gave a leap and began to race like an accelerated motor. But he said coolly enough, looking straight at Nugent, "I haven't the faintest idea. It was dark. There was only a kind of whitish outline."

"But you knew it was a hand?"

"Why—yes."

There was a little silence and I looked at my watch in a marked manner. Soper said, "So you think the same person that killed your father tried first to kill you?"

"I don't know," said Craig. "But I do know Miss Cable was in New York when I was shot."

"How do you know that?" interposed Soper.

Craig lifted eyebrows. "Obviously she wasn't here."

Nugent said abruptly, "It's all right, Mr. Soper. She was in New York; I checked that and the telephone call to the Nurses' Registry office."

Soper looked annoyed. Craig went on quickly, "In any case, it isn't likely that she would take a pot shot at me one night and the next night poison my father because she wanted to see me and he opposed it. The motives seem a little mixed."

Soper said, "Now look here, Brent, we are only trying to get at the truth. You needn't take that tone."

"I know," said Craig soberly and with the edge gone from his voice, so it was only weary and honest. "I understand your position and I appreciate what you are trying to do. I'll do everything I can to help you. But I really do think you are wasting time making out a case against Miss Cable; she was not anywhere near, the night I was shot. And she had no motive to kill my father. She doesn't want to marry me any more than I want to marry her. Our marriage is absolutely finished and neither of us regrets it."

"Do you mean to say," said Soper, glancing covertly in Drue's direction, "do you mean to say that if Drue Cable—your former wife, came to you and suggested that you remarry, you would refuse her?"

I didn't look at Drue; no one did but Soper. Craig's pulse was as steady as a clock. "At the risk of sounding unchivalrous," he said coolly and distinctly, "yes."

# XI

I said, "Time is up. I'll have to ask you to go."

I must have sounded a little vigorous about it, for instantly Nugent turned around and stalked toward the door. But Soper said, "Your father was a rich man, Brent. Who benefits by his death? I mean to say, what are the main provisions of his will?"

"You'll have to ask his lawyer. John Wells. In Balifold. Are you going to release Miss Cable?"

Nugent jerked around to look at Soper; Soper turned a fine magenta. "Release her! By God, no! She stays here under guard or in jail."

"But I need her," I said quickly, essaying a rally. "I need her to help me nurse Mr. Brent."

"You can get another nurse out from New York," snapped Soper. "She stays under guard or in jail."

Well, I didn't want another nurse bothering around. Anna could give me any help I needed. Soper waddled out of the room like an enraged and vicious duck. Nugent, however, drew me into the hall. "Miss Keate," he said in a low voice, "Who was here in the hall last night? When something bumped against the door and you went to look?"

"Why—why, no one! That is, oh, some time (perhaps half an hour before) I saw Nicky in the hall. But not after the bump on the door. There's a dent—here," I put my finger on it and he looked at it, his face as inexpressive as a Red Indian's. "But it's as I told you," I added. "After the bump against the door I didn't see anybody in the hall."

Something very queer in his eyes stopped me. But he said only, "I advise you to tell me. Think it over," and went away. Leaving me a little perplexed, for if I had seen anyone or anything I should have been only too glad to tell him and shift the burden of suspicion from Drue.

When I entered his room again, Craig was lying with his eyes closed. Wilkins advanced a little, tentatively, toward Drue, who was still at the window. "Wait outside," I told him, and with an uncertain look at me he did so and I closed the door after him. But if I had had, as I don't think I had really, any vague notion of a word of understanding between Craig and Drue I was disappointed.

Drue had turned so I could see only her back, slim and erect, and her lifted, white-capped head.

"Are they gone?" Craig said to me.

"Yes," I said. And then because I had to, I said slowly, "There was a glove on the hand, wasn't there? You couldn't have seen the color in the dark. Why did you think it was yellow?"

His eyes flared open. He looked very straight at me for a long moment. Then he said definitely, "I don't know what you're talking about."

Which was about what I might have expected.

"All right. I can't make you tell me. But there's one thing you'll have to explain, if not to me, then to the police. You said—half asleep yesterday—'there'll be murder done. Tell Claud.' What did you mean?"

He just lay and looked at me through half-shut eyes whose expression I couldn't read. And he denied it flatly.

"I don't remember it. I could have meant anything. Unless I was referring to the attack upon me. Go ahead and tell the police."

"I will," I said. And Drue whirled around then. Her hands were doubled up, her crimson mouth tight. "Craig, you needn't have lied for me!" she cried.

"I didn't," he said briefly.

"You didn't send me for the revolver . . ."

"Oh," said Craig, "that. But the rest of it was the truth, wasn't it? I mean, you didn't come here with the intention of —of"—he smiled a little, though his eyes were very intent— "of a reconciliation? I'm sure you didn't." The smile left his lips, but his eyes were still very intent, watching Drue. "It's something neither of us wants. That's why I told them . . ."

And at that instant the trooper, Wilkins, knocked on the door. He looked apologetic when I opened it. But Drue had to go with him all the same.

When the door closed behind her, Craig closed his eyes and lay there, very quiet, with a gray look around his mouth for a long time.

Well, after that the day settled into a smoldering kind of quiet. Eventually I bestirred myself to my duties. Craig was really on the mend, in spite of occurrences which, certainly, were not exactly conducive to convalescence. He must have been thinking hard, for he was unexpectedly docile, while I gave him a quick sponge bath and an alcohol rub, got him

94

into fresh pajamas and took a look at the dressing on his wound.

"Such a fuss about nothing," he said, but winced nevertheless as I worked. "If it had been a Jap bullet I'd feel as if I deserved some of this fuss."

"You'll be dodging Jap bullets soon enough," I said tartly. "Hold still."

"So long as I dodge them," he said, and grinned. While I thought of youth and war and the hideous waste of it.

I said, "When do you go?"

"I don't know. The end of this week sometime."

"With this? Nonsense!"

"I feel fine. I'd get up now if you'd let me."

"Certainly. Just try it. And start your wound bleeding."

"Would it?"

"Listen, young man, you just escaped with your life. Do you want to get well enough to leave or do you want to be an invalid for several weeks?"

"Okay, okay," he said but looked rebellious, so I realized I'd have to watch him. I said, "If you want to spend the spring at home or in a hospital, all right, get up. If you want to fight, do as I tell you. Stay in bed. I'll get you well."

For the first time he looked rather approving and pleased. "In time to leave when the orders come through?"

"It depends. I'll try. Do you know where you will be sent?"

"No." He moved restively. "I hope they get the inquest over satisfactorily and everything settled before I go."

"Yes, naturally. Does Drue know you are leaving so soon?"

"No," he said, and eyed me with sudden sharpness. "And you are not to tell her, either."

"But . . ."

"I mean that. Understand?"

"All right. If you don't want her to know, but I think . . ."

"I'm doing the thinking about this," he said, and then added with a touch of apology, "I'm sorry."

I eased him back onto the pillow. The wound was doing all right; but the pain of even the slight motion brought moisture to his forehead and around his mouth. Well, it was just luck that the bullet had missed his heart.

I said, "Have you been at home long?"

"Only a few days. There, that's better." He relaxed against the pillow and sighed and grinned a little. "The brave soldier!" he said, deriding his weakness.

"You're lucky to be alive," I said. And, as the shadow of perplexity and horror and sorrow came over his young face again, I said impulsively, "Mr. Brent, what do *you* think happened last night? This is your home. You know these people. What's your theory?"

He closed his eyes. Weakly? Or was it, I thought suddenly, to shut me out, so I would read no expression in his eyes that might reveal his thoughts. He said, "Theory? I haven't any. I don't know what to think."

"Do you think it was accident?" I persisted. "Or do you think the police are right?"

"Murder," he said thoughtfully after a moment. "No, I don't think it was murder. My father had no . . ." He had been about to say, I thought, that his father had no enemies. He stopped and changed it. "No one would murder my father." He paused again for a moment and then went on, his eyes still closed, "My father and I had our differences. Yet we loved each other. The differences we had didn't separate us in that way. I'm sure that he felt that. I'm sure he did."

"One knows things like that without words," I said. "I'm sure he felt as you do. I'm sure he was proud of you, too. And that he . . ."

"No," said Craig rather quickly. "No, he wasn't proud of me. Not that I've ever done anything to make anybody proud of me, or anything to be exactly ashamed of either—that is, I'm an ordinary fellow. But he wasn't proud . . ."

"I meant, about your getting into the air force. Having a son going to fight for his country." It's queer how the true things can sometimes sound trite. But Craig laughed a little, on an unsteady note, so he caught himself up quickly.

He said, "You don't understand. That was one of our differences. He wasn't afraid; it isn't that. He just didn't want me to go to war."

"Why not?"

"Because he—because . . ." He moved a little again. "Oh, it's nothing, Miss Keate."

He said it easily enough; yet something in his tone caught my ear and my interest. I waited, thinking of it and of what he had said—or rather had failed to say. And he added all at once, "It was nothing my father could help. He'd felt that way for years. And, anyway, he changed lately. I know that he changed. Since December seventh, I mean. Since we entered the war. Yes, he'd changed, I'm sure."

"But . . ." I began, wanting to get whatever it was he was trying to say clear in my mind.

He didn't want it clear for me, however; he said rather brusquely, pushing the subject away, "Pete will be going too, you know. Soon. He thinks in another few weeks."

"Pete? Oh, Peter Huber. What's he doing here, by the way? Did he come to see you?"

Naturally, it wasn't my business to know; still, I have seldom if ever scrupled to ask questions, particularly when I wanted to know. As in this case. Craig said, moving his shoulder a little and wincing again, "No, he's been here several weeks. Came on from the coast to try to get into some branch of the service. He's waiting now to hear; remembered we lived here and came up to Balifold and was staying at the inn when my father discovered him and made him come here. Ouch . . ." he said, moving his shoulder experimentally. "What makes it hurt like that?"

"It's doing all right. No infection. Did Mrs. Brent know Pete in school, too?"

"Mrs. Brent? No." The corner of his mouth twitched. "Pete's more or less susceptible."

"Susceptible! Oh, you mean . . ." There wasn't anybody to mean except Alexia. Craig said quickly, "Oh, it's only Pete. Alexia's so—beautiful," he finished rather dryly.

"But then . . ." I was struck by a sudden and rather far-fetched speculation. If Peter Huber had fallen madly in love with Alexia, there existed a motive for Conrad's murder.

Not however a very sound motive; certainly not a very pleasant one—but then a motive for murder is not likely to be pleasant. Mainly, though, there was little if any evidence to back it up. So I caught back my own words.

But Craig guessed my unuttered thought.

"He didn't murder my father to get Alexia! Peter's a good egg. Besides, Alexia doesn't go for him."

Which was true enough. Alexia had certainly wasted no time in making her intentions clear and they obviously had nothing to do with Peter Huber.

The trouble was however that Conrad Brent had been murdered; the police don't make mistakes about things like that.

It's very difficult, and I discovered it then, really to face and accept the fact of murder; yet it's inescapable too—like an ugly, invisible presence. Murder in that house. Murder in the night just past.

I put away my instrument case in silence. After I had made Craig comfortable and was sure he was warm, I pushed aside the heavy curtains and opened the windows and aired the room.

It was cold, much colder than it had been the day before, with the lowering kind of still gray sky that threatens snow. I could see then, as I couldn't the day before, something of the rolling landscape. Hills, everywhere, thickly wooded, rose gently up to the gray sky. Roads twisted here and there over and among the hills; and stone walls traced old boundaries. Near at hand, running along just outside the wall and appearing to pass the garden, a path wound downward and out of sight. It led, as a matter of fact, from the Brent house directly to the Chivery cottage about a mile away and was a short cut.

The hills and the trees gave an effect of isolation. As I looked, a snowflake, very white against the gray sky, fluttered past my eyes and then another. Shivering a little, I closed the windows.

The day went on quietly. Soper, I think, went away shortly after the talk with Craig. Nugent vanished, too, but I believe busied himself for some time, quietly, about the house. Once a policeman came to the door with an ink pad and slide and took my fingerprints; I must say I didn't relish the little attention but did not intentionally smudge one hand as he seemed to think. The glass slipped.

He would have taken Craig's fingerprints, too, but Craig looked convincingly asleep, and I wouldn't permit rousing him. The policeman went away, and I caught a glimpse of Lieutenant Nugent down by the stairs, listening but not talking to Beevens. We were to become well accustomed to Lieutenant Nugent's spare, silent figure, unobtrusive, yet ubiquitous. He did, indeed, a very good job of lurking.

There were, of course, things I wanted to do and just then couldn't. The thing that worried me more than anything else was the hypodermic or rather its whereabouts. Who had it and why—and above all else what did he intend to do with it? I use "he" in a general sense; it seemed to me most likely that Maud's bright little eyes had ferreted it out. And I could do nothing; to search the place for so small an object would be at best difficult. With the police about it was impossible.

Yet if found, it would be the District Attorney's triumph and vindication.

I had begun to wonder if Chivery had forgotten that he

still had a patient in the Brent house when he did finally arrive, late in the afternoon, looking very gray and drawn, and at least ten years older. After I had watched him examine Craig's wound and taken a few orders he told me to go. "Get some fresh air," he said, with a kind of glassy heartiness, looking at the corner of my cap. "You needn't come back for at least an hour. I'll stay with Craig." As I hesitated, he added, "I want to talk to him."

So I had to leave.

My room was orderly and quiet. I went through the bathroom between our rooms and knocked softly on Drue's door and, as she didn't answer, I opened it cautiously. She was sleeping; she looked very young and childish lying there with one hand pushed under her pillow and the shadow of her eyelashes dark along her soft cheek. The little dog, Sir Francis, lying on the foot of the bed, watched me intently and growled in a kind of formal way. It was a tiny growl, of course, yet as full of intention and sincerity as a police dog's growl. It didn't wake Drue and I retired quietly. It suddenly occurred to me that if I'd married and if I'd had a daughter she might have been something like Drue. But while I'm an old maid and make no bones of it I'm not a sentimental, dithering idiot; so I thought no more of that, changed to a fresh uniform, took my cape, passed Wilkins in the hall again and went for a walk.

No one was in the hall below, so we weren't then, all of us, under close guard. The front door closed heavily behind me and I walked along the driveway toward the public road. It was still gray and cold and the air felt moist, but it was not snowing. Dusk was coming on and it was very quiet. Twenty-four hours ago I had had my first indication of smoldering tragedy and terror in that house that lay behind me.

The drive went down a long curve among clumps of evergreens. When I reached the huge stone gate-posts I stepped out briskly along the public road which wound north and west with many curves and a little bridge or two.

Somewhere along the way Delphine, the cat, picked me up and I looked down at his battle-scarred ears and wondered what had roused him so suddenly in the night. A footstep? Clothing brushing against the door? Or had it been something more tenuous even than that; an awareness of movement outside that door that was denied to my own, merely human, ears? And I wondered, too, what had struck the door so sharply and so hard. Like a hammer.

Gradually, as I walked along, the Brent wall gave way to a low field rock wall beyond which an irregular, partially wooded meadow stretched away into the dusk.

And presently, having skirted two sides of the meadow and reached a little ridge, I could see the village of Balifold about a mile or two away. It was a cluster of white houses, narrow and irregular but pleasant streets, and a church or two, for I could see the white steeples rising among bare trees and against the dull gray sky. There were many trees, beautiful, strongly symmetrical maples and oaks, and again evergreens.

From there too, spreading casually away from the town, I could see here and there what appeared to be large country estates hiding behind trees and in valleys, like the Brent place. There was about all of it—village and wooded hills and the soft dusk—a stillness and repose that would have been pleasant, except that there was a definite chill and loneliness in the air. Delphine decided to leave and did so, on secret feline business into the meadow, where his gray body slid into the shadowy growth near at hand and vanished. Leaving me alone.

Murder by poison. Standing on that hill, leaning against the low stone wall, looking down at the village and across those silent hills and valleys, I began to think again of the means of Conrad Brent's death. The use of poison presupposed a murderer with some knowledge of drugs, accessibility to digitalis, and a certain amount of ingenuity in inducing Conrad Brent to take it. And to take it *before* Drue had returned with her unlucky hypodermic dose.

And that, of course, led me back again, irresistibly, to the circles my thoughts had traveled so many times during the day. Who had murdered Conrad?

Craig Brent had by no means told all he knew; there was that business of the yellow gloves; and he had merely, unconvincingly, denied words that were suspiciously prophetic. Against this he had told a story to account for the bruise on his temple which not only sounded true but indicated, in my opinion, a line of inquiry the police would do well to follow. And while there may be few real alibis for a poison murder, still he had been under my observation at the time Conrad was induced to take poison. He was also in a drugged state, which would have prohibited clear thinking or quick action. And he had been shot, himself, the previous night. It was not likely, as he had said, that two potential murderers existed in their immediate circle—both with the evident intention of cutting off the Brents, root and branch, so to speak.

Furthermore, he had so narrowly escaped with his life the night before that there was no doubt at all but that the shooting had been a real attempt at murder. Therefore, someone else had shot him; he had certainly not shot himself in any fantastic effort to induce just such a theory on the part of the police, and thus clear himself beforehand, so to speak, of his father's murder.

No, I didn't think that Craig had murdered Conrad Brent. And it was true that he had done his best to divert suspicion from Drue; I had to give him credit for that.

Nicky practically invited suspicion, but I had no evidence to back up any suspicions in that direction. Alexia was, of course, an obvious suspect; she was young, she was beautiful, she was married to a man she flatly declared she had never loved and that man was the father of a man to whom she had been all but engaged and for whom, apparently, she still cherished what appeared to be far from a purely stepmotherly regard. I thought of her kneeling beside Craig, and the things she had said. "You knew—you always knew I never loved Conrad." And then, ". . . all that is ended now for us both, my darling." Craig hadn't exactly said, "Oh, isn't that fine, hurrah, my father's dead and you are free!" Still, he hadn't said, "Don't be a fool, Alexia," or even looked it.

Yet there was no real evidence against Alexia. Nor, as to that, against Peter Huber or Maud Chivery. Maud had all but run the household during the long years of Conrad's widowerhood; it would not have been unnatural for her to feel a kind of jealousy for her young supplanter, Alexia. But that didn't mean that she had murdered Conrad! And certainly Maud fairly exuded an almost belligerent, tight-lipped respectability which did not go with whatever secret, horribly urgent emotion which, at last unbridled, finds its only relief in murder.

I stopped to think of that and then tried not to. It's a curious thing about murder, and I learned it during those days in the Brent house and among the low-lying Berkshire hills. Murder as a fact has a strangely insistent, wholly appalling quality; it is almost like a secret and terrible personality. At one instant you may be surrounding yourself with the commonplace, with reality, with everyday things—letting yourself think of the weather or what you had for lunch. And

101

then all at once, the next instant, you get a kind of psychic nudge, as if that grim presence stood invisibly at your elbow and said, mutely, *"You may try to evade me, you may try to pretend I have gone, but I'm still here. You can't see me, you don't know really where I am, but nevertheless I am here. I have struck and I may strike again. How do you know I won't? And how do you know whose body is possessed of me and whose arm will do my will?"*

It brings your heart to your throat and your breath stinging in your lungs. That's queer, too, and primitive, I suppose. As is the way your neck muscles, of their own accord, keep wanting to pull your head around so as to look behind you.

Well, that's the way it is. I felt it then and looked behind me, but there was nothing but hills and gathering dusk and silence.

So I went on in my little list to Peter Huber. Here at last was evidence. He had appeared on the scene almost as soon as I had, with a story to explain it which might or might not be true. He had fumbled around about the telephone call to the doctor; he had run straight upstairs at the sound of something falling and had disappeared. And while he was no relation and so couldn't profit directly by Conrad Brent's death, as all of the others might conceivably do, even the Chiverys, he might have a motive, that is, *if* he were in love with Alexia. Yet certainly no man is going to murder a woman's husband without making sure that he's going to get the woman and, if I had eyes in my head, it wasn't Peter Alexia wanted; it was Craig, and Craig, whatever he admitted and refused to admit, knew it. Besides, Peter Huber was only a friend happening to be there as an innocent bystander does happen to be on the spot and probably wishing heartily he were anywhere else.

Dr. Claud Chivery remained. He had prescribed the famous medicine which might have some as yet unsuggested significance; and somewhere in the history of that long friendship between the Chiverys and the Brents might lie seeds for murder. But again there was no evidence.

It had grown dusk as I stood there, although the sky was still light, so I realized later that, on the little ridge and in my swirling cape and hood, I was silhouetted from below against the clear gray light. A lemon-colored star came out above the eastern hills. It was colder, too, so I pulled my cape more tightly around me and pulled the hood over my head.

And it was just then that I heard somebody running heavily across the meadow toward me, through the dusk and the bramble.

And that wasn't all. Something sung sharply through the dusk over my head; I heard that before I heard the sound of the shot. I literally fell upon my hands and knees behind the stone wall just as both sounds came again. And whoever was running there in the meadow reached the rock wall a few feet away and began to scramble over it.

# XII

A singular thing about gun shots is this: no matter how little experience one has had at either the giving or receiving end, one recognizes the sound of a shot with really a peculiar facility and swiftness.

And just then another shot sung lower, over my head and over the stone wall. And I knew that that scrambling figure was at least thirty feet from me, but that the shots came from somewhere in the darkening, irregular meadow below, possibly from the wooded valley which seemed to outline the bed of a small stream.

I knew too that it wasn't the cat shooting at me. But that was about the extent of my knowledge.

Whoever had crawled over the stone wall had ducked; at least no figure emerged from the shadow of rock wall and shrubs.

I don't know what would have happened; perhaps in the end some car was bound to come along and rescue us. It takes a bold murderer to shoot anybody in cold blood on a public highway. But I was never to know because just then, with a loud whirring of the engine, a small automobile whirled around the bend in the road and began to climb the little ridge, its lights streaming ahead of it.

So I did what sounds dangerous and really wasn't. At least, I don't believe it was dangerous. I really remember very little of that moment or two during which I crept out, running low in the shelter of the rock wall and into those welcome lights and stopped the car. And it was Dr. Chivery.

He leaned out to look at me incredulously as, keeping the car between me and the dusky meadow, I approached him.

*"Miss Keate . . ."*

"Somebody's shooting at me! From the meadow! Somebody . . ."

And just then another figure loomed up from the shelter of the wall and it was the maid Anna. Her face was the color of an underdone muffin and her braids had slipped over one ear, giving her a rakish air which was belied by the terror in her eyes. She gasped, "Doctor—please, sir—someone's shooting—in the meadow. . . ."

Neither Claud Chivery nor I spoke; in the little glow from the dashlight his chin retreated still further and his slightly popped eyes seemed to take on a kind of reflection of the terror in the maid's face. Then the maid caught a long, rasping breath and said, still panting, "I mean—shooting rabbits, I suppose, sir. I—I was walking in the meadow, when I—I heard someone in the brush along—along the brook. It—it frightened me. I—I ran . . ." Her eyes shifted to me and back to the doctor. "And just then—as I got to the wall— the shots began. I don't know who it was, sir. But they—they often shoot rabbits in the meadow. People from town and— and . . ." She stopped again. And then said, "Doctor, would you mind taking me back to the house? I—I'm afraid I've taken more than my usual afternoon time off. Beevens . . ."

There was another little pause. Then without a word Dr. Chivery reached back, swung open the door to the rear seat of the car and I got in and so did Anna. Still in silence so far as speech went, he turned and reversed and started back for the Brent place. Nobody said anything. There was only the staccato sound of the engine waking echoes along the looming shadows of the hills all around us.

He took us all the way to the house, up the winding drive to the front door, where he deposited us. I thanked him and he drove off into the night again with, it seemed to me, that queer reflection of terror still in his eyes. Anna hurried to open the door for me.

"Anna . . ."

"Yes, Miss Keate." She had caught her breath now and straightened the fat blonde braids around her head.

"Who was in the meadow?"

"I don't know, Miss," she said flatly—and defiantly.

So I had to let her go.

But she knew as well as I did that unless the rabbit had jumped up in front of the gun and barked at him, our hunter wasn't shooting at rabbits. It was too dark to have taken a good potshot at anything smaller than a horse—or a human, silhouetted against the gray sky.

"Well. I glanced in the morning room and Nicky was sitting there, reading. His back was toward me but his small head and vividly checked coat were unmistakable. His coats were always a little alarming, being made up in very large checks or plaids and in an amazing range of colors—that day I believe brown and maroon again predominated. But however I felt about Nicky, it couldn't have been Nicky shooting at rabbits or at me. Nobody else was around and, feeling a little shaken by my recent experience, I went to my room, took off my cape, and again cast my mind back over the few things I knew of the murder of Conrad Brent. But after a while I had to give up; if those shots had been, by any stretch of the imagination, intended to remove me and at the same time any clue in my possession, then I didn't know what that clue was. The only conclusion then was, in a word, rabbits.

And since I couldn't quite believe this, either, it was only natural that I was a little uneasy. Perhaps wary is more descriptive. But in any case, hunting in the meadow was a good excuse; it was not unusual, Anna had said. So it was within the realm of possibility that any would-be murderer might count on that.

I didn't go in just then to see Drue, for, a little belatedly, I bethought myself of my patient and the fact that he had been presumably alone, with Dr. Chivery dashing about the roads in his little car and Anna fleeing from gunmen in the meadow. But on the way to his room I stopped and told the trooper on guard in the hall what had happened. I don't think he believed me; or perhaps he favored the rabbit theory, for he gave me a rather pitying and indulgent smile. But he did promise to tell Nugent when he saw him.

So I went on to Craig's room where I found Peter Huber with him and both of them talking of Chivery. "Who does Chivery think did it?" said Peter, as I entered the room and Craig looked at me, said "Hello, Miss Keate," and replied to Peter. "He says he doesn't know. He says it had to be somebody that knew about digitalis. How much to give and how. He says you've got to give enough to cause a heart block, as it does, right away. If you give too little there are all kinds of symptoms of poisoning—nausea and convulsions and—but that isn't what happened." Craig took a quick breath and went on hurriedly, as if to hide the pain in his eyes—yes, and the grief, for no matter what had happened between Conrad Brent and Craig in their adult life they were still father and son. He said hurriedly, "Claud has been looking it up in his reference books." He frowned. "He says he doesn't know who did it. But . . ."

"But what, Craig?"

"Oh. Nothing. . . ." He paused again, frowned into space and said, "If only I could get up and about! If I could even find out who it was that gave me this. . . ." His fingers touched the bandage on his temple. "I didn't see anybody— I didn't even hear anything. . . . Look, Pete, scout around a little, will you? Find out, if you can, exactly who was up and about till midnight or shortly before. Find out what happened at dinner. . . ."

"Nothing happened at dinner," said Peter. "I was there."

A touch of exasperation crossed Craig's face. "I don't mean did they throw things at each other or threaten anything. Just—oh, what did they say and how did they look and —oh, hell," he gave a flounce, and I clutched the light eider-down as it slid off.

"You'd better go now, Mr. Huber," I said, eyeing the tinge of scarlet that was coming up in Craig's lean cheeks.

"Wait, not yet, Nurse," said Craig quickly. "Listen, Pete, keep your eyes open and tell me if you see anything out of the way. And—and another thing," Craig hesitated, shot me an oblique glance and said, "Look through the house and see if you can find some yellow gloves. Loose—biggish. Don't let anybody know and if you find them, bring them here."

Peter nodded. "Okay," he said. And then I sent him away. But Craig said no more of the mysterious yellow gloves and, still aware of that touch of red in his cheeks and the feverish brightness in his eyes, I didn't ask further questions.

Dinner for both of us was sent up on a tray; no one came but the cat again. He meowed hoarsely and when I let him in he went to Craig's bed, jumped on the foot of it, purred loudly and hoarsely, but eluded my hand and Craig's and went to sleep, with his slitted grape-green eyes opening now and then to look at the door into the hall. It was only a wary look, though, normal one to one of Delphine's pessimistic nature, nothing like the silent, listening stare of the previous night.

Eventually I folded up like an accordion on the couch again. I thought a little pensively of the bed in my room which looked very comfortable.

Nothing happened that night. Alexia and Maud disappeared directly after dinner. Peter and Nicky went for a long night walk, for I happened past the stairway as they left and had a glimpse of Nicky's dark head and Peter's broad shoulders and leather jacket just as they closed the front door behind them. Later, because the house was so still, I heard their return. Or rather, I heard Peter's return; Nicky apparently got tired and returned first. I saw him as he passed Craig's room, for the door was a little ajar, on his way apparently to Alexia's room, and a moment later I saw him return. He glanced in both times and smiled airily, and looked exactly like a beautiful inquisitive young leopard on the prowl. It was much later when I heard Peter's return and by that time I had closed the bedroom door.

There was no chance to talk to Drue. Once or twice during the night I glanced into the hall. Mr. Wilkins or his double sat in a chair just outside her door.

The next morning, too, was without untoward incident. The police were about, for I saw them from my window, prowling through the grounds, and later Nugent questioned me about the affair in the meadow, so the trooper was as good as his word and had reported the shooting to him. The Lieutenant questioned me, too, again as to what or whom I had seen in the hall just after the odd little bump on the door, the night of the murder. This time I thought he believed me when I told him again that I hadn't seen anyone. But something to my alarm he suggested a motive for the shots of the previous night.

"Perhaps someone believed that you had seen more than you were willing, publicly, to admit. You gave me that impression, too. The way you stopped in the middle of a sentence."

"But I saw nothing! Besides, no one last night could have known I would be just there, above the meadow."

"Well. Can you suggest another motive?"

I couldn't, of course. "Rabbits," I said weakly, and Nugent said, "No doubt. But I'd not go for a walk alone again."

He went away, then, leaving me with mixed emotions. Chiefly it seemed a good idea to hang a placard on my back with the words on it, "I know nothing," which seemed just then a redundancy.

Alexia telephoned that morning to Bergdof's for a full mourning outfit, and I believe Maud assisted the police in going through the papers in Conrad's desk and in the safe. It was that morning, too, that reporters arrived; Chivery and

Nicky saw them. Later one of the papers had a picture of Dr. Chivery caught, apparently, as he was stepping into his car in front of his own white-picketed gate. His face, twisted over his shoulder, had a curious expression; there was a hunted, hag-ridden look about his eyes, taken unaware like that. Or it may have been the camera.

There was a picture of Drue, too, her graduating picture which someone had discovered. She looked very young and very lovely, her eyes steady and uncompromising above the stern severity of the Bishop collar our nurses have to wear on state occasions. Some of the papers made much of her brief marriage to Craig. "Nurse's Secret Romance" said one paper. But very few facts of evidence appeared; so I judged Nugent held his cards close to his belt, as a poker-playing patient of mine used to say.

None of the papers, however, reached us until after the next morning's train, which was just as well. And the reporters soon left.

Naturally, all that day I was like a hound on a leash about the hypodermic and still had to wait, what with the police there, to say nothing of Maud, Alexia and Nicky, and the maids cleaning the rooms.

Craig's condition was good, so far as the wound went; but there was a kind of nervous, fine-drawn look about his mouth and eyes. He said little but lay there, watching the door.

The police did not question Drue again that morning; she told me that when I went, about eleven, to her room. She was very pale and there were faint blue marks under her eyes. She wore a fresh white uniform like a signal of defiance and had touched her mouth with lipstick and brushed her soft, shining curls upward with a clean, childish sweep from her temples, but she could not hide the look in her dark gray eyes. We talked until I had to go back to Craig, but without any real or helpful conclusion.

She asked about Craig and some of the shadow in her eyes seemed to lessen when I told her he was better. She sent no message, however.

About one-thirty, Soper came to tell Craig there was to be an inquest that afternoon and to ask him if he knew a Frederic Miller.

"*Inquest?*" cried Craig. "Look here, Miss Cable ought to have a lawyer's advice before . . ."

"It's only a formality," snapped Soper looking sulky. "She's not to be asked to testify now. The doctor's the only necessary witness just now. And Nugent. What I'd like you to tell me now is, *who* is Frederic Miller? Your father has given him checks totaling fifteen thousand dollars in the last two years. You must know . . ."

"But I don't! There's nobody . . . See here, I don't understand!"

"Never heard the name before?" The District Attorney's eyes were little and suspicious.

"Never! And I don't think my father knew anybody by that name!" Craig looked honestly perplexed. "Did you ask Alexia—Mrs. Brent?"

"Certainly. She knew nothing of it either. Haven't any idea who it was that struck you that night?" His eyes were on the bandage still on Craig's temple.

"No."

"Are you sure it *was* anybody? You could have fallen."

"But I didn't," said Craig. "I was in the hall. Somebody hit me and dragged me into the linen room. So it must have been a man."

"Not at all. A woman could have done it easily. Good morning," said the District Attorney and went away looking remarkably like a stuffed frog.

And as he left Nicky came. I remained, in spite of the look Nicky gave me, which plainly invited me to leave. He was still limping a little.

"Hurt your foot, Nick?" said Craig and Nicky said, "Someone dropped a flashlight on it, in the ruckus the other night. Accidentally, I hope," and glanced at me and lowered his silky eyelashes so there was only a half-hidden but definitely malicious gleam back of them. I looked blank, as if I'd never heard of a flashlight and Nicky said, "Craig, look here. Oughtn't we do something?"

"Do something?"

"I mean—well, murder's murder. There's either a motive or it's a question of a—a homicidal maniac. I've given it a lot of thought, and that's my conclusion."

"It's in the hands of the police," said Craig. "They'll do everything they can."

"But, Craig," said Nicky, leaning forward suddenly, his pointed elegant face jutting into the light, "do you know who did it?"

"*No,*" said Craig. And added as bluntly, "Do you?"

"N-no," said Nicky slowly. "That is—of course the police think it was Drue."

"Thanks to your evidence against her."

"I didn't tell them everything I could have told them," said Nicky slowly and in a curiously tentative way.

"What do you mean?"

"Oh. Their conversation, for instance. Conrad's, I mean, and Drue's, just before he died."

Craig's eyes narrowed. "What do you mean? I suppose you listened."

Nicky shrugged; it was again tentative, only half-assenting.

"Well," said Craig, "what did you hear?"

If the library door had been closed, I didn't think he had heard anything, for it was extraordinarily thick and solid. Still, it might not have been quite closed. Certainly Nicky's handsome face looked extraordinarily disingenuous, almost, indeed, naive.

Naive like a rattlesnake, I thought abruptly. And listened.

Nicky hesitated then lifted his elegantly squared and tailored shoulders again. "Think it over, Craig," he said.

"You didn't hear anything," said Craig. "And if you did, it's nothing to me."

"Drue is nothing to you?" said Nicky softly.

"You heard me."

Nicky's bland face changed a little; his cruel lower lip protruded. He got up. "I see it's no use to talk to you, Craig. Oh, by the way, your divorce is still in good standing, I presume?"

Craig's straight, dark eyebrows made a line across his face. "What do you mean exactly?"

"Oh, nothing," said Nicky airily. "Except Drue is in circulation again. Prettier than ever. I'd forgotten"——he stopped, laughed a little and said——"well, no—not quite forgotten. After all, she did leave you once and I daresay you remember why. So if she is absolutely free . . ."

Craig said shortly, "Drue is perfectly free. As you know, Nicky. *Now get out.*"

When he'd gone, somewhat hurriedly, Craig lay for a long time looking at nothing, with a very grim expression.

Late in the afternoon Alexia came. She looked very beautiful and not at all like a recently bereaved widow, in a handsome tea-gownish dress, emerald green and trailing. It seemed to me that Craig's jaw set itself a little rigidly when he looked at her, but he promptly sent me away, which I must say was rather disappointing.

Drue was sitting at the writing table when I reached her

room but wasn't writing. Sir Francis lay like a little brown muff on the table beside her, his head on her arm.

"Sit down, Sarah. What happened? Did Dr. Chivery drive you away again?"

"Alexia, this time," I said a little grimly.

"Oh, Alexia." Her eyelids went down and she patted the little dog's vigilant head. And said suddenly, looking at the dog, her voice quite clear but completely without expression, "He's in love with her, you know. I suppose now—after a decent interval—they'll marry."

Well, if Alexia had anything to say about it, it was more likely to be an indecent interval. I repressed my evil nature to the extent of not saying it, and she went on, "I was wrong about everything. I thought if I saw Craig again—but I was wrong."

I said, energetically if ambiguously, "Nonsense."

"No. It isn't nonsense. You see, I know. He's still in love with her, Sarah. Nicky says so. Besides I—know . . ." She took up a pen and traced a circle with it slowly. "I'd better tell you, Sarah. I think that's what started everything. Alexia and Craig, I mean. You see—Alexia was in the garden with Craig a few minutes before he was shot. Nicky told me. And I think"—mindful of the trooper outside her door, she whispered—"I think Conrad shot him."

"Shot *Craig!*"

"Sh. He'll hear you."

"But—you mean Conrad was jealous?"

"Conrad made a kind of fetish of being old-fashioned," she said slowly. "And he was in love with Alexia."

"If his father shot Craig in a fit of jealousy and Craig knew it, he wouldn't tell—that's true." I was struck by a sudden memory. "Was that why you told Conrad you had found his revolver in the garden?"

"Yes. I knew it was his revolver; at least I knew he had one. And I knew him. I didn't know what had happened—I don't really know now. But I thought—you see, I was afraid. For Craig. If his father had shot him in a fit of jealousy, I wanted him to realize the horrible thing he'd done. Everyone else, I knew—Craig himself, and Claud and anybody else who knew or guessed the truth,—would try to cover it. Conrad was defiant; he said I couldn't have found it where I did find it. He said I was trying to blackmail him into letting me stay. But I wasn't—I really wasn't, Sarah. I never thought of it."

I knew that. And Conrad's defiance savored of guilt; it sounded as if he already knew of the revolver, for, if he didn't, his normal reaction ought to have been to start an immediate investigation.

Yet, again, I couldn't believe it.

"No, Drue, it's impossible! I can't think jealousy over Alexia would so blind Conrad. Don't believe Nicky. Don't believe anything he tells you. He's in love with you himself. . . ."

"Nicky in love with me!" She laughed shortly.

"But why then—Drue, he asked Craig if you were perfectly free. From your marriage to Craig, he meant."

"He asked Craig that?"

"Yes."

She didn't look at me. "What did Craig say?"

"Nothing," I said hurriedly, perceiving shoals too late.

"What did he say?" she repeated.

So I said reluctantly, "He only said that your divorce was final. But, my dear . . ."

Her lips had closed tightly. "Quite right and correct of Craig. *And* Nicky."

"You can't really think of marrying Nicky!"

"He hasn't asked me. But if he does, why not?" she said, and began making circles again, rapid ones now, jabbing the pen into the blotter.

"But . . ."

Her mouth and chin were set, there were two scarlet spots on her cheeks. I stopped and took another course.

"Drue, you said you intended to find out what really happened here. When Craig came back, I mean, at the time you left this house and went back to New York. And Conrad said Craig wanted a divorce. Did you?"

"It's too late for that."

I was about to say tritely and not at all truly that it is never too late. But she flung down the pen. "It's too late, Sarah! I was a fool to try it. I . . ."

The abrupt motion of her hand had knocked over a little blue jar of pebbles intended to hold the pen that rolled across the desk. And we both looked just as a little pasteboard box fell out upon the desk amid a shower of colored pebbles. It was a medicine box; there was the prescription sign and Conrad's name and Dr. Chivery's and directions and it held digitalis. Rather it had held digitalis. It was empty now, for I picked it up and opened it.

# XIII

Drue had made one quick, stifled motion to snatch the box, but I had it in my hand.

"*Drue . . .*"

It was dreadful to see the color simply drain out of her face until she looked like a ghost.

"I found it," she whispered. "Sarah, I can't tell you. I can't tell you any more. I've said too much now. Don't ask me—don't . . ." She stopped. And put her face down on her arms and against the little dog and began to sob. Dry, long, shuddering sobs, as if every one of them fought against her will. I think I put my hand on her shoulder. She said, in a stifled way, "Go away. It's all right, Sarah. Only go away. *Please.*"

Drue never cried; it wasn't her way of facing trouble.

After a moment I went. I took the medicine box with me; I had to. And I had to try to think, not that up to then I had got very far in that direction. But first I hid the little flat box in a handkerchief and pinned it inside the blouse of my uniform with a good, strong safety pin.

It turned me cold to think of the danger it had been to Drue. But there was only one explanation for her possession of the box, for her tears, for her refusal to explain it to me, and that was that she was protecting someone. There was a corollary to that, too; the only person she would protect was Craig.

Well, then, why hadn't she destroyed the box? And did she have some reason to believe that Craig had killed his father? As Soper had said, there is really no alibi for a poison murder. Craig could have done it by ingeniously (how, I didn't know) using his father's own medicine, fixing it (somehow) so he knew his father would take the poison that night, and at the same time (by faking an accident on the previous night, really shooting himself) arranging an alibi for himself that couldn't be shaken. An alibi that covered actually twenty-four hours (and might easily be made to cover much more than that) thus allowing a margin of time. So that if, say, he had put poison in the brandy (or in anything else his father was in the habit of taking) it didn't matter when Conrad voluntarily took the stuff, for Craig still had an alibi.

The flaw was his wound; nobody in his right mind would have come so near killing himself, when he could (with exactly the same effect) wound himself less dangerously and less painfully. And I still didn't believe Craig had killed his father—*but Drue was afraid he had, because she believed Craig had a motive*. I saw that, then; she believed that Conrad had shot Craig, so Craig's motive might be self-defense, or it might be a long-standing jealousy between the two men over Alexia!

When I reached that point, I got up and put on my cape. I had to get outdoors. I had to reach some sensible conclusion about that box and Drue and Craig.

In the hall, as I was starting for a walk, I met Anna. She had an enormous black eye, a perfect mass of black and green and purple bruises. I stared and she said quickly, "I ran into a door, Miss."

"Really, Anna. Dear me."

"Yes, Miss."

Of course one does encounter a door sometimes. It doesn't make a round mark, however; and there is almost always a sharp red line on the eyebrow made by the edge of the door. I said, "You're sure you didn't see anyone in the meadow last night?"

"Yes, Miss. That is, no. I didn't see anyone but you."

Certainly I hadn't given her a black eye. But I couldn't think of anyone who might have done it, either. With the possible exception of Delphine who was of a jaundiced enough nature but much more likely to scratch. However, I persisted. "I thought you might have seen someone in the meadow. Someone you were afraid to tell the police about."

But she didn't blush or show any change of expression; she just stood there neat and respectable in her long black uniform and white apron and cap. "No, Miss," she said stolidly.

But Nugent had been sufficiently impressed by my story of the shooting to question Anna. For she added unexpectedly, "The Lieutenant says it must have been someone hunting—last night, you know. Someone from the town, perhaps. He searched the house and he says the only guns in the house that any one knows about belonged to Mr. Brent. A revolver," she said flatly, "which the police took from Miss Drue's room yesterday. And a shotgun which hasn't been fired for a long time. They said they could tell. So you see, Miss, I—I was right."

"I see, Anna." Her eye looked terribly painful. "Try alternate hot and cold packs for your eye," I told her and went for a walk.

I had walked along the driveway down to the public road, meeting no one, deep in thought of Drue and the little medicine box, before it occurred to me that if I had been the possible if extremely unwilling target for gunshots the previous evening, I might well be again. This time perhaps more successfully from the hunter's point of view. It was getting on toward dusk again and the February landscape was very quiet and deserted, but there were plenty of little thickets of brush and evergreens, to say nothing of the opportunities for concealment offered by the walls and hedges. So I turned back, but before I had gone more than a dozen steps, Peter Huber came along in a long and very handsome gray coupe and stopped. He'd been to the inquest, he said, leaning bareheaded from the car. "Is everything all right at the house?"

I told him yes, and that Alexia was staying with Craig while I took a rest.

"Good," he said cheerfully. "How about a little ride? I'll tell you, we'll drive back to the village and get a drink. Hop in."

It suited me perfectly, for I wanted to hear about the inquest. So I got in beside him, looking with rather stunned admiration at the inconceivably luxurious car. It didn't have platinum handles and diamonds set in the wheel, but it had everything else. He saw me looking at it.

"A beauty, isn't it?" he said, backing expertly and swiftly so as to head the long gray hood toward the village. "My means don't run to cars like this, though. It's Alexia's."

His voice didn't caress her name in loverly fashion, certainly; but then there was no reason why it should, even if, as Craig had hinted, he was actually rather infatuated with her. Craig hadn't said how he knew, but then one can usually tell these things about people one knows very well, without words and without definite proof; it's something in the eyes, something in the air. But it occurred to me that if Peter intended to wait, discreetly, until he could press his suit with propriety, then he was reckoning without Alexia's singular directness.

In any case, whether or not there was anything in what Craig had told me, certainly both Peter Huber and myself, chance wayfarers, really, in the Brent house, were yet inexorably and inextricably bound up with the things that had happened there.

I sighed a little at that thought and he glanced at me.

"Tired? They've kept you going. I don't suppose you've really rested since Conrad died. Well, since before that really. What with Craig sick and all the goings on before Conrad died."

"There weren't . . . Oh, you mean the bump on the door and seeing Nicky?"

"*Seeing* . . ." The car swerved toward the stone wall at the edge of the road, jerked back to the middle, and Peter said, "What do you mean? Was it Nicky you saw in the hall when you opened the door?"

"No, no. I didn't see anybody. I opened the door after there was that—well, bump against it. But not right away. So whoever went past the door, carrying Heaven knows what, was out of sight by that time. It was earlier when I saw Nicky. And he wasn't doing anything, really. Just coming out of some room along the hall."

"Oh," said Peter. "I thought the way you spoke you had seen Nicky in the hall."

"No, no! Not then." Nicky! If he'd hurried, the night before, taking a short cut through the meadow to the house, he might possibly have arrived before me. In any case I made it clear. "I didn't see Nicky then. It was earlier." Suddenly I remembered Conrad's white starched shirt front and black tie. "Nicky must have changed after dinner again. Unless he didn't change for dinner. Do you remember?"

"Do I—oh, I see what you mean." He frowned, seemed to think back and said, "Why, yes! He wore a dinner jacket at dinner that night. So did Conrad; he always did. I changed, too. But I believe—yes, you're right. It must have been my room you saw Nicky come from; he'd been in to get a book I was reading. And I remember now, he had changed back to, I think, tweeds; a brown checked coat, anyway. But I . . ." He drove in silence for a moment, watching the road ahead. "I thought nothing of it then. And I don't see now that it makes any difference."

"Well," I said, "I don't either."

We had already topped the ridge where I stood the previous night; now we turned into the main traveled road. We could see the village ahead, very snug and peaceful and rather distant in the gentle dusk. And then all at once, neither of us speaking, we were there. The little main street lengthened, the white houses attained sudden height, and we turned and parked along a street of small, low-roofed shops, in front of a small haberdashery, in fact, and a clerk lounging in the doorway recognized Peter and spoke to him. "Evening, Mr. Huber."

"Hello."

"Hear there was an inquest this afternoon." The man's eyes were curious.

"Yes," said Peter shortly and helped me out.

"H'm," said the clerk and, as Peter offered no comment but steered me along the sidewalk in the direction of the inn (a long, sprawled, white building with the sign Coach Inn, 1782, hanging above its door), the clerk called after us, "You look fine, Mr. Huber. Glad the things fit."

"Oh, thanks," said Peter. "Yes, they were all right."

"I'll never forget what you looked like when you came to the store that morning," added the clerk with a chuckle that carried clearly through the winter twilight and silence of the little street.

Peter grinned back at the chatty (and curious) clerk and we crossed the narrow white porch of the inn.

It was a hospitable and warm old tavern. We went along a dark passage so narrow that my cape brushed the walls and entered the tap room, all smoke-stained rafters and age. Aside from nearly braining myself on a low rafter, I reached a table without misadventure and looked around me. Except for the bartender, no one else was there—or at least I could see no one, although the highbacked settles along the side walls cut off my view of one corner of the room.

Beside the bar was the kind of machine where one drops in nickels (or dimes or quarters, if one is really just a gambler at heart) and takes what comes, if anything. With this machine it had to be nickels. It was very quiet; I had had a kind of expectation of some kind of repercussion from the inquest, but if the police or Soper were still in town, I saw and heard nothing of them then.

The bartender knew Peter, too. He came forward, wiping his hands.

"Hello, Mr. Huber."

"Hello, John. I guess we'll have a—what do you want, Miss Keate?"

I took ginger ale. Peter ordered whisky and soda. And suddenly the bartender chuckled much as the haberdashery clerk had chuckled. "You certainly look different, Mr. Huber," he said. "Ever find your baggage?"

"No," said Peter. "Guess it's gone forever."

"Too bad. You looked as if you'd been shipwrecked," the bartender laughed.

"Felt like it, too," said Peter. He unbuttoned his short leather jacket, untied the white scarf around his throat and said, "Anybody been in here from the inquest, John?"

The bartender's face sobered instantly. "That's a bad business, Mr. Huber," he said. "First murder in Balifold since—well, I can't remember another and I've been here a long time. Ginger ale for you, Miss? And whisky and soda." He ambled away.

Peter leaned his chin gloomily in his hands. "I lost my baggage," he said ruefully. "I arrived here in what amounted to fancy dress. The natives can't forget it. They all but burst into hysterics whenever they see me."

If he was trying to divert me, he didn't succeed.

"You were at the inquest, then," I said. "What happened?"

"Nothing, really," he said, staring at the bare table and biting his knuckles. "They didn't intend anything to happen, I suppose. It was a formality. Dr. Chivery was there; he and the police doctor both testified as to what they had found. The police testified, too—that is, Nugent and one of the troopers. Then they had the lawyer that had drawn up Brent's will tell something of its contents. I suppose that was only to show that Brent was a rich man and that there might have been a motive for his murder."

"Was that all?"

"That was all. Or about all. They adjourned then."

"Then they said nothing of—of Drue?"

He shook his head, rubbed his hands across his thick, curly blond hair and then put them flat on the table. "Not a word. And Soper can't ask for a Grand Jury indictment until after the inquest reconvenes and delivers a verdict. Or so they tell me. So Drue is safe till then. They had to hold an inquest in order to give the police a kind of ticket to go ahead. Soper can go back now to the county seat or wherever his office is. And Nugent stays here and goes on with the investigation, calling on Soper whenever he needs him. The inquest can't be concluded, I understood, until they have more evidence. There couldn't be a verdict, but they made no bones of calling it murder."

The bartender ambled toward us and set our glasses on the table. Peter cupped his hand around his own with a welcoming sigh. "Alexia wanted me to go and hear what was said, so I went. She didn't want to go herself." He took a long drink, put down his glass and said unexpectedly, "He had really a lot of money. Conrad, I mean. And it won't come to Drue, so that ought to help out your little friend. I mean, she hadn't money for a motive."

He looked very gloomy. I said, a little gloomily myself, "Unless they think she hoped to remarry Craig and thus get money. That is, if Craig does inherit."

"Oh, yes, he inherits. Conrad wouldn't have cut him off; Conrad was strong on family, you know. A little cracked really on the subject. Had all kinds of grandiose ideas."

"Yes, I know," I said dryly, remembering what Conrad had said of Drue. "Anybody's wife, yes," said Conrad, "but not *my* son's." I added, "He seems to have felt that Alexia fitted into his family particularly well."

Peter glanced quickly at me, and I felt the way you do when you've said something that sounds more disagreeable than you meant it, and a man gives you that look of "So-it's-true-about-women-and-cats." He said slowly, "Perhaps he married her because Craig had as good as jilted her. The honor of the family—all that."

"Nonsense," I said. "He was in love with her; he . . ." I hesitated and then went rashly on, "Perhaps he'd been in love with her, really, without knowing it, for a long time. But that doesn't matter, anyway, and it's nothing to me."

"Nor to me," said Peter, and added thoughtfully, "But there's Mrs. Chivery. An extremely handsome and brilliant woman. I should have thought somebody like—well, like Mrs. Chivery, would have attracted Conrad."

"Mrs. Chivery!"

"Oh, I didn't mean anything," he said hurriedly. "It's only that she's very—well, attractive, you know."

I stared at him. He had a pleasant face; his calm blue eyes were well spaced above high, rather sharp cheek-bones; his blunt chin and his wide mouth and thick blond eyebrows suggested a certain uncompromising strength. He was no Adonis, certainly, but he was not bad-looking, either. And I was visited by a more or less fantastic idea. Perhaps it was Maud he'd fallen in love with and not Alexia, so Craig was right in guessing his emotional temperature, so to speak, but wrong in his diagnosis of its cause. True, Maud was at least twenty to twenty-five years older than he, but what with all the liberties playwrights and scientists are taking with time these days, that might not make so much difference. Time might be actually a sheer question of relativity; and I might be skipping rope again at any moment. Which was a fairly blood-curdling thought and shocked me back into a semblance of common sense.

Peter said, "Chivery knew about Conrad's will; we sat together and before the inquest began he told me about it. Dr. Chivery himself inherits fifty thousand dollars."

"Fifty . . . Good gracious!"

"They were old friends. And Mrs. Chivery managed the house for Conrad for years. Until he married Alexia. Then there were a few bequests to servants, something like five thousand to the butler, small sums to the others. The library rug was willed to a museum. A blessing, that; it ought never to have been put on the floor. There were smallish sums to one or two charities. The rest was divided between Craig and Alexia."

So Alexia had that for a motive. But if money were a motive for murder then it was widespread, for it included everyone except—suddenly I remembered Nicky.

"Nothing to Nicky Senour?"

"No. But Nicky'd already had his share."

"Nicky! But he's only Alexia's brother. He . . ."

Peter said, in a matter-of-fact way, "The police have already got to that. For two years or so Conrad has been paying Nicky Senour fairly substantial sums. At irregular intervals. By check."

If that was true then Nicky Senour had every motive to keep Conrad alive. Peter went on calmly, "But I don't think that it was blackmail. "It . . ." His head jerked around and his eyes fastened on something behind me. I hadn't heard a sound or a rustle, but Peter got quickly to his feet. And I turned around just as Maud Chivery emerged from the high-backed settle in the corner.

She wore a long black cloak and no hat on that neat, high, black pompadour. She floated toward us, noiselessly, her small white face suspended above that black cloak, her bright, peering eyes upon us.

The bartender materialized too, beside us, but more noisily. "That'll be for three brandies, Mrs. Chivery," he said, and Peter began to dig quickly into his pocket. Maud said to Peter, "I thought Claud would come in here after the inquest. I wanted to know what happened." (I thought, parenthetically, that she had heard that, and some other things too.) She went on quickly, "Have you seen him?"

"He left the inquest a few minutes before it was ad-

120

journed," said Peter. "Ten or fifteen minutes before, I imagine. I don't know where he went."

"Oh," said Maud. "Well, then I'll go home with you, if you don't mind." She folded her cloak around her, fixed her bright dark eyes upon Peter and said, "Are you sure about the money? Conrad's money, I mean. Doesn't any of it come direct to me?"

"Dr. Chivery told me the money comes to him," said Peter. "But Conrad must have meant it for both of you."

Maud's lips set tightly. "Yes. Yes," she said with an odd effect of resolution, as if she were casting a vote or making a vow. She pulled her cloak closer around her and let Peter pay for her drinks and I got up and prepared to go. I didn't leap to the conclusion that Maud Chivery was a dipsomaniac because she chose to retire to the depths of Balifold's bar for a little private drinking. I did think that in spite of her clear speech, her eyes were a little glassy. And I thought too that it was time for me to go back to the Brent house.

On the way out I stopped at the slot machine.

Peter and Maud had gone on ahead when rather unexpectedly I found that my fingers had explored the pocket of my cape and found a nickel. So I put it in a slit in the machine and then, as directions said to do, turned a kind of crank. I can see why these instruments have a certain attraction, for instantly a veritable shower of nickels shot out of the machine. Being unprepared, I didn't catch all the nickels and they went everywhere, rolling merrily on the floor. Peter and Maud came back quickly in a startled manner, and helped me gather up nickels. At least Peter did. Although I'm not sure that Maud didn't pick up one or two in spite of her aloof attitude, but, if she did, she didn't give them to me.

But it was owing to the nickels (and perhaps a little to the brandy she'd drunk while waiting for Claud Chivery) that Maud said just what she said.

Peter had pursued several spinning little disks behind the bar and he and the bartender were talking. And Maud leaned over toward me, touched the nickels in my cupped hands with positively loving fingers and said suddenly and low, her face all at once aglow, "Money—gold, silver, jewels. I'm going to have lots of money, soon. As soon as they can get the jewels. Heaps of jewels. All behind the church."

"Ch—church!" I said in a kind of gasp, clutching nickels.

And Maud nodded briskly and brightly, with a shimmering hard glaze over her eyes.

"Truckloads of jewels. Spanish. Castles in Spain—*my* castles in Spain . . ." she said in a dry whisper. And then Peter came back with the last of the nickels.

I didn't have time then to count them; we went directly out to the car, Peter laughing a little and Maud suddenly as silent and uncommunicative as a little black shadow. As well she might be, I thought a little tersely, if brandy affected her like that. Castles in Spain and truckloads of jewels! Truckloads. Well, really! In the car the odors of brandy and Maud's violet sachet were quite marked.

It developed shortly, however, that she had an errand at her own house and Peter offered to take her there and bring her back to the Brent place. "Alexia insists upon me staying on," said Maud.

So they let me out at the corner where the main road to Balifold branched onto the road past the Brent place. "You're sure you don't mind?" said Peter politely and, when I had to say I didn't, Maud said suddenly,

"There's a short cut to the house through the meadow; you'll see the path just beyond the wall."

So I got out and stood there, weighed down with nickels, watching the red tail-light of the car disappear along the main road south and east, in the direction of the Chivery cottage. And I didn't at all fancy the walk I had so airily undertaken, simply because I didn't want to refuse and then explain why. My road wound westward, skirting the northern wall of the meadow, and then, still winding, southward and eventually reached the Brent gate. A path through the meadow would be roughly the hypotenuse of the triangle and much shorter.

But I didn't like the meadow and the shadowy patches of woodland and brush; I didn't like the dense strip of brush and trees outlining the little valley of the brook; I didn't like the time of day. I remembered too well the hunter of the previous night, and I still didn't think it was rabbits.

Yet I couldn't stand there in the chill, silent loneliness of the approaching night. And the road must be nearly twice as long a way as the path.

So in the end I scrambled over the wall and took the path. I guessed it would come out somewhere about the garage and kitchen end of the Brent house.

Until I had got quite a distance into the meadow I didn't realize exactly how dark it was. I went along hurriedly, my ill-gotten gains making a small chinking sound in my pockets.

The meadow was rocky and the path twisted around weed-grown boulders and up and down tiny valleys and mounds; I hadn't realized either, looking at it from the road, how irregular the meadow was. I neared the belt of woodland and the strip of dark shadow which seemed to edge the brook.

What, really, had Anna run from, the night before?

The meadow, the strip of woods and thickets down by the brook were all clothed now in silence and in dusk. The sky was dark again and there were no stars an only a faint purple glow of lingering daylight in the west.

Once, somewhere in the shadowy distance, it seemed to me there was a kind of rustle and crackle of twigs, but when I stopped to listen there was nothing.

The path entered the strip of trees and sloped downward toward the brook. A twig caught at my cape and I jerked it away with a sharp tug, as if it had been fingers. And then I stumbled.

Something was in the path, lying like a sack in the middle of it. I fell on one knee, flinging out my hands to save myself, my cape swirling around me. My hand encountered the sack. Only it wasn't a sack. For my hands came away and they were wet with a kind of stickiness.

I knew by that viscous stickiness what was on them. I leaned over, trying not to touch him again. The twilight was deep but still I could make out the outlines of Dr. Chivery's anxious face and popping eyes, for once fixed and direct. His throat had been cut.

Then I heard again a rustle and snapping of twigs. This time it was clear and definite. This time I knew what it was.

It was the soft sound of something moving in the dense brush beyond the brook, on the slope between me and the Brent house.

As I listened it stopped. There was just silence and night coming on and the bloody thing at my feet.


# XIV

With every second it was growing darker; I don't know how long I listened like that, but it seemed all at once fully dark. There was no further sound from the thickets on the slope ahead. And I had to get to the house.

I got awkwardly to my feet, tripping on my cape, spilling

nickels. There was nothing I or anyone could do now for Claud Chivery. And I was afraid.

All at once I started to run—back, along the way I had come, for I couldn't follow the path into those shadowy thickets where something had moved. I ran as Anna had run, gasping for breath, listening behind me, running.

Eventually, after an eon of time, I reached the wall and nothing came out of that black and haunted meadow behind me. Then I was on the public road and I still had to circle (on the road now) around that dark and horrible meadow in order to reach the house.

Yet nothing, really, seemed to have a meaning except the hard-packed, winding road, the loud sound of my feet upon it, the dark lines of wall and hedges, the trees on either hand, the silence of the night sky above. It was as if I was suspended in a strange and ghastly world, cut off from everything I'd ever known, aware only of the road—and the grotesque and horrible thing I'd left in the little thicket, flung down like an empty sack.

Well, I got to the gateposts which loomed sudden and huge in the dusk. I could then see the lights of the Brent house, glimmering through the trees.

My throat and lungs smarted and stung. Yet I was horribly watchful and aware of the shadows and shrubs along the driveway. But there was a light in the hall; the many-colored stained glass window was garish above me. The door was unlocked, for I flung it open. And fell, literally, into Beevens' arms.

He caught me and his face seemed instantly to sharpen, so lines stood out and it turned the color of skim milk. I knew I was talking, trying to tell him.

He cried, "Dr. Chivery—Dr. Chivery . . ."

Someone else said, *"Where? Where?"* sharply, and there was a flash of color and Alexia, in her long green tea gown, came hurrying from the door of the library. Nicky floated into my vision too and seemed to have followed Alexia. Then Anna came from somewhere, and it was Anna who screamed.

She screamed so sharply that Beevens turned to her and said in a voice of snarling authority, "Get back to the kitchen. Shut up."

Someone—Nicky—was helping me to a chair. Beevens ran to the telephone beyond the stairway and Alexia was telling him what to say, her pointed face a white, vehement mask.

And then the trooper (Drue's guard; not Wilkins but another man) came running into the library, and wrested the telephone from Beevens' hand. "I heard you! I heard everything. Are you sure he's dead? What happened exactly? Operator, operator . . ."

He jiggled the hook and I tried to reply and he finally got the police. Alexia came back. "Where is Peter?" she cried. "Have you seen him? Where is he?"

"I don't know. Yes, I do. He took her home."

"Took who home?"

"Maud Chivery. In the car. They left me at the corner. Someone was on the meadow—don't you see—someone was there! Tell them that."

The trooper was already shouting the news of murder ("Another murder! Dr. Chivery! In the north meadow down by the brook . . .") presumably into Nugent's distant ear. We all listened. "She doesn't know who did it. Well, that's what she says. Just now, five minutes ago. No, the Cable girl's still in her room . . ."

Alexia looked at Nicky and Nicky looked at Alexia in utter silence, as if they didn't need words; it was a secret look, communicative, with a kind of mutual question and answer. It was baffling, for I could feel those elements in it, yet there was nothing I could really interpret. The trooper said, "Okay—okay—okay," and emerged into the hall again. "They'll be here right away. Now then . . ." I'd never noticed what big and extraordinarily substantial-looking revolvers the troopers wore strapped to their trim waists, until I noticed the revolver this one held poised in his hand. He said, "Don't leave the house, any of you," and ran into the hall and up to the landing where he stopped instead of at Drue's door. It was evidently an order from Nugent and it was a fairly strategic spot, for he could see the whole of the lower hall and part of the upper.

Alexia looked down at me. "Do you know who did it?"

"*No. No . . .*"

Nicky said, almost dreamily, "Claud—well, he must have got in somebody's way."

"Suicide," said Alexia, all at once. "It must have been suicide!" And Nicky said sharply, leaning over me, "What's she got on her hands?"

"I fell—I told you. He was on the path . . ." I began jerkily. Alexia and Nicky drew a little together and just looked at me, so their faces, so alike, and the eyes shining from behind those long silky eyelashes, were almost like one face, seen in duplicate, with one expression.

It was Beevens who came forward, clucked disapprovingly and exactly like a hen when he saw my hands and said, "This way, Nurse. You'll want to wash them." I followed Beevens through the library and into the narrow little washroom adjoining it. There was soap there and I scrubbed my hands and then saw a small stain on the hem of my white skirt and I took that out with cold water too and shook myself and felt better. Although I'd lost my cap somewhere. Probably in the woodland and the police would find it and say I killed him.

And then I thought of Craig. Alexia hadn't been with him, she'd been downstairs and in the library. So he was alone.

When I came back into the library Beevens was gone, and Alexia and Nicky were talking.

"Beevens said Maud walked into town about three-thirty this afternoon; she said she would wait in town and come home with Claud after the inquest. The inquest took place in the hotel," Alexia was saying.

"But she must have missed him," said Nicky. "Otherwise she and Claud would have come home together." He turned to me. "You said, didn't you, that Peter took her home in the car?"

"Yes." I went to the couch to gather up my cape. "I rode into town with Mr. Huber; we went into the bar and Mrs. Chivery was there."

"*Maud?*" cried Alexia.

"Claud must have walked from town," said Nicky. "He often does. And he must have intended to stop here; everybody takes the short cut through the meadow."

Alexia said, "Somebody's got to tell Maud. I'll telephone." She started briskly for the telephone, quite cool and unperturbed.

I said, "It's going to be a shock," and looked at her trailing green tea gown—not a costume for walking in the meadow. Yet Chivery had been dead for some time when I found him, so she or anybody else would have had time to get home and change. And just at that moment I suspected

126

anybody and everybody in the house, even Anna and Beevens and Craig.

But Drue had an alibi; she'd been under police guard. *And now they'd release her, for this proved, didn't it, that she hadn't murdered Conrad!* For, as Craig had said, simply on the basis of averages and logic, there weren't likely to be two murderers, mysteriously converging in our midst.

At that thought and its implications I took a long and thankful breath.

Alexia had reached the door when Nicky said, "You'd better let me do it. I'll have Peter bring her here. . . ."

As Alexia paused, I walked past them quickly toward the stairway. The trooper let me pass; he didn't speak or try to stop me; it was his presence there (uniformed, armed, waiting because he had to, alert as a coiled spring with only the excitement in his eyes betraying the man) that was a threat of power to come. Investigation, evidence, accusation. One attempt at murder: Craig. One murder by poison: difficult to prove. One murder by stabbing. Outright, cold-blooded, horribly feral. Wolfish.

Drue's door was unguarded and I wanted to go to her, but that would have to come later. I hurried to Craig's room; the door was open and he was sitting bolt upright, wrapped in a dressing gown, in the chair near the fireplace. His eyes blazed at me; his face was stiff and white. And I knew by the look on it, that he already knew. He said, "Shut the door."

I did. "What are you doing out of bed? Who helped you . . . ?"

"Come here. Put down your cape. Sit down—no, over here on the couch. Tell me about Claud. I heard the trooper at the telephone, and you when you came in the door. I know Claud was murdered."

"But you . . ."

"Listen," he said savagely. "I'm up. It didn't hurt me to get up. Nobody let me; it was my own idea. And as soon as you tell me everything about Claud I'll go back to bed. Not an instant sooner."

Well, there was no use struggling over it; I was still shaky and my knees were unsteady. I just sat there looking at him and wishing I could smack him and above everything else not really caring much about anything, I was so tired. And he said suddenly, in a less hard and terse way, "You'd better lie down a minute, Miss Keate. What about some brandy?"

The brandy made me think of Maud and her violet sachet and what had happened afterward and I refused it with a shudder. But I told him about Claud Chivery. Told him the whole story, and watched the gray, drawn look tighten around his mouth.

"Now then," I added wearily, "you'd better get back to bed. I thought Mrs. Brent was going to stay with you; I wouldn't have left you alone so long."

He was looking at the rug with narrowed, intent eyes that didn't see it. "I thought you ought to have some rest. That's why I didn't send for you. Alexia went away only a moment or two after you left. Miss Keate . . ." he looked at me then. "Do you have any idea who did it? Tell me what you saw, everything. I'm tied here. I have to depend on Pete to get around for me. And you. If I could only get out of here . . ." He started impatiently to rise, turned a blue-white, and I sprang forward just as he sat down again on the edge of the chair, clinging to the arms of it rather desperately.

"Well, you can't," I said.

"I've got to. I know I could do something."

"What?" I asked. It was a pungent question.

He said, "I don't know. But something. There must be clues. There must be something the police have missed. There must be—well, somebody. Somebody we don't know about . . ."

It was not a nice suggestion. It conjured up a lurking, homicidal figure hidden in some forgotten room or outbuilding, waiting to pounce. Something seemed to crawl along the back of my neck, and I shot a rather nervous glance toward the door, which was closed, and into the corners of the big room where there were only empty shadows, and said rather sharply, *"Who?"*

He stared at the fire. "Nobody," he said finally. "It's just that murder—is so unaccountable. So—well, so hideously erratic. You can't hook it up with anybody you know."

There was another little silence. I agreed with him altogether too heartily. At last I said, "If you were able to get around, what would you do? Where would you look for what you call clues?"

"I don't know," he said slowly, his eyes somber and brooding, watching the fire. "I don't know. Pete is doing what he can. But I—if only I could be sure that Drue is safe!" he burst out all at once and looked at me with a sudden appeal in his glance that was boyish and direct and touched with anguish.

"She's all right," I said quickly. "That's one advantage of being practically under arrest. She is protected by being guarded."

His eyes clouded again. "Yes," he said. "And that's another danger. If they arrest her—Miss Keate, I can't move. I couldn't get as far as the door without collapsing. Don't you see you *must* help me? Be my *eyes*, my—my *ears*. If I could only get out of here!" He struck the arms of the chair and gave a kind of groan. And said, "Tell me everything you saw or heard. Everything. You can trust me."

Which, for no reason at all, made me wonder if I could. Indeed, after seeing Claud Chivery as I had seen him I would have had a mental reservation about trusting my own image in the mirror.

Still Craig was the one person (besides Drue) who couldn't have killed Chivery. He might be able to get out of bed by himself and reach the chair; he might even—the night his father was killed—have walked as far as the linen room and collapsed. But he couldn't (at least I was fairly sure he couldn't) have waylaid Chivery at the brook; and he couldn't have hurried up that slope back of the house, along the rest of the path (the short way I had not dared attempt), reached the house before me and got back to his room unobserved.

Although someone could have done just that, and it didn't improve my state of mind to realize it. The path was a short cut; there would have been time. And certainly whoever it was in that shadowy brush had gone somewhere.

But I didn't know who it was nor why he was lingering there so long after Chivery must have died. I had no idea who, and telling Craig that, I almost said *what* as if the thing in the meadow had only horrible being and not humanity. Which in a dreadful sense was very near the truth.

Well, I answered his appeal as fully as I could answer it by simply repeating, in detail, the events that had taken place since I had left him with Alexia in the late afternoon. Or rather, since I had left him alone, for he'd said that Alexia stayed in the room only a moment or two. He listened intently but asked only a few questions. And eventually I got him back to bed; he didn't resist; he seemed indeed scarcely

129

aware of me. But he spoke of Drue, and he thought the same thing I thought. "They can't prove anything against her now," he said suddenly looking up at me. "They had her under guard at the time Claud was murdered."

"Thank Heaven for that," I said, meaning it. And just then, with the ironic neatness of life's little coincidences, Drue herself opened the door and walked in.

Rather she hurried in, closing the door quickly behind her. She was breathing rapidly; there was scarlet in her cheeks and lips and her eyes were bright. She wore her long cape with the hood over her head. She slipped the hood back; the light shone on her short, brown curls, catching gold highlights; her hair was disheveled and she'd been running. She came quickly toward us and Craig cried, *"Drue! For God's sake, where have you been?"*

"Is it true?" she asked breathlessly. "About Claud Chivery? Is it true? I heard them in the servants' living room. I came up the back stairs. What happened?"

I couldn't answer; I really couldn't; disappointment was like a vise on my throat, for I had so counted on her alibi. Craig said heavily, "Oh, it's true enough. He's been murdered; in the meadow, north of the house, by that little brook. Drue . . ." She was very near us and Craig caught her hand, pulling her down to sit on the bed so he could look in her face. "Drue, where were you?"

"I was out, Craig. I had to get out . . ."

"How did you do it? There was a trooper. You were under guard."

"It was easy—he thought I was Sarah. Oh, it doesn't matter . . ."

"It does matter. Tell me exactly what you did. Hurry . . ." His tone was as savage in a queer way as the tight, hard grip of his hands, and as demanding. She said, "Wilkins, the other trooper, was relieved. I heard him tell the man who took his place that there were two nurses and not to stop the other one—he told him which door entered your room, Sarah. And from the way he spoke I was pretty sure that the new guard got the idea we were both in our rooms. I had to get outdoors. I was stifled and sick with thinking and myself and—oh, I had to get out of this horrible house. It's brought nothing but unhapp—" She checked herself abruptly and her eyes met Craig's fully. There was a fractional instant when a small flame seemed to leap between them and pause tentatively as if waiting for breath to live.

Then Drue looked away. She said stiffly, "So I tricked him. It was very easy. I simply wrapped myself in my cape and pulled the hood over my head, walked out Sarah's door and along the hall. He saw me, but he didn't see my face—(he may not have been here with the others; he may not have seen either Sarah or me before)—but anyway whatever it was, he didn't stop me."

The little flame was gone. Drue looked at her hands. Craig's eyes were veiled. He said, as stiffly as Drue but quickly and urgently, too. "Where did you go, Drue? Did anyone see you?"

"I walked along the little path toward the Chivery cottage. I don't think anyone saw me. I . . . Suddenly her voice broke and she cried, terrified and despairing, "Craig, Craig, what is it? Who is it? What dreadful thing is happening here?"

The stiffness that had been like a wall between them broke down with that. Yet probably neither of them was aware of it. She leaned forward simply and swiftly and his arm went around her and drew her down close to him so her face was against his, and he cried softly and shakenly, "Oh, my darling, don't be afraid . . ."

And then, in the queerest little hush as if everything in the world had stopped for an instant, waiting for that very thing to happen, she turned her face and their lips, met and clung and he held her there against him.

Which was, it seemed to me, an extremely good idea.

But being in my softer moments (fortunately rare) a little on the sentimental side, something tight got into my throat and I got up quietly and went to the window and looked out into the winter dusk.

I did rather wonder after a moment how his wound was making out. Still he had one good arm. And the main thing was that they had come together again and now the course of true love would run smoothly. It would be now only a question of a few words and possibly a number of kisses which do seem to have their place in life. I was sure of that.

But the next instant I wasn't so sure. For the door opened again and I whirled around and Alexia came quickly into the room and stopped. Drue must have heard it too, for she sat up quickly, her face radiant and her eyes shining until she saw it was Alexia standing there.

Craig said, "Come in Alexia. What is it?"

Drue with a single sweeping motion so the cape fell about her like a shield rose from the bed and turned to face Alexia, her golden head high.

Alexia's lovely face looked sharper and more pointed; her underlip was full and cruel; her eyes gleamed softly from between those drooping eyelashes. She paused only for a moment then she came straight to the bed. Her soft white throat was as white as her pearls. She stood as near to Craig as was possible, as if by her very physical presence she could separate Craig and Drue. She said, "Drue, you'd better know the truth now. Craig loves me. Not you. He belongs to me and I belong to him. It's always been that way. You came between us once, but he didn't love you even then."

Drue's eyes blazed. "I was his wife," she cried. "We loved each other!"

Alexia's voice, husky and vehement, rose over Drue's. "No, he didn't love you. I knew it then. He married you, yes. We'd had a misunderstanding; he did it to hurt me. As I, later, married Conrad to hurt Craig. But Craig never loved you."

"I was his wife. . . ."

Again Alexia laughed. "He never loved you. He told me so. He asked me and his father to help him get the divorce."

Craig was as colorless as the pillow; his eyes were closed, his mouth a straight white line. And he didn't say a word.

He didn't tell Drue that Alexia lied, he didn't defend Drue, he didn't even look at either of them.

I said, my hand on Drue's arm, "Go back to your room, Drue. I'll come to you. Hurry."

"I'm free now," said Alexia. "And Craig is free and . . ." It was then that Alexia's eyes fastened on Drue's cape; a quick look of speculation changed to one of frank and glittering triumph. She cried, "So you weren't in your room under guard when Claud was murdered! You were out of the house! You have no alibi! The police are going to hear of this. . . ."

Craig opened his eyes then. "Drue," he said, in a voice that was as cold and chill as if she were a stranger to him, "I'm sorry. Alexia is quite right about everything. You'd better go back to your room now."

Drue stood perfectly still for a moment, terribly still and erect, in her long blue cape with her golden-brown hair shining, and the lining of her hood a scarlet banner over

132

her shoulders. Craig met her eyes across barriers that now, I thought, could never be dissolved. Then Drue said clearly, "I'm going, Craig. And I'm never coming back."

# XV

She turned so swiftly toward the door that I had to run to follow her.

No one was in the corridor. Drue swept along it like a queen with the folds of blue cape swirling around her, so the red lining was like her insignia of royalty. I didn't speak to her; I took only one look at her blazing white face, her small lifted chin, the poise of her head upon her slender shoulders. At the stairway I hurried ahead to look down to the landing with some vague idea of stopping Drue so the trooper wouldn't see her—although I could as easily, I fancy, have stopped a whirlwind. But he was gone, luckily, for Drue swept past without looking and on down the corridor and into her room. I followed her and said then, "Drue— Drue . . ."

"Sarah, don't!"

The little dog was there and came quickly, his tail wagging furiously; I saw her take him into her arms as I turned away and press her white face down upon the wriggling, little brown thing.

I closed the door behind me. Funny how seldom you can really face anything with anybody you love, no matter how hard you try. It's the everlasting loneliness of life; you are born alone, die alone, go up and down the winding road alone. Only in love do you ever really share, and I suppose that's why it's so important.

Well. I went back to Craig's room. Alexia was sitting in a kind of sulky silence beside the bed, and Craig was lying there looking straight ahead; neither of them spoke when I came in, although Alexia's eyes shifted toward me, measuring me again, I thought. Wondering, planning perhaps. And after a while she got up and walked out of the room. As she went Beevens came to the door; he still looked sick and his color was a pale blue-gray, but he said punctiliously enough: "The police are in the north meadow, sir; I thought you had better be informed of their arrival."

Police in the north meadow.

But it was at least two hours before they came to Craig's room and brought the things they brought.

It was a queer two hours which I remember in patches. Mostly we waited. Craig said nothing to me of Drue or of Alexia. Naturally, I said nothing of it to him and indeed made the few remarks I had to make as short and crisp as I could make them. He noticed it, for once I caught his eyes upon me in the oddest look; it had a kind of understanding, yes, and liking, and I don't think I imagined it. If it was liking, however, I did not reciprocate; on the contrary, for I thought he had treated Drue abominably. Indeed, I thought a lot of things, none of them pleasant, and looked coldly back at him and asked him what he wanted for his dinner tray. My suggestion would have been, at that moment, a sprinkling of cyanide, but it isn't really considered ethical for a nurse to poison her patient even though he richly deserves it. Which somewhat vigorous but merely fanciful line of thought brought me quickly back to unpleasant reality. Murder had actually happened in that house.

And on a dark and silent meadow.

It must have been about then, or earlier, that Peter Huber brought Maud back to the house. Alexia helped Maud to bed and later I gave her a sedative. Pills; nothing could have induced me to give her anything by way of a hypodermic. Maud said almost nothing; yet she seemed in a queer way to know everything we did, her eyes were so bright and knowing in her little sallow face. It may have been shock or brandy or sedative or all three—whatever it was, she went to bed docilely enough and then all at once to sleep. Alexia stayed with her for a while and, when she left, I think Nicky took her place.

We all had that curious feeling of haste that goes along with tragedy as if there's a great deal to do (hurry, see to things!) and yet there's really nothing you can find to do.

Every so often someone would bring a bulletin from the police in the north meadow and once Peter and Nicky and Beevens went to the back door and down into the meadow until they encountered a policeman who sent them back. There were by that time quite a number of police and cars; we could see lights (the long steady streams from the cars and searchlights, and the glancing, busy gleams from small flashlights going everywhere) like the lights of ushers in some darkened, dreadful theatre. Someone knew and told us when Chivery's body was at last removed.

A trooper again was outside Drue's door, and this time when I attempted to enter my own room and then go to Drue, he stopped me. "Orders, Miss," he said. And when I said, "Orders nothing; it's my room," he removed my hand from the doorknob in a very muscular way and then put his hand on his revolver holster. So I had to give up; not that I thought he was going to shoot me, I just thought I'd wait a better chance.

Beevens gave us a kind of dinner, served from the buffet in the big elaborate dining room, with its crystal chandeliers and stiff, green and silver brocade draperies. It was an elegant room, too big and too cold. Anna didn't help him serve; she was having hysterics in her room and I sent her some spirits of ammonia.

But before dinner Peter came to Craig's room; I was there and remained so I heard everything they said. Peter told him of the inquest and of our visit to Balifold where we found Maud, and when and where he had left me.

"I'm horribly sorry, Miss Keate," he said. "It must have been a terrible shock finding him like that. I ought to have taken you to the house. Craig, what's your idea of this? Why do you think he was murdered? If it was because he knew something that was a danger to whoever it was that killed your father, then what was it?"

It was the only motive for his murder that had as yet occurred to any of us; I suppose because it was so obvious. But I thought Craig hesitated. If so, however, it was barely perceptible. He said, "It's hard to say; Claud was very secretive. Pete, what about these checks to Nicky? It does look like blackmail, but there was nothing anybody could blackmail my father about. *Nothing!*"

Peter shrugged. "The police found the canceled checks. That's all I know."

Craig said suddenly, "I knew about the will, of course; Maud inherits now from Claud."

And she would inherit fifty thousand dollars; I'd forgotten that. I remembered Maud sitting quietly in the bar while we talked, drinking steadily. And an ugly picture presented itself in my mind: Maud in her dark cloak waiting for Claud in the meadow—and then afterward walking in to Balifold, trying to establish a kind of fumbling alibi, and drinking because she had to, to steady herself for the discovery. She had told me to take the short cut which was the path through the meadow and led inevitably to the discovery of the murder; was that, again, to give herself a semblance of an alibi? Or had it merely happened; everyone knew of and used the path.

And what of the time? Claud had left the inquest ·fifteen minutes before it adjourned, which would have given him just about enough time to reach the meadow. So what of Maud? How long actually had she been in the bar? And how long had Chivery been dead? Everything would depend upon that, and I didn't believe that anyone could fix the time of his death with real exactness.

Craig and Peter were probably thinking very much the same thoughts for, after a longish silence Peter said suddenly, "I don't think she did it, Craig. A woman . . ."

Nicky came in just then to say there was a dinner of sorts in the dining room. A little to my surprise, Craig tackled him then and there about the checks.

"What were those checks for, Nicky?" he said. "It couldn't have been an allowance. My father wouldn't have given you or me or anybody an allowance."

Nicky answered instantly, promptly, smilingly. "He would have, if Alexia asked him to. As she did for me."

A slow flush came up into Craig's face, but his voice was quite level and steady. "Do you know Frederic Miller?" he asked.

This time Nicky didn't answer promptly; he seemed to stop and think, cautiously. Then he said, "No. What about him? Are there canceled checks to him, too?" There was an eager light in his eyes that baffled me; it was as if he really wanted an answer. But Craig shook his head and made us all go to dinner. Gertrude, the little waitress, popeyed with excitement, stayed with Craig while I ate hurriedly with the others.

I·was alone with Craig when the police finally came. Lieutenant Nugent and two other officers. And asked me to bring a towel from the bathroom.

When I spread it out on the foot of the bed so Craig could see, they put down upon it two objects. Neither was exactly pleasant to look at. Quite· the reverse, in fact, for one was a small knife, a kitchen paring knife, quite ordinary except its blade was sharpened razor-thin and bright, and it was spotted, especially about the wooden handle, with a dark, dried substance, now turning brown.

The other was a yellow string glove and it, too, was stained in thick reddish brown patches, dry now and stiff.

Both had been found near Claud Chivery's body, but not near enough for him to have used and dropped, so it did not indicate suicide.

And there were no other clues, except my own white cap and some nickels, which they returned a little ceremoniously to me, Peter already having explained them.

They let me stay; in fact, they requested me to stay, for they wanted to question me, and thus I heard the whole thing. And beyond the fact that they had found no one yet who had seen Claud Chivery after he left the inquest, I knew no more than I had already known.

Except, of course, about the matter of alibis. For it was developing even then that there was a troublesome lack of alibis for that hour or so during which the murder had taken place. They couldn't, or at least they hadn't yet been able to fix the time very definitely. They asked me about rigor mortis, I remember; and the temperature of the body when I found it and I could tell them simply nothing. I'd had a kind of impression that he'd been dead for a time when I'd found him; but had no way of giving them a really accurate answer.

They asked me too, for I told them of it, about the rustle I had heard in the brush. I'm not sure, however, that they believed the little I could tell them; it was too tenuous, too unsubstantial a thing.

Nugent told Craig again, briefly, of the inquest, except he didn't mention the checks Conrad Brent had given Nicky. Mainly they asked Craig about Dr. Chivery: when had he seen him last, what had Chivery said, could he suggest a motive for the murder?

"Did he know anything—any clue or any evidence, about your father's death?"

"Claud didn't tell everything he knew," said Craig obliquely.

Nugent's green eyes sharpened. "Why do you think he was killed, Brent?"

"I don't know. But I'd stick to the knife if I were you—for a clue, I mean. The glove . . ."

"What about the glove?"

"Oh, nothing. It doesn't seem to mean anything."

"You're not being very frank, Brent."

"I can't do anything to help you like this. In bed."

Nugent said slowly, "I'd better tell you that it would help if you had an alibi for this afternoon."

*"I!"* Craig lifted himself abruptly on his elbow, winced and lay cautiously back again.

"An alibi always helps," said Nugent. "But the fact is people are saying—that is—well, it's like this, Brent. Everyone knows now that you and Mrs. Brent inherit practically all of your father's money. And everyone knows that you and Mrs. Brent . . ."

A slow flush was creeping up over Craig's face; his eyes narrowed. "Well? Say it."

"You know as well as I do what I mean," said Nugent. "Everyone thought you and Mrs. Brent were to be married over a year ago; then you married the little nurse and Alexia Senour married your father. Now they're saying . . ."

"Listen! I didn't kill my father! Get that into your head! I didn't kill Claud, either," said Craig bleakly. "I've no alibi for this afternoon, unless you consider it an alibi not to be able to walk without getting dizzy."

Nugent leaned forward. "Are you sure of that, Brent?" he said quietly.

An angry flush came over Craig's face. "My God, do you think I'd stay here if I could help it?" he cried angrily. "Don't you think I'd get out and do something! Don't you . . ."

"What would you do?" broke in Nugent softly.

Craig stopped abruptly. "I don't know," he said wearily, after a moment. "I don't know."

I said, merely in the line of duty and not to defend Craig, "He couldn't have murdered Dr. Chivery. He couldn't have walked that far and back again. I'm sure of that, Lieutenant."

Nugent's gray-green gaze plunged at me. "Are you, Miss Keate?"

"Yes. And as to that, Mr. Brent had an alibi the night Mr. Brent—that is, his father—died. I was with him."

"I know," said Nugent without any expression at all in his face. "Still, sick people have been known to walk incredible distances. And there really is no alibi in the case of murder by poison."

Craig made a quick motion forward as if to expostulate, and I said hurriedly, "I can't let you question my patient very long, Lieutenant." And put my hand on Craig's wrist. Not, again, to defend Craig but merely because it was my obvious duty. His pulse seemed steady enough, however. And Nugent said,

"All right. Just a few more questions. The night your

father died, Brent, you were found in the linen room. How did you get there?"

"I told you everything I knew about that."

"You said someone struck you. Who?"

"I don't know. I've told you. I didn't know anyone was near me."

"You say you were in the hall, starting downstairs, your back to the corridor. How did you get into the linen room where your wife—I mean Miss Cable—found you?"

"I don't know. That's the truth. You've no case against me."

Nugent looked at him slowly. "I'm not saying I have," he said. "But where there's murder, there's motive. And everybody knows that you and Mrs. Brent . . ."

"Can't we leave Mrs. Brent out of this?"

"Not very well," said Nugent. But after a moment's thoughtful silence he said no more of Alexia and went on instead to Conrad Brent's will, asking Craig if he knew its main provisions. Craig said he did. "My father told me."

"How did he make his money?"

Craig glanced at the Lieutenant with a little surprise. "It's no secret. He inherited from his father, quite a lot; I don't know how much. He invested it—oh, a long time ago. Before I was born. Anyway, everything he touched prospered. In the summer of 1929 he sold; everything was almost at its peak. Since then he's done very little buying or selling of stocks."

"He was a very rich man."

"Yes," said Craig, "he was. That is, it wasn't anything fantastic. But more than enough."

Nugent, hard and sinuous as a whip in his trim uniform, leaned over the railing at the foot of the bed. Lights touched his narrow high cheekbones and reflected in small points in his gray green eyes. "Brent, there was a queer codicil to your father's will. I mean, he'd lived in America all his life . . ."

"Oh, that," said Craig abruptly. "You mean he wanted to be buried in Germany. At Stuttgart. Yes, I know. It was an odd notion of his. When it struck him years ago, he had it written into his will; then, after his recent marriage, when his new will was written I suppose that was just carried over. I am sure that he'd changed his mind about it."

"Why did he want it, in the first place?"

"You'd have to understand and know my father to understand that," said Craig slowly. "I'll try to explain. He once had a kind of hobby for family; he dug into his genealogy, oh, away back when. Unearthed a single direct line, and clung to it. Got hold of the coat of arms, all possible records and history, everything. He was of German descent; although I think his father came to America and made his fortune sometime before the Civil War. My father had time on his hands; the study of genealogy interested him."

"A hobby," said Nugent. "I see. He didn't take it too seriously, did he?"

"What do you mean?"

"Well, did he consider going back to Germany to live, for instance?" said Nugent.

"Good God, no," said Craig. "He was a little hipped about family, that was all. He thought a lot about pure Nordic blood . . ."

"Approved of some of Hitler's ideas, in other words?"

"*No!* It was only at the beginning of the Hitler regime that he was rather taken with some of the ideology it claimed—resurrecting the old Teutonic family life, improving the race, keeping family blood pure, that kind of thing. But he got over that right away. There was nobody more loyal to America than my father. I'm sure of that. He much regretted that he'd been even briefly taken in by anything Hitler claimed."

"I see," said Nugent. "Forgive me, Brent, but he did disapprove of your marriage, didn't he?"

"He thought we hadn't known each other long enough. That was all."

"Oh," said Nugent. "I had an idea that you had rather quarreled with him about your marriage. I mean when you married a girl he didn't think was good enough to marry into his family."

"That," said Craig dangerously, "is enough of that. As a matter of fact, Miss Cable was too good for me and the Brent family. If that is all, Lieutenant . . ."

"No, it isn't," said Nugent. "It's this way, Brent. Soper thinks the girl—your former wife—did it. I'm not sure. Until something clinching and material turns up I'd like to hold off an arrest. And I've tried to give her a fair break. But she's not telling everything she knows."

"Well?" said Craig, still with a dangerous look in his face.

"For one thing, she disclaims having taken the missing

box of medicine. Yet her fingerprints were on the drawer of the desk where the medicine was kept; they were on the wooden handle and the panel across the front. She wouldn't explain how they got there."

My heart sunk, quite literally and heavily down toward my white oxfords; yet I'd been afraid of it. Craig said evenly, "That doesn't prove anything."

"And she got past my man late this afternoon and went outdoors. He . . ." Nugent stopped there and left us to conjecture what had happened to the trooper on guard in consequence. "It won't happen again," he said briefly. "But she was out of the house at the time Chivery was killed."

"A woman couldn't have killed him! Like that," said Craig.

"Mrs. Brent told us Drue Cable had been out of the house," said Nugent slowly, and looked at the ugly things that still lay there on the towel—the bright, sharp paring knife, the yellow glove.

And abruptly then, after a few more questions about Claud Chivery, they went away. As they left, Craig asked a question.

"Oh, by the way, Nugent . . ."

The Lieutenant turned. "Yes . . .?"

"Did you find only one glove?"

For an instant something very deep and intent stirred again away back in Lieutenant Nugent's green gray eyes. "Only one. See you in the morning, Brent. The District Attorney may be here then, too. I'm leaving a man in the house tonight."

They went away then, rolling up the towel and taking it and the things inside it along with them.

Craig lay in silence, his eyes closed, after their departure. And I can't say that I felt exactly chipper and talkative myself.

And presently Beevens came; he'd stay with Mr. Brent he said, while I got some rest. "And the Lieutenant spoke to the trooper on guard in the hall. I heard him, Miss. He's to let you enter and leave your room whenever you wish to."

"They're still holding Miss Cable, then," said Craig.

"Yes, sir. I'm afraid they are. Is there anything about medicine, Miss?"

I told him there wasn't and went away quickly; there were things I had to do, for somehow, now, everything was different.

It was an ugly difference too, something in the air, in the

stillness of the house, in the shadows in the corners and around the stairwell. In our meeting eyes.

There was no possibility of evasion this time; no way to deceive ourselves, no glossing of the grim and terrifying truth. Murder had been in that house, murder on the black and silent meadow. A thing that struck swiftly, out of nowhere and might strike again as swiftly, as silently.

An opened door, with the room unlighted beyond it, was a threat.

Well, I hurried along the corridor. The trooper, the same one who had stopped me earlier in the evening, let me enter my room, this time without a word. But I didn't go straight on to Drue's room, for the first thing I had to do was write a letter to the police.

I didn't really think I had done any harm or obstructed their inquiry in the least by hiding the hypodermic syringe. But I also felt a responsibility about it, to say nothing of the empty medicine box. So light in my hand when I weighed it and looked at it, so heavy on my heart. Perhaps now that Claud Chivery was dead Drue would tell me what she knew of it.

But just now I had to write my letter.

Since the shooting episode, not unnaturally perhaps, I had felt a remarkably unpleasant sense of personal danger. This was now very much stronger. I had seen Claud Chivery with his throat cut, huddled like an empty sack. The only motive for murder so far attributable was that he'd known something that was a danger to the murderer of Conrad Brent, or to whoever it was that shot Craig. And I, accursed with the Keate nose and a mentality that would have startled and delighted any psychiatrist, was simply reeking with clues. I had been led astray by my affections and softening of the brain; it was impossible to avoid the conclusion that if I didn't end as Claud Chivery had ended I'd be lucky.

True, I was none the wiser for any of my clues, if clues they were, for I didn't know who had murdered Conrad or Claud. But still there they were, and suppose something happened to me. Not that I intended to let anything happen to me; but I did want a clear—or fairly clear conscience. Just in case.

And it was equally conceivable that the little I knew might later, in some way, clear Drue or another innocent person, rather than convict anyone.

So I wrote it quickly, a bare statement of facts about the

142

hypodermic—*not the medicine box*, for that was still Drue's secret—put it in an envelope, and, as I didn't know what else to do with it, I pinned that too to the under side of my uniform, just below a pocket so it didn't show, and patted it down flat. Although, as to that, mine is not exactly the kind of figure which reveals an extra bulge or two.

Even then, however, I didn't go to Drue. I had nothing to tell her, nothing at all to offer that would give her support, except my affection for her and she knew she had that.

Besides, I'd have had to ask her again about the medicine box.

But I was beginning to be thankful for the trooper on guard at her door. Whatever the intention was, the result must be a degree of safety for Drue. After that twilight moment or two down in the meadow, a queer and horrible *unsafeness* was everywhere in that house, among the shadows of driveway and garden, across the stretch of lawns, around every corner. Even the encircling, shadowy hills seemed to know it and wait and watch.

I went first in search of Anna's room. The narrow hall that crossed the main corridor near the stairway led to the back of the house and I turned into it, passed the entrance to some rather steep back stairs, turned again and brought up in a wing that was obviously the servants' wing. I walked along, passing one or two open doors beyond which Anna obviously was not, and came to a closed one.

And just as I knocked someone inside the room spoke. It was a murmur, further muffled by my knock, but it sounded masculine. And it stopped abruptly at the sound of my knuckles on the door.

But it was Anna's room; for, after a longish pause, I knocked again and then Anna said quaveringly, "Is that you, Gertrude? I—I'm asleep."

"It's Miss Keate. I want to see you."

There was another sudden silence on the other side of the door. This time however there was a quality of consternation about it. Anna was not the type for tender dalliance; I didn't even think of that. But I didn't imagine the consternation either for it was plain in Anna's voice when she said suddenly, almost at the keyhole, breathlessly, "I—I'm all right now. I'm not upset any more."

And when I insisted, she just kept repeating it, "I'm all right. Thank you, Nurse. There's nothing wrong—nothing wrong . . ." with her voice growing thinner and more

143

frightened at every word. It was exactly as if whoever was there with her, and had stopped talking when I knocked, was standing beside her holding a club over her head.

But it wasn't really till sometime the next morning that they found the other yellow glove, bloodstained and stiff, hidden under the mattress in Anna's room. And by that time it was impossible to question her.


# XVI

Well, luckily in a way, I didn't yet know about that. And I couldn't break down the door to Anna's room and I couldn't see through hard pine.

I said, "Open the door, Anna. Beevens said you were ill. I'd like to get some medicine for you."

"Thank you, Miss Keate. No, I'm all right now." There was another slight pause, and she added, "I don't need medicine, thank you. I don't need anything."

So in the end I was obliged to retire to the end of the hall, loudly, and return on tiptoe to the open door of a room opposite Anna's. But after five minutes no one had emerged and there was no further sound of a (possibly) masculine voice from behind the closed door on which my eyes were glued. I was eyeing the keyhole thoughtfully and, indeed, had tiptoed nearer and was bending over (merely to see if a key was in it; as there was) when I heard footsteps behind me and straightened and whirled around and it was Beevens.

Who said "Ah" and coughed, giving me a chance to pull myself together. Not that I needed it; I said "Yes, Beevens?" as calmly as if keyhole investigation were my everyday and normal activity.

"Dear, dear, dear," observed Beevens, and again coughed and choked and choked and coughed so wildly that I saw that he was agitatedly concerned with something else and possibly had scarcely noted my posture and pursuit. His eyes were bulging and his throat palpitated like a fish's gills, quite noticeably, above the little white wings of his collar.

Craig wanted me—at once, quickly, he said.

Not even by a look did he question my presence just where I was and where I had no business to be. There was silence in Anna's room. So I followed Beevens back to Craig's room and Craig was waiting impatiently, watching the door, harassing the folds of blanket and coverlet across him with nervous fingers.

"There you are," he said. "Come in. That's all, Beevens. Shut the door."

Beevens hesitated. "If you please, Mr. Craig . . ." He looked uneasy but determined—so determined that it checked Craig's impatience.

"What is it, Beevens?"

The butler cleared his throat and came nearer the bed. "Two things, really, Mr. Craig. I've been in some doubt, but I—if you feel quite able . . ." He glanced anxiously at me as if for my permission and Craig said quickly, "Yes, of course. What is it?" Beevens swallowed. "A large blue vase has disappeared from the hall."

Craig frowned, his eyes perplexed. Beevens said, "No one knows anything about its disappearance."

After a moment Craig said: "What else?"

The other item Beevens had to relay was more serious. "It's a question of alibis, sir," he said. "Mr. Nicky told the police he spent two hours this afternoon in the morning room; he said he didn't leave the room at all during the time Dr. Chivery was killed. And Gertrude—the housemaid—saw him there twice."

"Well, go on."

"But he did leave, sir. I saw him."

Craig sat up abruptly. "You saw him! When? Where?"

Beevens looked quickly over his shoulder and lowered his voice still further. "He went out the side door, sir. Walking toward the garage. I thought nothing of it, naturally. Until the police . . ."

"What time?"

Beevens swallowed hard. "Not more than half an hour before the nurse found Dr. Chivery and reached us with the news. Scarcely half an hour, as a matter of fact."

There was another silence. Beevens' intelligent blue eyes watched Craig and reserved conclusions. And I thought, was it Nicky then in the meadow? But Claud Chivery had been dead for some time when I found him. Then why, if it was Nicky, had he lingered? Or had he returned for something? The glove? The knife?

Craig said, "Are you sure it was Nicky?"

Beevens permitted himself a slight shrug. "I saw him walking toward the garage and thus toward the meadow. Besides,

I couldn't mistake his checked coat; I was looking out the pantry window. But I didn't see him return. I was busy then in the dining room; he could have returned by the door just opposite the back stairs, gone upstairs and then down again by the front stairs. There's no doubt he had returned by the time the nurse reached the house." He paused. "Shall I tell the police, sir? I heard them question him and he definitely did not admit his absence from the house."

"Yes . . ." said Craig, and changed his mind. "No! No—I'll tell them. Is that all, Beevens?"

It was apparently all. But after Beevens had gone, closing the door carefully behind him, Craig lay for a moment in thoughtful silence; he looked perplexed—but there was something else in his eyes, as if Beevens' story had given him the barest glimpse of some new idea. Well, Nicky had been one of my choice suspects all along. And there's no doubt there was something queerly feral and inhuman in his very grace and lightness, as if behind his pointed face a graceful jungle beast might well inhabit.

Craig finally shook his head in an impatient and perplexed way and looked at me. "See here, Miss Keate, I've been thinking. You're fond of Drue, aren't you? Never mind answering, I've got eyes. Well, then . . ." He paused, his gaze plunging deeply into my own as if to test some quality within me. "Look here," he said. "I've got to trust you. You're pretty discreet—aren't you?"

I lifted my eyebrows and nose and he said, "Oh, yes, I know, but this is murder . . ."

"My dear young man," I said. "I have been a nurse since you were in rompers. The exigencies of my career have not failed to include a brush or two with the law."

"Oh," he said and looked at me speculatively for a moment. I did not see fit to explain, however, for one reason, the memories induced were a little unnerving, particularly just then and in that murder-ridden house. And for another reason, what is past is past and usually a good thing. So I merely waited in silence and presently he frowned and said, "I know. But it's not me or you that's in danger. It's Drue."

And at that, though it was not a new thought, I sat down on my patient's bed for the first time in my professional career. "*What do you mean? What new . . . ?*"

"Oh, it isn't new! I guess I'll have to tell you. You're her friend. It—well, what I want you to undertake, Miss Keate, is a little second-story job."

I digested that for an instant. "Exactly what do you want me to steal?"

His eyes were very intent; he put his hand tight and hard on mine as if to compel my understanding. "This is important, Miss Keate. It means everything to her. If they get hold of material evidence against her . . ."

"All right. Tell me quickly."

He was still reluctant to share the thing with me. "If I could only do it myself. I'll be up tomorrow. I *must* be. I tried to get up just now, while you were out of the room. Beevens helped me. It was no good."

"Don't be a fool," I said hotly. "Do you want to work up a fancy temperature?"

"I've got about as much strength as a kitten," he said angrily. "It's a hypodermic, Miss Keate. It's Drue's hypodermic syringe."

"Oh . . ." I said a little weakly.

"You see, Alexia's got it. She is sure it belongs to Drue. She found it somewhere . . ."

"Never mind—I know . . ."

"You know!"

"I put it there. In the fern."

He started abruptly upright, clasped his free hand quickly over his wounded shoulder and cried, "You, for God's sake! Why?"

"Never mind that either; I thought I was doing the right thing. Where does Alexia keep it?"

But he lay there staring at me. "She didn't tell me you had put it there," he said, and muttered something which sounded more or less profane. Then he said more sensibly, "Do you know what happened? Why did you hide it? Did Drue really give my father the hypodermic?"

"Yes, she did," I said, sighing and very cross. "But she didn't kill him with it. I'll tell you anything I know later. But I think everybody but Maud is downstairs now. If I'm to search Alexia's room I'd better do it quickly."

He was still anxious and frowning but agreed with me at once. "Right. You'll have to hurry. Look in her dressing room, and in the cupboard in her bathroom. Then also, there is a kind of cupboard built into the wall beside her bed. You'll see. She says she puts jewelry and stuff in there when she doesn't want to bother to put them in the safe. Look there. Look . . ." He moved restlessly and impatiently. "If only I could go! I suppose there's not a chance of your finding it. There's no telling where she's put it and it's so little . . ."

I was on my feet. "When did Alexia tell you this? How long have you known?"

A subtle change came over his face; his mouth tightened a little, his lean jaw hardened; his eyes went past me and looked very remote and uncommunicative. "Not very long," he said. "She wouldn't tell me where she kept it. You'd better go. It's the second door to the left across the hall. I hate to ask you to do this . . ."

I didn't tell him I only wanted the chance. I went at once to Alexia's room and the trooper was the only person in the long, wide corridor and he was away down near Drue's room with his back turned toward me and thus didn't see me.

But I didn't find the hypodermic. I found Alexia's room with no trouble and I searched it, and her tiny, luxurious dressing room as quickly as I could; and, while I don't happen to have the underworld training really requisite for such a task, still I do have a native aptitude for thoroughness. Indeed, the cool way I went through that glittering little dressing room confirmed a kind of impression I've had from time to time in a perfectly lawabiding life that I'd chosen the wrong era and sex to be born in and of. I mean, well, I wouldn't have been a successful courtesan but, after all, there were pirates.

I felt it even more so when, giving up the dressing room and going back into the beige and rose bedroom with its deep rugs and great leopard-skin hassocks and huge sheets of mirrors, I went directly to the little bookshelf and found the cupboard. And found not the syringe but something else and that was a little cluster of checks made out to Frederic Miller.

There were three of them, for five thousand dollars each, signed by Conrad Brent, dated in July, September and October of 1938. They were canceled and endorsed "Frederic Miller" in an ornate and curly handwriting and pinned together with a little steel pin. They were lying flat, under a soft suede case, the kind you use for jewelry when traveling.

The multitudinous nurses reflected in the mirrors (all in white, all inclined toward embonpoint, all with great wads of red hair and white caps which were in every case a little crooked) gave a simultaneous and rather theatrical start.

There was no shadowy pirate forebear standing behind each one of them, but there might well have been for, after only a few seconds meditation, I took the checks, adding them to my already substantial little hoard of clues. I'd have to tell Nugent. But I'd tell Craig first.

I didn't go then into the intricacies of explaining to Nugent how I'd got hold of the checks. And perhaps five minutes later I had to give up; it seemed more like an hour what with watching the door with one eye, looking for the syringe with the other, and listening with both ears in case someone came—which sounds involved but wasn't and had no really permanent effect upon my eyesight.

When I heard voices somewhere in the distance I thought I'd better give up. I ducked out of Alexia's room and into my patient's room as Alexia emerged at the head of the stairs and was followed by Peter Huber.

Craig was watching for me eagerly but still looked a little startled at my possibly precipitous entrance. "Somebody chasing you?" he said.

I straightened my cap and caught my breath and he got up on his elbow. "Did you find it?"

"No." I hated the disappointment in his eyes, the tenseness of sharpened anxiety, almost as much as the admission itself.

He lay back against the pillows. "Oh. All right, Miss Keate. Don't look like that. You did your best. She's given it to the police, then. She said she would. She hates Drue. It's because of ∴ ." He stopped there, abruptly, his face a kind of mixture of anger and discomfort and, queerly, sadness. There was no embarrassment about it and no fatuous or flattered look. I said crisply, "Because of you, I suppose. She makes it clear enough."

He wriggled his feet under the covers and scowled at them, but there was still a sad, altogether mature and grave look in his face.

"I hurt Alexia's pride one time. I didn't realize I was doing it; I was in love with Drue, you see. I was so in love that"—he paused and then said, simply—"so in love that there wasn't any other woman in the world. There wasn't anything but Drue." He stopped again and then went on, "Alexia just didn't exist for me. Nothing did really."

There was another silence; I was wishing Drue could hear him and resolving to tell her. I also realized that this was the time to put in a word or two with a view to clearing the situation between them. That is, while I am neither meddlesome or sentimental, it did seem to me that interference was practically invited at that point.

However, just as I was preparing to come out with something really clinching, he moved suddenly and restively and said in a different tone, "I tried to humor Alexia. She has the whip-hand. And my father loved her—he did, you know. She married him and he loved her."

"Don't get excited," I said, automatically rearranging the covers he had twisted around. "You'll get a fever. . . ."

"Oh, for God's sake shut up," shouted Craig suddenly, explosively, and gave a flounce which sent the eiderdown on the floor.

"Don't talk to *me* like that, young man!" I picked up the eiderdown and put it over the foot of the bed.

"I've got to think! I've got to do something. . . ."

"Well, it doesn't help to shout."

He glared at me and I glared back at him. My fingers itched to come into smart contact with his ears, but such a gesture seemed rather to exceed my nursing duties. And then just as we were staring at each other like two enraged cats looking for an opening, he grinned. The anger went out of his eyes and an odd, amused and, which was really remarkable, a rather affectionate look came into them. It really was that, and I couldn't help seeing it. He said: "I'm sorry, Miss Keate. It's only that it makes me savage, being helpless like this."

"You're lucky you're not dead," I said crisply.

The shadow came back into his face. "Yes, but it's Drue that's in danger. If she gave him digitalis . . ."

"She tried to save his life. She didn't give him enough digitalis to kill him. Unfortunately, though," I added grimly, "there's no way to prove that. That's our whole trouble. Are you sure Alexia gave the syringe to the police? Perhaps it was only a threat."

"I think she meant it. I was a fool. She knows I still love Drue. I tried not to let her see. I was afraid of what she would do to Drue. Sounds queer to say you're—afraid of anybody. But Alexia's not like other people." He paused and then thoughtfully, quietly, as if he were explaining something to himself as well as to me, talked of Alexia. "We've known each other since we were children, you know: Nicky and Alexia and I. They used to come here for summers when

150

their mother was alive; then she married again and went abroad to live. Nicky and Alexia were pushed around anyhow, schools in France and Italy, camps in Switzerland, hotels everywhere. After their mother died they were shipped back here. They hadn't really much of a chance and never enough money. My father always liked Alexia."

"Your father was in love with her."

"Yes, later. Perhaps all along without realizing it. At any rate Alexia married him. She's ruthless in a queer way, you know; she doesn't seem to comprehend pain. If it doesn't touch her it doesn't exist. She—I can't describe it exactly. She's the same with animals. It's like a kind of blindness."

"She could murder anybody."

He looked up at me quickly. There was a short silence. Then he said slowly, "Not unless she was so angry that she didn't stop to think. But that's why I'm afraid of what she might do to Drue."

There was a sincerity in his voice that didn't give my spirits what you could call a lift. But I did decide (provisionally) that Craig Brent had not murdered his father. And I must talk to Drue and among other things tell her that. Perhaps, then, she would explain about the medicine-box— that is, if her determined silence regarding it really was, as I thought it was, to protect Craig. Which meant obviously that at some time it had been in Craig's possession and she knew it. And that reflection brought me around the full circle again and in spite of myself I wondered whether Craig's continued and repeated statements of regret at not being able to get around were as sincere and frantically frustrated as he made them sound!

I was thinking that (and it was definitely not a happy thought) when he said abruptly, "That shooting in the meadow night before last; you remember?"

"How could I forget?" I demanded with some earnestness.

"Nugent thinks it was a kind of spur-of-the-moment attack on you."

Just an idle impulse, no doubt," I said, bitterly. "Well, I didn't like it just the same."

"Anna was sure it was only a hunter. Hunting in the meadow is not uncommon, you know."

"Besides being a fine alibi!"

"Yes. There's that too. But are you *sure* he shot at you?"

"I'm sure two bullets whizzed over my head. Of course, he may have been aiming at Anna. Or he may have been just a little prankster, bent on having his fun and giving us both a scare." I said it sarcastically, but he looked perfectly sober.

"Perhaps," he said, and added, "Anna's honest and loyal." And before I could remark upon the curious way Anna, terrified, with a mysteriously black eye, kept obtruding herself at every turn (to say nothing of a masculine voice, hurriedly hushing, drifting out of the keyhole), he went on, "I suppose there'll be traces of digitalis in the little—what do you call it, barrel?—of the hypodermic?"

"Yes. Unless it's been cleaned. Did Alexia see me put it there?"

"She didn't say."

I thought back rapidly to the hurried moments following Conrad's death. "She was walking up and down in the library, just behind the big desk. She must have seen me put it under the fern. Beevens was coming down the stairs just ahead of me. When I turned I saw no one. But—yes, the stair landing is visible from the library; she must have moved out of sight just as I turned. Then I suppose she took it—later, on her way upstairs, immediately after she left the library."

"Miss Keate, *who* telephoned for the police?" It was of course a pointed and significant question and had been from the first. But it was still without an answer.

"I don't know. I simply don't know."

"If we could find out who did that and why. If I could do anything—anything . . ."

I looked at him, decided to meddle, took a long breath and said, "Look here, you still love your wife."

"She's not my wife. You forget that."

"Fiddlesticks. There's no law against remarrying. If Nicky . . ."

"What about Nicky?" The question was like a pounce.

"I'd hate to see her marry him."

"You'd hate . . ." he stopped. "Listen, Miss Keate, there's something you don't know. That's why she left me. Because of Nicky."

# XVII

The breath simply went out of my lungs, so I couldn't say a word.

"Oh, yes, it's perfectly true," said Craig quietly. "She loved him. There's no other explanation for it. I didn't blame her. How could I? It's nothing you can help or do anything about. Love, I mean. I knew Drue. No cheap emotion would have made her do it. It was the real thing."

"But *Nicky!*" I gasped, incredulous.

He smiled a little. "That's another thing about love; you don't choose. If you're in love and it's the wrong man or the wrong woman, still you can't help it."

"N-nonsense," I exclaimed, rallying a little. "Of course you can help it! You can nip it in the bud! You can —why, that's a very immoral statement!"

He shook his head a little. "They went away together. Only a little while after she became my wife. It's been Nicky all along; only he wouldn't marry her because of the money. My father was grateful enough to Nicky for breaking up our —the marriage . . ." He said it swiftly. "He paid Nicky regularly for that, all this time. That is, I'm sure, the explanation of those checks to Nicky. But my father wouldn't have given Nicky a cent if he'd married Drue."

I wanted to shake him. Stupid, blind young idiot. I said, "She is in love with you. She always has been. She . . ."

He interrupted sharply, "There's no use talking of that, Miss Keate. She went away with Nicky while I was in Washington, shortly after our marriage. She asked for a divorce through a lawyer. She never tried to communicate with me."

"She wrote to you."

"No."

"Yes, she did. She told me."

"She . . ." He looked slowly at me. "I never got it. Are you sure? My father wouldn't have . . ."

"Your father would have tampered with St. Peter's mail if he wanted to. But it's too late now. What happened then?"

"But I can't believe . . . Well, then I went into training. She had gone with Nicky; she didn't even just go away and

153

then meet him later; she actually left the house with him. My father told me. She didn't write to me. . . ."

"Look here," I said in exasperation. "Five minutes talk with Drue would clear up everything."

"No," he said stubbornly. "All that's in the past and done with. Drue wanted a divorce. . . ."

"You wanted a divorce."

"No, it was Drue. . . ."

"Nonsense. She only wanted it so you could get into training."

"She . . ." He stopped and gave me a long look and then said very slowly, "Exactly what do you mean?"

"Are you trying to make me believe that you know nothing about that?"

"I haven't the faintest idea as to what you're driving at. What do you mean?"

"Now, see here," I began incredulously and then, at the look in his face, gave up. "Oh, all right. Drue said that your father explained to her why you wanted her to ask for a divorce."

"But I didn't . . ." Again he checked himself and said, "For God's sake go on. Why would *I* want a divorce?"

"To get into the training school, of course. Your father told her they wouldn't take married men."

"They wouldn't at the time. But I could have gone to another . . ." He broke off again to question me. "He told her that?"

"Yes. He said it was the thing above everything else that you wanted to do—or at least he succeeded in making her think that. He convinced her so thoroughly that she consented to ask for a divorce—believing that you didn't want to ask her for it yourself. And that once the training was over you would come back and marry her again. He told her," I added, quoting, "that it would be merely a long engagement."

Craig's eyes were very intent and very bright—and a little sad. He looked at me for a long moment or two as if to test the things I had said and measure them in his mind against what he had formerly believed. "So," he said at last, "he did that. And then I suppose if she wrote to me, he . . ."

"Obviously," I said, seeing that he was reluctant to say it. "Obviously your father got the letters. And Drue being the

154

kind of girl she is, I don't think she would write very many letters without a reply."

"No," he said slowly, staring at the mound his feet made under the eiderdown. "No, she wouldn't write very many times without a reply."

I said, "I'm going to get Drue. I think I can manage somehow to get her past the guard; perhaps I can't but . . ."

"Wait a minute," he said sharply. And stared at his feet, frowning. And finally said, "No."

"But . . ."

"No, don't. You've forgotten Nicky."

"*Nicky!*" I cried. "Drue's not in love with Nicky and never was! You're as stubborn as your father!"

"He had to finish what he'd begun. He couldn't help being the way he was."

Nor you the way you are, I thought in furious exasperation.

"Oh, Good Heavens! Can't you see she's in love with you? That's why she came here. She wanted to find out what had happened, why you demanded a divorce without even seeing her again. They drove her away—your father and Alexia and Nicky. Your father planned the whole thing. He paid Nicky for whatever he did to help."

He stopped my headlong flight into conjecture—yet, knowing Drue, knowing something of Nicky, it seemed to me reasonable conjecture. But he said, "So she went away with Nicky. Willingly."

"But she—there's an explanation for it. Give her a chance and give yourself one. That—why, that's why your father meant to send her away. The night he died. She told him, I heard her; she warned him. She said she was going to find out the truth about the divorce."

There was a little silence, then he shook his head slowly and deliberately. And I lost my temper. "All right," I snapped, "think as you please. It's your loss. You can fix your own pillows and dress your own wound, too, because I'm through with you. I wash my hands of you. If you'd even tell the truth about the things you know it would help. You know who shot you, don't you? And you knew there'd be another murder. And you know about the yellow glove— the glove that they found beside Claud Chivery. And I think you know why he was killed."

"If I knew anything I could tell the police I would do so.

But you see, Miss Keate, that's the trouble. If I tell who shot me, it'll make it that much the worse for Drue. It wasn't the same person. The person that shot me, I mean, was not the person that killed my father—or Claud Chivery. If I tell the police that they'll say she murdered my father."

After a moment I said heavily, "Was it your father, then? Why? Was it a quarrel over—well, was he jealous of Alexia?"

I couldn't read his eyes. He drew up his knees and clasped his unbandaged arm around them. "Forget that, Miss Keate," he said decisively. "The thing for us to do is to insist upon Drue's alibi for that night when I was shot."

"You said 'There'll be murder done.' You said that the afternoon before your father was murdered."

"I remember, vaguely. I wasn't sure—I'm not sure now exactly why I was shot. But I had a vague notion that I ought to tell Claud that it was an attempt at murder."

"But that isn't what you said. You didn't say 'There *was* an attempt at murder.' It was in the future, as you put it. You said 'There'll *be* murder . . .' "

"I know. You see, I had sense enough to know that since the first attempt had failed another attempt might be made."

"Do you mean you wanted protection?"

"In a sense. Yes. I wanted someone to know. I wasn't clear in my head. I only knew there was danger—everywhere."

"Why?" I demanded.

"Because," he said.

Which was not exactly illuminating. "Why Claud?" I persisted, getting nowhere fast.

"Because Claud was Claud. He wasn't much in the way of force. Yet he—he knew all about us; he smoothed things over, he could always manage my father; he was in the queerest way devoted to him. I think," said Craig slowly, "it was partly because of Maud; she thought there was no one like my father. In many ways Maud has a much stronger character than Claud had; he gave in to her about everything but money. Maud's a little overfond of money and would have been a sucker for get-rich-quick schemes if Claud had let her!"

"Oh, she wouldn't have murdered Claud on account of the will," said Craig quickly. "They did have a quarrel lately about money. Claud told me. But it was only about some money they had invested, twenty thousand or so; Maud wanted the cash in order to make another investment. Claud didn't know—or at least didn't tell me what it was."

"I suppose," I said on a wave of astuteness, "that Claud knew who shot you. And got rid of the bullet so it couldn't be traced." (As he would have done, I thought, for Conrad, to keep a family secret.)

But Craig's face was instantly blank and hard. "Do you?" he said flatly. So I got nowhere with that. And, as I lifted my arm to look at my watch, something rustled in my pocket and I remembered what, actually, I'd forgotten, the Frederic Miller checks. I gave them to him at once. "They were in Alexia's room, in the cupboard . . ."

He snatched them out of my hand; he looked at them and examined me and questioned me and then lay for a long time staring at the sprawling gilt figures on the dark wall paper, a queer look in his eyes, his fingers tapping the checks, an expression in his face that I couldn't read. I tried to question him.

"Do you know who Frederic Miller is, is that it?"

"No—no—that is, perhaps I do. I'm not sure. Let me think. . . ."

But he didn't want to think any longer, for almost at once he turned quickly to me, excitedly. "Look here, Miss Keate. Will I be able to get out tomorrow?"

"You may be able to get out of bed and walk around the room—that's about all," I said slowly. "You've done extremely well, as a matter of fact."

"Can I get to the Chivery cottage?"

"No."

"But I've got to."

"All right. You're free, white and twenty-one. Go ahead and kill yourself."

"I'll keep these checks."

"Are you going to give them to the police?"

He hesitated. "I don't know. I've got to think. If they arrest Drue, I'll do anything—everything. . . ."

I gave as jeering and mean a laugh as I could contrive— and succeeded so well that it startled even me. Craig jumped and stared at me. I said, "Anything, yes! Except tell her you still love her. And use your common sense about Nicky."

"If she loves me," he said slowly, "that's enough."

"I'll bring her here," I cried again. Practically with eagerness. "I'll get rid of the trooper on guard—I don't know how. But I'll get her . . ."

"No," he said again and firmly. "You'll bring Alexia here. Now. If you please, Miss Keate."

"Alexia! What on earth for?"

The queer look of speculation was in his face again. He said quite coolly, looking remarkably like his father in his more unpleasant moments, "Because I'm going to ask her to marry me."

"Marry Alexia! But, good heavens . . ." I broke off. "If you think you'll keep her from giving them the hypodermic that way . . ."

"Please go, Miss Keate."

"But I . . ."

He lifted himself on his elbow; his eyes flashed and his chin and nose seemed to grow hawkier, if you understand me. He snapped crisply as a drill sergeant, "Do as I tell you! Bring her here!"

Well, I did it. I've never met a man yet that could make me change my mind; I obeyed him only because—oh, because I did. I was furious, too. I caught a glimpse of myself marching back out of the room with my red hair flaming and two bright spots of anger on my cheeks. But I got Alexia. She was in her room, undressing, and I had to watch her select a diaphanous creamy lace garment that set my teeth on edge and not because it courted pneumonia and, as to that, every possible rheumatic ailment. I only hoped, following her lovely figure and noting how seductively the creamy soft folds of lace and chiffon melted into it, that she would be thus attacked and succumb quickly. In fact, before she reached Craig's room.

It was a wild hope. The trooper down at the end of the hall saw us and even at that distance I could see him snap to interested attention when his gaze fell upon Alexia. We reached Craig's room and she swept straight to the bed and Craig said, "Alexia, did you give the police the hypodermic?"

"Why, I . . ." She settled down on the bed, sitting very close to him, her short, dark hair cloudlike and beautiful about her pointed, delicate face. "Yes, I did, Craig," she said softly. She shot a glance toward me. "I thought I ought to. It was my duty. I gave it to Nugent tonight. He's taking it to be fingerprinted. And to have the sediment inside the barrel tested for digitalis. I'm sorry, Craig, but I had to do it."

"Yes," said Craig slowly. "I suppose you had to. Well, you've done it now. Alexia, there's something I want to ask you."

"Yes, Craig."

"Will you marry me?"

I shut my teeth so hard that I bit my tongue and uttered a stifled ejaculation which turned out, after I'd said it, to be highly profane. Alexia didn't hear it, not that I would have been anything but pleased if she had, but she was leaning over toward Craig as if she couldn't believe her ears. *"Why, Craig!"* she cried.

"Will you?" he demanded, his eyes holding her own intently and his profile exacly at that moment like a belligerent young hawk's.

"Why, I—oh, Craig darling." She hesitated. Then she seemed to get a kind of hold on herself and leaned over nearer him, lace and chiffon and all. "Oh, my darling," she breathed. "At last . . ."

He pushed her away, rather abruptly, so I hoped she'd fall off the bed, but she didn't. He said, "I don't mean just sometime in the future. I mean now. Right away. Tomorrow."

"But your father—Conrad—what will people say?"

"It doesn't matter. They'll not know. I can fix everything. Will you, Alexia?"

Which was just exactly more than I could bear. I whirled out of the door and gave it such a good hard bang behind me that the trooper away down at the end of the hall jumped three feet in the air, and came down facing my way and running, with his revolver in his hand.

We met at the stairway.

"Don't hurt yourself with your revolver," I said waspishly. "It was only a door." And sat down on the top step to brood. Which was an unwise move because the more I brooded the more discouraged I got about it, and the more suspicious the trooper, eyeing me distrustfully from before Drue's door, looked.

But it wasn't long that I had to wait; in fact in a surprisingly short time Alexia came swirling out of Craig's room, gave me the fraction of a glance and went quickly to her own room. I couldn't see the look on her face very distinctly because of the distance between us and the dimness of the night lights. But it did strike me then that there was something surprised, yes, and a little disorganized in her usually poised and self-possessed manner.

I didn't go to see Drue, then, either; I didn't want to have to tell her anything. Morning would be all too soon for it to break over her head.

Well, I went back to Craig's room because it was my duty as a nurse. And neither one of us actually spoke another word that night. I arranged his pillows, gave him one of the pills poor, dead Claud Chivery had left for him, and turned out the light beside his bed. He watched me—the queer, thoughtful look still in his eyes. He didn't give me back the Miller checks, and I didn't ask for them. I had enough clues on my mind—or rather, pinned to my anatomy —that I didn't know what to do with without adding to them.

Again I folded up like an accordion on the couch. But not to sleep for a long time. Craig didn't sleep either; I could tell by the way he turned and twisted. But I wouldn't have given him an alcohol rub for all the emeralds in Barranquilla.

About three, Delphine turned up and yelled at the door, so I had to let him in. He created an unwelcome diversion by bringing in what looked like and was a newly deceased mouse. Before I could bring myself to dispose of the creature, Delphine did it for me with really horrid zeal and sat there licking his chops and enormous whiskers while Craig grinned from the pillows and looked all at once young and boyish and rather nice. Which paradoxically made me crosser than ever.

I went back to my couch without a word and eventually I slept. I neither knew nor cared about my patient's slumbers, except I hoped they were troubled.

And in the morning early, just after Beevens brought in a breakfast tray for each of us, the police came.

It was as I had feared and known it would be. They came directly to Craig's room and told him. The hypodermic had Drue's fingerprints on it and mine. There was a very small residue of digitalis in the barrel—but enough to identify. They had informed the District Attorney of it and of her fingerprints on the drawer of the desk where Conrad had been accustomed to keep the missing medicine box (the medicine box that to me was anything but missing; I only wished it had been). Soper, over the telephone, demanded an immediate and formal arrest on a murder charge. But that wasn't all. For it was then, when they sent a trooper to bring Drue into the room to be questioned (Craig, looking terribly white and drawn insisted upon hearing them question her), it was then that they found she was gone.

160

She had disappeared during the night; nobody knew when or how. In her cape and without her shoes.

I knew that, for it was I that counted the row of slender, sturdy little pumps and oxfords. She'd brought four pair, including some stub-toed red bedroom slippers. They were all there in a row.

You don't go out into the night on purpose without shoes.

# XVIII

The trooper, questioned, seemed dazed but insisted, looking frightened, that she couldn't have passed him. There were no other exits from her room unless she got out the window and it was a sheer drop for nearly twenty-five feet with no shrubbery at that point to break a fall.

At noon they still hadn't found her; the household was nightmarish that morning—at fantastic sixes and sevens, with Beevens red-eyed and Craig like a crazy man, his eyes blazing out of a hollow, drawn white mask. We made peace somehow, Craig and I, without knowing it, conscious only of Drue and that little row of slippers. No matter what the police said, I knew it wasn't escape. Craig knew it, too.

Nugent gave orders, however, that started a wideflung, hurried search by telephone, radio and police cars, with alarms sent to neighboring states and hurriedly reinforced squads of state troopers searching the hills.

Much of the inquiry itself took place in Craig's room; he made Nugent stay there so he could hear everything. Soper telephoned frantically with a dozen different theories and directions; he believed that Drue had escaped. Very cleverly, he said; how, he didn't know; there were no cars gone from the garage. But he suggested that she'd got a ride with a passing motorist. And he blamed Nugent for letting her get away.

I listened and watched and kept going back in my mind over and over again, seeking for any small thing Drue had said, any hint of an intention to leave, anything at all that would serve to show she had gone of her own accord, willingly. There was nothing. Yet she must have got past the trooper somehow.

I kept going back into her room, too—and looking and finding nothing, except for the little dog, Sir Francis, who was still there; he had been there when they knocked and called to her and opened the door at last and she was gone. He wouldn't leave, but sat on the foot of her bed, bright eyes terribly watchful and worried. About noon, I think, I took him outdoors and tried to feed and pat him and he struggled away from me and took up his post in Drue's room again, watching the door, listening. I thought she would have taken him with her if she had gone voluntarily. And she would have told me.

It was a horrible, nightmarish day. Yet things happened. The police inquiry, for instance. Nugent's questions when I gave him the letter I had written about the hypodermic syringe; I was glad then that I'd written it, for I'd put down all the facts about the hypodermic syringe so it explained her fingerprints on the desk drawer; I'd said that Conrad begged her for his medicine and she looked for it but it was gone and it was only then that she'd remembered she had digitalis and had got it and the hypodermic syringe, and given it to him. But I still didn't tell them about the medicine box; I didn't want them to know she had so much as touched it.

Nugent did everything he could do short of sending for bloodhounds, and I'm not sure he wouldn't have done that. And I was in the room when Craig told him that Beevens had seen Nicky going toward the meadow (or at least toward the garage) just before the discovery of Claud's body.

Nicky, questioned, flatly denied it.

I heard that, too, for the Lieutenant had Nicky come to Craig's room. And the curious thing was the flatness and boldness of Nicky's denial. It sounded true; his eyes were bright and inquisitive, but he wasn't frightened, even when Beevens, summoned also, said he couldn't have been mistaken and seemed very nervous but certain. Nugent finally dismissed them both.

Sometime that morning, too (thinking of what I knew and what I only guessed of the attempt upon Craig's life) it occurred to me that if the person who tried to kill Craig was not the same who had killed his father, then an alibi for the time Craig was shot did not automatically constitute an alibi for the time of his father's or Claud Chivery's murder. And once, when we were alone, I asked Craig again about that meeting with Alexia in the garden just before he was shot. After a moment's thought he said, "It was an unintentional meeting. She was walking there too; she was there when I went down the

162

steps. We walked up and down the paths for a little and then she went back to the house."

"*Was* it your father who shot you?" I asked him again directly. And again he wouldn't answer.

And Nugent came back into the room, shook his head to the anguished question in Craig's eyes and, that time, sent for Maud. When she came, looking horrible with great dark pockets around her eyes and her face the color of wax, he asked her about the decanter of brandy that stood habitually on Conrad's desk. For her fingerprints were on it, it developed, and so were mine.

I explained my fingerprints on the decanter quickly; I had touched it. I was shocked, I started to take a drink of brandy, and then didn't. And Maud said in a tight, strained voice that was exactly what she'd done. "It was a shock to me; Conrad —dead like that. The brandy was on the tray and . . ."

"It was on the desk," I said.

"No," said Maud, "it was on the tray. I stood right beside it. I would have noticed if it had been on the desk; that decanter drips and alcohol ruins the desk top; I bought the tray for it myself."

"How much brandy was in it when you touched it, Nurse Keate?"

"I'm not sure I remember—not very much—the rim of the brandy came to not more than an inch from the bottom of the decanter."

Maud said, "You're quite wrong, Nurse. It was more than half full. . . ."

Nugent said, "Perhaps you are both right. If poison was in the brandy . . ."

"Did you find poison in it?" I cried. "Did you find digitalis in it?"

"No. Not in the brandy that was in the bottle when we arrived that night. But we can find no other way by which Conrad Brent might have, without knowing it, taken poison. He had a habit of drinking brandy at odd times; it's why he kept it constantly on his desk. Poisoned brandy may have been put in that decanter while he was out for his walk. In that case, he returned, drank it and died. Then in the time during which the room was empty the poisoned brandy was removed from the decanter (there's that little washroom on the other side of the panel; the poisoned brandy could easily have been poured down the drain and washed away with water from the faucet) and ordinary brandy put back in the decanter. It *could* have been done, like that. It's a good thing you didn't drink any, Miss Keate," he said a little drily.

I was thinking that myself, rather vehemently. He went on, "Conrad had to get the poison, somehow. It's the only way that hasn't been eliminated—so far as I can discover, at any rate. All that method needed were three things—the digitalis, a knowledge of the household and where to get more brandy, and opportunity to make the change after Conrad was dead." He looked at me gravely; I think he felt sorry for me. I know he was almost as frantic as I was, and as Craig was, about Drue's disappearance; he only controlled himself better and went on about his job.

Constantly, every few moments, there would be a report from someone—somewhere—looking for Drue. Troopers mainly, tall and well built and military-looking in their dark, trim uniforms, in the way they snapped into the room, snapped to attention, took their orders, snapped out again. But still time went on and there was no news.

He stopped then to listen to a report of a girl picked up near Northampton. It wasn't Drue; this girl was five feet eight and had black hair and wore a lambskin coat. (She turned out, as a matter of fact, to be an innocent Smith College Senior out for a walk and was highly indignant.)

And then he went back to Maud. "Mrs. Chivery, I *must* ask you again. If you know you *must* tell me. Why was your husband killed?"

Maud shrank back, her eyes sunken deep in her face, her black dress like heavy mourning. "I tell you I don't know. I've told you that many times!"

And Craig, watching and listening, gray with anxiety, leaned forward. "Maud—Claud said you quarreled. Lately. About money. What was it?"

She whirled on him. "I didn't murder Claud," she said.

"Why did you quarrel?"

She eyed him for a moment, her little face taking on a deep, queer flush. Then she told him. "It was an—an investment I wanted to make. He thought it unwise and refused to sell some bonds we owned together. That's all. It was nothing."

"What investment?"

She refused to tell. "It's a secret," she said. "It has nothing to do with this."

I said, rather absently really, for I didn't think Maud or

anybody in his senses was out to buy a Spanish castle just then. "Truckloads of jewels."

Maud whirled around toward me then—silently as always —but there was alarm in her eyes. "I don't know what you mean!" she cried sharply.

I didn't either; but I could and did quote her words to me over the nickels, and quite explicitly.

"Nonsense," said Maud flatly. "I said nothing of the kind —or if I did, it meant nothing."

There was a silence—and again that look of concentration in Craig's eyes. And another trooper came in to say that the knife that had killed Chivery came from the Brent kitchen; Beevens, he said was willing to swear to it. But no one knew just when it disappeared.

It was all written down in shorthand.

Maud silently disappeared and I think it was just after that that Beevens himself made his not inconsiderable contribution to the thing.

"It's about the vase, sir," he said to Nugent, his blue eyes worried. "Or rather, I mean about the noise—the sound of something falling, if you'll remember, the night Mr. Brent— died."

"What do you mean?" said Nugent. Craig got up on his elbow to listen. I stood there, in my starched white uniform, at the foot of the bed. I couldn't seem to settle down and it did no good to prowl the corridors and look out the windows and keep going back to Drue's room.

"I think I know what it was, sir," said Beevens and told his queer little story. He'd felt all along, and Mr. Craig had agreed with him, he said, with a side glance at Craig, that whatever that sound had been it had not indicated an intruder in the house and that therefore it must have some special significance. It was not, in other words, accident.

"So I took a look around," said Beevens. "This morning I found it."

"Found what?"

"The vase, sir, broken in fifteen or twenty pieces, all of them gathered up and wrapped in brown paper and shoved into the bottom of one of the ash barrels. The ash barrels," said Beevens austerely, "are removed once a week by a truck from the village. There was also a large, thick twine—at least twenty feet long, and one end of it was tied around the lower part of the vase. The kind of twine that I keep in my pantry for tying up parcels; anybody could have taken it."

He went on to elaborate, and he had a theory. It was a large vase, at least three feet high, he said, and heavy. Its rightful place was on a table in the second-floor corridor. He hadn't missed it because the household had been so upset that he hadn't really taken a look around the upper hall as he usually did (regularly) just to be sure it was all in order, but had left it entirely to the housemaid. And she had apparently assumed that he had removed the vase. But when he had missed it, he had looked for it with the result that he believed it had been placed at the top of, possibly, the back stairs.

"With the other end of the twine at the bottom of the stairs, perhaps," said Beevens, and stopped significantly.

Nugent's green eyes were narrow. Craig said, "You mean somebody placed it there and hung the string down the stairway and then gave it a jerk at the right time from below."

"It would fall, I believe," said Beevens, "in a series of thuds upon the treads which would sound extremely loud at night. It broke, perhaps at the bottom of the service stairs—which accounts for the crash the nurse mentions and which I myself heard. However, the pieces of the vase must have been picked up at once and hidden." He looked a little bleak. "I don't know who could have done it. But it was a very heavy vase."

Craig turned to Nugent. "Why? Why would anyone . . ."

"To get Miss Cable—or Miss Keate or both of them out of the library, of course." Nugent's green eyes were intent. "So whoever was waiting to dispose of the poisoned brandy could do so. But who picked up the pieces and hid them before we got here? There was nothing there when we looked, and whoever changed the brandy had to work fast. It's impossible for anybody to be in two places at once."

"Yes, sir," said Beevens respectfully and stubbornly. "You might look at the pieces of the vase for fingerprints, sir."

"Well, naturally," said Nugent. "The wrapping paper, too. Although I doubt . . . Where was the vase, as a rule?"

"On a table at the south end of the corridor, sir."

"South. Then anyone carrying it to the back stairs would have to pass this door. H'm—the back stairs and the front stairs are not far from each other; both in the middle part of the house. Well," Nugent looked at me. "You heard something bump against the door shortly before Drue Cable screamed. When, presumably, the murderer realized that there would have to be a sure-fire device to get her out of the

166

library before anyone came in order to change the brandy. Was it the vase?"

"It could have been. Yes. It must have been an accident . . ."

"Naturally. But when you opened the door you really saw no one?"

"But I've told you that. There wasn't anyone."

"Did you go to the door immediately?"

"Yes," I said. "That is, no. I mean I was a little surprised. I waited for a few seconds and then went. . . ."

"You waited long enough for whoever was there to have time to get away?"

"Yes, I suppose so."

He didn't say "What a help you are" but he looked it. "No more rabbit hunting in your vicinity lately?"

"No," I said. But thought nevertheless of the sense of threat that had crept like a live thing, like a wolf prowling and secretly waiting for prey, into every corner and every shadow and every empty room of that ill-fated house.

Well. Nugent sent for Nicky then and Peter. Peter came first and when he heard of the hypothesis of the broken vase, said he thought it very likely. I watched him closely, for by that time I suspected everybody, but his boyish, blunt face looked merely worried and sorry and perplexed.

"But I didn't see anyone," he said. "I glanced down the back stairway, too, and all along the corridors in the back of the house. I thought a window had been broken, from the sound."

"Did you see any pieces of the vase?" asked Nugent.

"No. But I wasn't looking for that. I was looking for a person."

"Pete," said Craig suddenly, "did you see Nicky anywhere? I mean, in the corridor, on the stairs—anywhere?"

"No. But I kept thinking there was a thief or some kind of intruder. I opened a couple of windows and hung out each one trying to see someone but didn't. It's the dark of the moon and was cloudy. Finally I heard voices and came back downstairs. Everybody was very upset. Maud was crying at the telephone. Nicky was in the library when I got downstairs again."

Nicky, when questioned, again simply denied knowing anything of vase, stairway or twine. "Why would I do anything like that?" he said calmly. "I didn't murder Conrad. I

167

know nothing about it. I didn't fix up anything like that to get Drue and Miss Keate out of the library. Why should I? I was sound asleep when the sound that you say was the vase rolling downstairs and breaking awakened me. Have you any news of Drue?"

And of course there was none.

I got up and made another fruitless trip around the house —to her room, up and down the stairs, into the library. I don't know what I was doing, really. When I got back Peter and Nicky were gone and Craig had given Nugent the Frederic Miller checks. I don't know why he hadn't given them to him sooner, unless it was because all that day Craig was fighting a queer kind of battle inside himself. He was like a man groping in the dark for a formless thing he had never seen, whose presence he could only surmise. And whose existence, even if he proved it, was still not evidence of murder.

But he told Nugent everything he dared to tell him.

"I didn't know this till last night," he said, their heads close together over the endorsed, canceled checks made out to Frederic Miller. "But I think I know what they are. And I think it may have something to do with my father's death."

Nugent's eyes glittered green fire. Craig said wearily, "I didn't at first connect it with my father's death. I can't really connect it now—except the checks ought not to have been found where they were found."

"Where ought they to be?"

"In his desk, of course," said Craig. "He kept all cancelled checks for five years. He kept them together, by the month and year, in one of the big drawers of his desk. Obviously they were removed. He may have removed them himself. Or Alexia may have done so. Certainly she must have known they were there, below the suede jewel case."

Nugent looked at me. "Exactly how and where did you find them?" he asked, although Craig had already covered the main points of my discovery. I told him, however, in detail. When I'd finished he looked for a long time at the checks.

"Do you know the handwriting?" he asked Craig.

"No. So far as I know, I've never seen it before. Of course, one doesn't remember handwriting accurately. But I've been thinking of that, too."

"We can investigate; we will." He turned the checks over again to look at the cancellation. "They've been cashed at different banks."

"Yes, I noticed that," said Craig. "Two in New York City and one in Newark. Presumably this Frederic Miller was well enough known at each bank to cash the checks. Obviously he either had accounts in these banks or some other means of identification."

"M'm," said Nugent, which was not illuminating. With me the thought of time was uppermost. Time and Drue. I said, "By the time you investigate those checks and, if luck is with you, identify and locate Frederic Miller—well, anything could happen. You can't do it in a day."

"No," said Nugent slowly. "But almost in a day. The F.B.I. are always ready to help with anything like this, and they have a vast system of records."

"What's in your mind, Nugent?" asked Craig suddenly.

"I'm not sure that anything is there," said Nugent. His words were candid but his look evasive. Craig said, "Do you think this Miller has got involved with the law at some time?"

"It's always possible," said Nugent.

"But . . ." began Craig and then stopped, and Nugent said, "What were you going to say, Brent?"

"Well, it's—it's nothing really. Except I've had all night to think about it, you see, and to wonder why those particular checks were removed from the others, yet not destroyed. And why they were found just there. If Alexia knows, she may tell and she may not tell. I don't see how she could help knowing that they were there; it's possible that she put them there. But why?"

"Exactly. Why? I'll talk to her. But in the meantime, there's something you want to say, Brent. Isn't there? Better get it out."

"All right," said Craig slowly. "It's not very pleasant. But it was only a—a prejudice on his part. It didn't last long. It's comprehensible. And I know that after the war began he had an abrupt change of heart. He still didn't—well, didn't really want me to go into the air force; that is, he used my wish to do so as a lever for something else he wanted. . . ." Craig glanced briefly at me, and Nugent said nothing. Craig went on, "But the fact is for—oh, for years he has been—or rather *had* been—well . . ."

"Germanic in sympathy," said Nugent quietly.

"Yes," said Craig as quietly. "How did you know?"

"Obvious," said Nugent. "Coat of arms in his study was of early German origin. I looked it up in a history of Heraldry. There are numerous books about genealogy in his study, too.

I questioned the servants in detail. He was very proud of his family line and of his descent."

"Yes," said Craig, "but it didn't mean anything, really. It was only a kind of hobby with him. He read German history, you know; loved it when some early robber baron, or later statesman, or title was connected with his family. He was always like that. During the First World War though, he swerved instantly around; he was all on the side of the Allies and against Germany. I knew he would do the same thing when this war came and he did."

"But in the interstice?" said Nugent.

"In the interstice," said Craig, "he lined up with Germany again. It was mere theory on his part. Merely a hobby. He was very proud of family, you see. And, as I say, had made a kind of study of German history and legend. When Hitler began his rise to power, my father was very taken with the ideas of encouraging the youth movements, bringing back the old German ideas of family life, that kind of thing. It was purely theoretical on my father's part. He had no faint idea of the real brutality and ruthlessness which lay behind all their talk. He wouldn't believe it for a time, even when it was increasingly evident to everybody else in the world. He was like that, you know; once he took a stand he—well, he clung to it. Blindly."

Nugent said nothing; I thought of my early impression of Conrad Brent and the obstinacy I had suspected resulted from an inner and ashamed weakness. Craig said, "He had changed. Believe me, Nugent. As soon as the war began he knew where his real sympathies lay. The other was merely a notion; nothing that really meant anything to him. He was patriotic and sincere. It was only that it was hard for my father to retreat publicly from a stand he had taken."

"Do you mean," said Nugent, "that these checks were somehow connected with sabotage or anything of the kind?"

"Good God, no," cried Craig. "He'd never have done that."

"What then?"

"I tell you I don't know. But that night—the night he died—you remember the clipping."

"The clipping that was in his desk and that Mrs. Brent went and got for him, during the bridge game? Certainly. It"—Nugent's eyes were bright, dark slits—"it was about the arrest of some Bund members."

"Right," said Craig looking very tired. "Alexia might know where the clipping is now. What happened to it, I mean."

"Your idea then, briefly, is that before the war began your father may have donated this money to some branch of the Bund, here in the United States."

"I don't know," said Craig. "But it would have been like him. He had money; he was curiously idealistic and curiously blind to reality until something happened to—well, give him a jolt. Make him see the truth. I don't know whether that actually happened or not. But I don't know of anybody by the name of Frederic Miller. I can't think of any reason for my father to give anybody such substantial sums of money. It seems to me that it must have been quite outside his business affairs."

"You must have some definite reason for connecting the checks with the Bund."

"No," said Craig. "I don't have. I knew nothing of it. I can't remember hearing him talk of the Bund—in any special way, I mean. Everybody at some time or other has commented pretty strongly and adversely about it. It was only the existence of that clipping and the mystery of these checks that started me thinking and putting them together with my father's previous—and lately altogether changed—views. The dates on the checks, too, would have corresponded with the period during which my father was theoretically favorable to the announced German plan. That was the year before the war; he never believed there would be a war. He swallowed everything the Germans then claimed, false though their claims were. It was when war actually began that abruptly again he came out in his true colors. He was honestly patriotic; the sympathy he thought he had for Germany was a completely unreal and assumed sympathy. When it came to the pinch he realized it himself."

"But you think that before the war he gave these checks to the Bund and that Frederic Miller was a Bund member."

"I don't know," said Craig. "I was only trying to think of some explanation for the checks. There may be a completely different explanation. I may be shooting very wide of the mark. But the clipping had some special interest for him. He wouldn't have kept it otherwise. And somebody said—I think Pete told me—that it was about the arrest of some Bund members."

"That's all you know?" said Nugent.

"I don't know that," said Craig. "It's only a guess."

"It's one I can easily check up," said Nugent. "I'll get on the telephone right away. And I'll send these checks in for investigation right away, too. And since it's fairly safe to assume that somebody in the household removed these checks from the desk, the next thing to do is to inquire about that. If you're right in your theory, Brent . . ."

"It's not a theory exactly," interposed Craig. "It's just the only thing I could think of to account for them."

"So you said. If you are right, then someone in the household knew of it. And blackmail is the answer to that. Could your father have been blackmailed in that way?"

"I'm not sure. Yes, I think he could have been. If most men had made a mistake like that, they'd have no compunction about it later. I mean they would be ashamed of it, and probably wouldn't want it known. Still, they wouldn't permit themselves to be blackmailed on the strength of it; they'd prefer making a clean breast of it, and trying to make amends for their mistake. But not my father. He was very proud. Yes," said Craig slowly, "I think he might have let himself be blackmailed. Up to a point, that is."

"A point that stopped short of murder?" asked Nugent.

"Certainly," said Craig. "But it was my father who was murdered. So that doesn't square with the blackmail theory. I mean, he was of no value to a blackmailer dead. That's the brutal truth of it."

"M'm," said Nugent aggravatingly. And just then in the corridor outside I heard heavy, quick footsteps and knew it was another report and, as always that dreadful day when someone came to speak to Nugent, my heart got up into my throat. Craig's did, too, I think, for his head jerked toward the door. But again it was only a trooper to say they were searching the north meadow and there was nothing to report except a rifle.

"Rifle?"

"Yes, sir." It was an old rifle which had belonged to the handyman; he'd used it now and then for shooting squirrels or rats, but he hadn't used it for over a year, he'd told them, and he'd left it, he was sure, in the old loft over the garage. It had been found in some brush in the meadow, as if it had been tossed there. There were no shells in it; but they believed it had recently been fired.

Nugent gave brief orders about it (they were to go over it for fingerprints; he would talk to the handyman), then he looked at me. "Your hunter," he said.

And then Nugent sent for Alexia and she, too, came as the others had done and sat there—composed and calm but with

172

a face so pinched about the nostrils, so curiously hard about the mouth and eyes that she looked ill and not at all beautiful. And she said flatly (as flatly as Nicky had made his own denials about the vase) that she knew nothing of the checks. Said it straight out, promptly, and looked as if she were going to die then and there. Which struck me as singular; it was the first time I had seen Alexia look as if any of it really affected her.

Nugent persisted. "Did you ever see these checks before?"

"No."

"Do you know what they were for?"

"No."

"Fifteen thousand dollars is a substantial sum of money."

"Yes. But I knew nothing of Conrad's affairs. Besides, as you see, these were written in 1938. Before my marriage."

"Mrs. Brent, are you willing to swear that you did not take these checks from your husband's desk and put them in the cupboard of your room?"

"Certainly," said Alexia quickly.

"When did you last open the cupboard?"

There was a short pause. Then Alexia, her eyes shadowed and secretive, said she didn't know. "Perhaps several days ago. I really can't remember. Except that if the checks had been there when I last looked, I would have seen them."

"Do you know Frederic Miller?" asked Nugent point-blank.

"No," said Alexia.


# XIX


And they could get nothing else out of her. Anybody in the house, she said, could have known of the little cupboard. She gave me a long, bright look when she was told that I had found the checks and there was something in her look that actually started a kind of chill up my back. Anybody could have put the checks there, just as anybody—again she looked at me fixedly and brightly—could have taken them. Conrad's desk was never locked. And when questioned about Conrad's former sympathy for the German cause she said that, of course, everyone knew where his sympathies had lain.

"Had he ever been interested in the various Bund organizations?" asked Nugent.

"I don't know."

"Do you remember the clipping you said you took from his desk? At the time you said you saw the box of medicine."

"Yes. Certainly."

"Did you read it?"

"Yes. I read it aloud. He asked me to."

"Can you remember what it was about?"

"I told you. It concerned the arrest of some members of the Bund."

"Their names were given, I suppose."

She hesitated but only briefly. "No, I believe not. I really don't remember. So much has happened since then. And it was not important."

"What did you do with it?"

"With the clipping? Why, I—really I don't know. My husband asked me to read it and I did. I believe I gave it to him then. Or perhaps I put it on a table. We were having coffee in the library. I don't remember. Why are you asking me about it?"

"Who was in the room at the time?"

Her slender black eyebrows drew together. "I'm not sure that I remember that, exactly, either. My husband and I, of course. It was immediately after dinner. Mrs. Chivery was there. I suppose my brother and Peter Huber were there, too."

"Can't you remember definitely?"

She gave a little shrug. "That is as I remember it. I don't believe I'd be able to swear to any one of them except, of course, my husband. But I think the other three were in the room."

"Mrs. Brent, try to remember this. Was it your impression that anyone in the room had a special interest in hearing the clipping read?"

I could read nothing in her beautiful, delicate face. She said very promptly, "No one but my husband. And I've no idea why he was interested," and looked at Nugent with a touch of silken and adroit defiance.

It did not, naturally, satisfy Nugent. He waited a moment and then said directly, "What about your brother?"

"My brother?" asked Alexia.

"It's much better, Mrs. Brent, to answer me truthfully and as fully as you can. Much better for everybody, believe me."

"But really . . ." Her voice was cool and polite; her eyebrows arched in delicate question. "But really, Lieutenant,

174

my brother had nothing to do with the arrest of any members of any Bund. He has never had any sympathy for Germany. He is not interested in politics."

"How old is your brother?"

Her voice was still cool, and polite. "My age, of course. Twenty-five."

"He's registered for the draft?"

"Certainly. I've forgotten his class. He can tell you."

"You and your brother lived abroad for some time, didn't you?"

"When we were children, yes. I don't understand your question, Lieutenant."

I was under a slight and I trusted erroneous impression that the Lieutenant didn't know exactly what he was getting at either; he only kept digging in the hope of unearthing something. He said, "What of Peter Huber?"

Craig started to speak, but Alexia replied, "You know everything I know of him, Lieutenant. He's been here about a month. He's waiting for his call to the army."

"Let me see. According to his story he went to school in Southern California."

"I believe so," said Alexia. "Didn't you check his statements? I understood that was part of your job."

"You are quite right," said Nugent, unruffled. "I'm afraid I've forgotten his home. I mean the name of the town. What was it, Brent?"

"Pete's home?" said Craig. "I don't know. I know where he went to school. I think he lived somewhere near Monterey. I'm not sure. Does it matter?"

"Do you remember his most recent address?" asked Nugent.

"Well, he had to come from somewhere," said Craig. "I think he said Hollywood. He was trying to get a job in the movies. I do remember that. I suppose a Hollywood address is the logical surmise in that case. Besides that's where he knew Bill Sheridan."

"Bill Sheridan!" said Nugent. "Who's he?"

"Fellow Pete knows. And I know. Went to school with Pete; that is, university. He—Bill, I mean—was in my class at prep school. Yes, I'm sure Pete came from Hollywood here."

"Is that your impression, Mrs. Brent?"

"Really," said Alexia. "If you've forgotten, I'd suggest

175

your asking him. Peter is nothing to me, you know. I never saw him before Conrad met him at the inn, in the village, and brought him here."

"That was about a month ago."

"Yes," said Alexia. "Lieutenant, why are you asking *me* about Peter? I was under an impression that you had not omitted him in your general inquiry. *I* can't confirm anything about him, if that is what you want."

Nugent got out a little black notebook and turned a few pages. "Ah," he said. "Yes, you were both right. It was a Hollywood address he gave us." I was sure somehow, in spite of his quiet voice that he had remembered all along and thus had only been testing Craig and Alexia—but testing them for what (aside from their knowledge of Peter and of Nicky) I didn't know. He said, "Yes, of course, how could I have forgotten! And Nicky"—he turned another leaf. "Nicholas Senour, brother-in-law to deceased. M-m-m. Apartment on East Fifty-sixth street in New York. Lives mainly at Brent home. Traveled extensively in Europe as a child; last trip made in . . ." He squinted hard at the writing, although from where I stood it looked perfectly neat and legible and said, "Can't make this out. When was his last trip abroad, Mrs. Brent, and where did he go?"

"It was in 1937," said Alexia, "and he went to Italy."

"I don't seem to have his occupation down here either. What does he do for a living?"

Alexia bit her full underlip. "He doesn't do anything," she said.

"Oh. You inherited money, I presume. You and your brother."

She hesitated and then said, "A little. Not much."

"I see." He closed the book suddenly and leaned forward. "Mrs. Brent, what about those checks made out to your brother? Were they for any specific service? Please answer."

She waited a few seconds, her eyes shadowed again by her dark eyelashes, then she looked up. "Lieutenant, that has nothing to do with my husband's death, or with the murder of Dr. Chivery. Nicky needed some money, of course; he's young and has no source of income. My husband knew that it would please me if he saw to it that Nicky had a little money, that's all."

"And Nicky lives here, mainly?"

"Yes. Since my marriage, at any rate. Before that we shared his apartment in New York."

"So you know most of his friends?"

"Why, I—yes, I should think so," said Alexia.

"Did he know Peter Huber?"

"No, of course not. None of us knew him."

"Were any of your friends at all interested in politics?"

"Why, I—really, I don't remember." There was a tinge of uncertainty in her voice, yet it was nothing that seemed exactly significant. It was more as if she could not discover the trend of Nugent's questions.

If so, she was soon enlightened however. For Nugent leaned forward, his lean face suddenly as sharp as a hatchet. "Who is Frederic Miller?" he asked again, abruptly.

But he got the same answer. "I don't know," said Alexia. "I don't have the faintest idea."

And again looked white and intent.

In the end, Nugent seemed to accept her denial. He said, "Try to think back, Mrs. Brent; try to remember." And added, "You told me that you had not seen Druc Cable since last night when you saw her going from this room to her own room. You are sure you didn't see her at any later time?"

"Perfectly sure," said Alexia.

"You don't know where she is?"

"Certainly not. She wouldn't have taken me into her confidence before she escaped, I assure you."

"Did you send her a message of any sort?"

"No," said Alexia, and rose. "If that is all, Lieutenant . . ."

He nodded. "Send Mrs. Chivery in here, will you please?"

Alexia went away rather abruptly. She looked a little shaken, it seemed to me, but by no means ready to break down and tell all. If, that is, there was anything for her to tell. It was entirely possible that the habitually secretive look in her small, beautiful face was merely a look and nothing else. Still, it seemed to me that she must have known something of the Frederic Miller checks. After all, they had been found in the cupboard in her own room. That was not, however, proof and I realized it.

Maud must have been in the hall, for Alexia had scarcely gone when Maud appeared silently in the doorway and, at Nugent's gesture, came in. She was preceded by a wave of violet sachet; her taffeta petticoat rustled sibilantly and her little dark eyes had brown pockets around them.

"May I ask a few more questions, Mrs. Chivery?" began Nugent and, as she gave a brief, birdlike little nod, he asked

177

her pointblank, as he had asked Alexia, if she knew anything of a man named Frederic Miller. And when she thought for a moment, fixing her bright eyes upon him and tilting her black pompadour to one side, and then finally said that she didn't, he told her of the checks and showed them to her.

She looked at them for a long time and very thoughtfully; studying the dates, the endorsements, the cancellations. She looked at them indeed for so long a time and with such an intent and thoughtful expression in her whitely powdered face that I was suddenly conscious of the fact that I was watching and listening intently for her reply. And so were Nugent and Craig. I glanced at them and they were watching her as intently as she was examining the checks. But when she looked up she said flatly, "No, I don't know anything about them."

Nugent said slowly, "Mrs. Chivery, is there anything those checks, or anything about those checks, reminded you of? Just now when you first saw them?"

"N-no," she said, and handed him the checks.

"You're sure?"

"Yes. That is . . ." she hesitated. And then said with a kind of plunge, "That is, for a moment I thought—but I was quite mistaken."

"What did you think?" said Nugent very gently.

"I was mistaken," said Maud. "The dates are wrong."

"Wrong for what?" asked Nugent.

"Wrong for—well," said Maud again with a kind of burst, "wrong for the kind of investment I thought he might have been making."

Nugent leaned back in his chair. "You'd better tell me exactly what you mean, Mrs. Chivery."

"But it—it has nothing to do with the murder. I can't tell you. I . . ."

"What investment?" said Nugent. And I remembered Maud's fuzzy phrases about Spain and jewels and said suddenly, surprising myself, "Spanish jewels?"

At which she shot me a dark, intent look. And said simply, "Yes."

Which further surprised me.

And before anyone could question or say anything she got up. "I can't tell you the whole story," she said. "But I do know that I was approached about an investment, and I believe that Conrad might have been approached, too. But these

178

dates are all wrong. The Spanish jewels—well, never mind that . . ."

Nugent got up, too. Craig watched intently, yet with no expression whatever in his face. Nugent said, "You'll have to explain what you mean, Mrs. Chivery. At once."

"No," said Maud. "I don't have to. That's enough. I don't know anything about your Frederic Miller checks. Have you heard from the girl?"

"Miss Cable? No," said Nugent, and looked quickly at Craig and said, "That is, not yet."

Maud said, "Look here, Lieutenant. I've been thinking. I'm not sure that I've been on the right side of the—of this affair. I've thought from the beginning that the girl, Drue Cable, killed Conrad. But somehow I—well, I don't think she killed Claud. I don't know what to do. That is, I have no knowledge that is a clue. I don't know who killed Conrad or who killed Claud. The only thing that I know of and haven't wanted to tell you is the matter of the investment I spoke of just now. But I did not make the investment; obviously these checks were not connected with that, either. I'll tell you all about that, if you want to know. I'll tell you tomorrow. But not . . ."

"Why tomorrow?"

"No reason," said Maud after a moment. "I—no reason. You'll have to believe me, for I"—she thought for another second or two and then said firmly, "I merely prefer it that way. And it really has nothing to do with the murder of Conrad or the murder of Claud. And it has nothing to do with Drue's disappearance." Her lips set tightly together.

And Nugent could not shake her. She merely shook her head obstinately with its high black pompadour and refused to tell him, even when he brought all the force of law and argument against her.

Craig said wearily, "You can't withhold information, you know, Maud."

And Maud said, "Can't I?" And did.

So in the end, only to save time, I imagine, Nugent let the thing rest and asked her what she knew of Drue's disappearance, and she said and insisted that she knew nothing and had not seen or talked to Drue for at least twenty-four hours.

Finally they let her go. Nugent looked baffled and Craig angry.

"There are points," said Nugent, "to the earlier forms of medieval torture."

Craig said slowly, "But Maud is honest, as a rule. And I think Claud's death has changed her view of the whole thing. I think what she was trying to say was that now she was on the side of—of . . ."

"Law and order," suggested Nugent.

"Yes. In a sense."

"Well, she's not doing a very good job of cooperating. Whose Spanish jewels? And where are they?"

"Probably in Spain," said Craig. "Maud was made for a sucker's list. The point is to find Drue. All these other things can wait, can't they?"

"Unless they can be made to point the way to Drue," said Nugent. "I'll do what I can with these checks."

"For God's sake, do it quickly," said Craig with a kind of groan.

It was, I believe, just then that the trooper who'd been on guard in the hall the night before came to Nugent. I hadn't realized until I saw him in the direct gray light from the windows how young he was. A boy, really, bony and tall with a thin, angular face which wore just then a look of desperation. But he had the courage to tell Nugent the truth—and then stand there biting his lip, but with his young eyes direct, waiting what came. I don't know what his punishment was; even then I felt sorry for him. But the point was that Anna had gone to Drue's room about eleven (to turn down the beds, she'd told the boy who'd believed her); she'd stayed with Drue, talking, for a while. Then she'd gone away but later—very much later, perhaps two in the morning—had brought him some coffee. He drank it, of course; and presently remembered sitting in a chair which faced Drue's door.

And that was all he'd remembered until he awoke, with a queer taste in his mouth, about six in the morning.

Nobody knew what Anna had put in the coffee; until I went and looked in my little instrument bag and some sedative I'd had—harmless in itself—wasn't there.

And when they sent for Anna, she was gone, too.

They found then—something after noon it was, I think—the bloodstained, yellow string glove—the mate to the one found near Claud Chivery; it was hidden under her flat, narrow little mattress.

But they didn't find Anna.

Oddly enough no one had missed her—oddly, but still comprehensibly. She had been ill and hysterical the day before; Beevens had told her to take that day off, to stay in her room and rest; Gertrude was to do Anna's work for her. In searching for Drue they had not (consequently informed of Anna's illness by Gertrude) entered Anna's room. It was an oversight, which only went to prove that such things (homely, trivial, perfectly understandable things like that) do happen and do complicate any police inquiry.

Nugent was furious and so were the troopers responsible for the omission, especially when they found the glove, which certainly ought to prove something and didn't, except it pointed suspicion toward Anna in a definite, material way that all my own odd encounters with the maid had never suggested.

Certainly, however, Anna's disappearance completed our demoralization.

Craig said, "They went together. They must have gone together. So Drue's—not alone . . ." and something like hope quickened in his eyes.

But I was afraid. So I told Nugent in detail all I knew of Anna—footsteps running from the meadow in the dusk—a black eye—an impression that someone was in her room with her and that she was frightened.

It was too little, however, and too tenuous a story.

Nugent looked at the small, black notebook again. "We've questioned the servants," he said, "over and over. Anna was nervous but she seemed to know nothing . . ." he stopped, frowning, and then read aloud: "William Fanshawe Beevens —British birth, age fifty-four; Gertrude Schieffel, American birth. Mrs. Lydia Deithaler—that's the cook; here we are—Anna Haub, German birth, age thirty-six, came to America from Bavaria fourteen years ago, in employ of Conrad Brent since 1929, no former police record. That's all." His lean dark face was so concentrated with thought it made me think again of a dark, sharp hatchet with glowing green eyes—which I realize however would be more or less in the nature of a phenomenon. "No former police record. No suspicious facts. She lived a quiet, hard-working life, apparently perfectly honest and devoted to the Brent family. Devoted . . ." he said thoughtfully, and looked at Craig who shook his head.

"I don't think she had any interest whatever in Germany or in the Bund. She must have left some kind of family in Germany—but if so I can't remember ever hearing of any of them. No, I don't think Anna would be likely to know anything of the Frederic Miller checks. Even if our surmise should turn out to be the answer, and Frederic Miller actually was somebody interested in the Bund. Anna wasn't smart enough, in just that way, I mean. She was shrewd but not—not scheming. Not clever."

"What do you think has happened to her?"

"God knows," said Craig. "If they're together though, she and Drue, there's some hope . . ."

I had let him get up again and sit in a chair, wrapped in a long camel's hair dressing-gown; he put his face then in his hands with a kind of desperate gesture.

It was after he knew about Anna that he redoubled his efforts to do something that, he was convinced, only he could do.

Twice already, that day (when I was out of the room) he'd tried to walk—once getting as far as the linen room again and the second time halfway down the stairs where he was found sitting, dizzily clinging to the bannisters, by one of the troopers and brought back.

The third time, late in the afternoon, with still no news, he sent me on a pretext to the kitchen, and this time he got as far as trousers and a sweater, and the fireplace bench of the lower hall. I found him there myself grimly upright, clinging to the bench with his eyes shut as if the room was going around him.

Peter helped me get him back to his room. And it was then that we had our long and curiously illuminating, and at the same time curiously baffling talk. It was long, that is, in content, not in time. All of us, I know, were strongly aware of the passage of time. It was growing dusk in the room, I remember, although it was still light outside with the clear, cold light of a late winter's afternoon. And Drue's disappearance was still unexplained.

Peter eased Craig down into a chair and then stood there looking rather ruefully down at him.

"You'd better go back to bed," I said, but Craig shook his head obstinately.

"Well, then," said Peter, "let me be your leg man. Just tell me whatever you want me to do and I'll do it. If I can."

"Find Drue, of course," said Craig, his head back against the cushion and his face white. I got some spirits of ammonia and in my agitation held the bottle too close to his nose. He sat up abruptly, gasping, and Peter said soberly, "I wish I could. I've helped look, you know. She's not in the house. She's not in the barns or the greenhouse. I looked myself and the police looked, too, of course. My opinion is, Craig, that she went away of her own will. Voluntarily. She must have gone like that because otherwise she would have been heard in the house. Even if the guard was drugged he would have roused, I should think, if she'd screamed or made some kind of struggle. I would have heard it. All of us would have heard it. She went of her own will. I feel sure of that."

"But what happened afterward?" said Craig. "Why did she go like that? Why is Anna with her?"

"Are you sure that Anna went with her?" asked Peter. "Or do we just feel that they must be together because they are both gone?"

"I'm not sure of anything," said Craig, and pushed away the bottle of ammonia. "For God's sake, get that thing out of the way! If Chivery was murdered because he knew too much of my father's death, then maybe Drue knew the same thing. Maybe she . . ." He stopped as if unable to say it. And Peter said quickly, "Craig, if anything had happened to her, they'd have found—well, found her by now."

"Then why doesn't she telephone? Why doesn't she let me know where she is? Why doesn't she . . ." Craig stopped again and put his hand over his face.

I said, "Why didn't you tell her how you felt about her? Then she wouldn't have gone away without telling you."

"She doesn't love me," said Craig from behind the hand that shaded his eyes. "It's Nicky she was in love with. She feels sorry for me now; and she feels it her duty to take care of me."

I started to expostulate and then stopped. What was the use! The more desperately I worked to get the two blind young idiots together the farther they swung apart. Everything, it seemed to me, combined to separate them. Even though they were actually in the same house, Drue had been made to stay in her room, and Craig couldn't move ten feet under his own steam, so to speak, without collapsing. And now they were in truth separated and there was no way of telling where Drue was, nor why (if Peter was right and she had gone of her own volition) she had gone. I felt as Craig did, however; if she could have telephoned to me I was sure she would have done so.

It didn't lift my spirits to reflect on that. I said waspishly to Craig, "You ought to have told her you wanted her to stay. Instead, you asked Alexia to marry you."

Peter lifted his eyebrows. "I thought it was Drue you liked," he said.

"Alexia said no," said Craig after a pause.

"Oh," said Peter.

"Do you want Alexia to marry you?" I asked directly, and Craig said after another pause, "No."

"Good God," said Peter. "What's the idea?"

"I wanted to see if she would," said Craig simply.

Which got me nowhere. I was staring at Craig in furious exasperation, and Peter was staring rather blankly at him, too, and Craig just sat there with his hand over his eyes when someone knocked and came in and it was Nugent.

"I got a report on the Frederic Miller checks," he said abruptly. "Do you want to hear?"

Did we want to hear! Peter's rather large ears stretched another fraction of an inch and Craig snapped, "Go on. What'd you find out?"

"Frederic Miller," said Nugent, "was a member of the New Jersey Bund. He lived in Newark at least for a time. He appears to have lived in New York, too. Sometime during the fall of 1938 he disappeared. Probably got wind of the fact that the activities of the Bund members were being watched pretty closely by the F.B.I. At any rate he disappeared and covered his tracks pretty thoroughly. The checks however were credited to his account at the Newark bank—the bank whose stamp appears on the back of one of the checks. The account was closed before he left the country, which is what they believe he did. That's as far as they could tell me at a moment's notice. They will investigate further."

Craig said quickly, "Were there any pictures of Miller?"

"I asked that, too," said Nugent. "No. But they said they'd be able to find somebody who could identify him."

"Then Mr. Brent was helping the Bund," said Peter.

"Presumably. Unless Miller used the money himself. However, that end of it comes under the jurisdiction of the F.B.I. They'll run the thing down if anybody can. As a matter of fact, this angle interests them in the whole case and I don't mind telling you it'll be a help. The trouble is it'll take time."

"But don't they know anything else about Frederic Miller?" asked Craig.

"No," said Nugent. "He was just one of the Bund; all of the ringleaders were kept under pretty close scrutiny. They knew of him mainly through the records. They didn't know whether he was young or old; born in Germany or in

America; anything in fact about him except what I've told you. The point is that it could have been an assumed name."

"Frederic Miller," said Craig thoughtfully. "The trouble is too that there's nobody around here who could be Frederic Miller."

"And if there were," said Peter, "why should he murder Mr. Brent? And Dr. Chivery?"

"The checks bring him into it," said Nugent. "If I knew how, the case might be ended here and now. And again," he added, "it might not be. But if it was an assumed name it could be anyone. You, Brent. Or you, Huber. Or Nicky. Or even a woman . . ."

"It's not me," said Craig, and Peter said, "Gosh," in a heartfelt manner. And Nugent said, "It might even be you, Miss Keate."

"Well, it isn't," I snapped. "You can check back over my whole history if you want to."

"Thank you," said Nugent coolly. "I have."

"But it couldn't be a woman," cried Peter, looking a little stunned.

"Remember," said Nugent, "there's only the name and the checks to go on. Women have managed to assume a man's name before now. As to that, it has often struck me that Mrs. Brent and her brother could easily exchange identities. Especially considering the way she wears her hair."

There was another silence and then Peter said again in a rather stunned way, "Gosh," and stared at Nugent as if he'd pulled a rattlesnake out of his hat. And Craig said wearily, "But what of Drue, Lieutenant? All the rest of this will take time. You may be on the right track and you may be on the wrong track. Certainly there's nobody around here whose whole past isn't known."

"I've checked on everybody," said Nugent. "Insofar as I could. But Frederic Miller could have had a quiet and infrequent existence in name only, so to speak, for some time. However, there's another thing that has just come out; nothing to do with the checks. The gloves that were found, one beside Chivery and the other in Anna's room, were sold to your father. He bought them at the little shop in the village the day of the attack upon you, Brent."

"Oh," said Craig. And looked at Nugent. And said suddenly, "I suppose you want me to tell you why he shot me."

# XX

Peter whirled and cried, "*He* shot you!"

I said, "You knew. All the time, you knew who it was."

And Nugent said quietly, "Yes. Why did he shoot you?"

Craig took a long breath. "It's not very pleasant, you know. But I know that he didn't mean to do it. I saw his hand, you know, with the glove on it. I suppose he—he got the gloves so his fingerprints wouldn't appear on the gun. But I don't think he meant to kill me; in fact, I think he believed me to be somebody else."

"Who?" said Nugent.

"I don't know," said Craig slowly. "I've thought and thought and I don't know who. It was dusk, you see; my father's eyesight was failing somewhat, although he'd never admit it. I was talking to Alexia, as I told you; then she went back up to the house and I walked up and down there for a little. And I saw the gloved hand showing behind the hedge, and I was pretty sure it was my father. There was something about him—you know how it is—a familiar line even when you can't see a person's face. And just then the shot came. Naturally—the next day—I wasn't going to explain it; I had sense enough even under the drugs Claud gave me, to know that. There was no reason for my father to shoot me; I knew that. So I knew there must be a mistake somewhere. That day I was too fuzzy and drugged to think clearly. But I did think I would tell Claud enough to put him on guard; he was devoted to my father and if my father told anyone, he would have told Claud. I think he did tell him; and I think he told him why he shot at me; and I think that is why Claud managed to lose the bullet that he extracted. It may have been why Claud himself was killed; he knew too much; I've always thought that."

"Why do you think your father shot you?" asked Nugent.

"I tell you, it was a mistake. He thought I was somebody else."

"Who?" said Nugent again.

And Craig said again, "But I don't know. I had on a lightish raincoat I had taken out of the hall closet. I think it belonged to my father; but anybody might have a light raincoat; there was nothing about that that would make my father think I was somebody else. And we're all about the same height—I mean you, Peter, and Nicky, and even Claud Chivery. We were all about the same height and in the dusk my father might have easily mistaken one of us for the other."

"But my God," said Peter. "Why would he shoot me? I scarcely knew him."

"Why would he shoot anybody?" said Nugent. "Unless it was a question of shooting or being shot."

"Yes," said Craig. "That's what I thought later when it was my father who was killed."

"You mean," said Peter, "that whoever he thought he was shooting when he shot at you was actually after your father?"

"Yes. In other words, I think it was a question of self-protection on my father's part. Somebody was after him and he knew it and he thought he'd get him first. And he got me and—and couldn't tell anybody but Claud what had happened and why. And then the other person, whoever it was, saw that action had to be taken at once. I mean it was—well, it was the same thing: kill or be killed."

Nugent said nothing. Peter said, "But, my gosh, why didn't they go to the police? I mean all your father had to do was ask for police protection. And whoever he meant to shoot . . ."

"That's the point," said Craig. "Whatever the disagreement, quarrel, whatever it was, was about something that neither the murderer nor my father wanted to tell the police about. That's why I keep thinking the Miller checks come into the thing. I mean—well, I don't think Miller himself is lurking around the countryside somewhere, although of course he might be—but I do think that the checks might have been used to blackmail my father. To keep him, perhaps from going to the police. My father would have hated the fact that he had given money to the Bund to come out. He'd have done anything to prevent it; he was that kind of man."

"Murder," said Nugent softly, "is usually done either in blind rage or from some very strong and personal motive."

And I said suddenly, "Alexia had the checks. Alexia was in the garden just before your father shot you."

"And Alexia," said Nugent, "is very like Nicky and Nicky very like Alexia. How was she dressed that night, Brent? I mean she didn't happen to be wearing, say, slacks? Women do."

"You mean he might have seen her going to the garden, happened not to see her leave the garden and go back to the house, and thus that he mistook me for Alexia?" said Craig frowning.

"M'mm, roughly," said Nugent. "You are sure it *was* Alexia you talked to?"

"Yes," said Craig. "And she wasn't wearing slacks. She had on a dinner dress, I'm sure; a black dress she wore at dinner, and a long coat."

There was another silence during which I thought back somewhat confusedly to the times I'd seen Nicky and the times I'd seen Alexia and wondered whom I'd really seen— Alexia in a checked coat and slacks, or Nicky. I could fancy Alexia in Nicky's clothes and, at a distance, even a short distance, so like him that one would think it was Nicky. But I couldn't somehow see Nicky in Alexia's trailing feminine clothes. And then I saw what I suppose Nugent had seen from the beginning and that was that the whole question of alibis was threatened, at least, so far as the twins' alibis went. Was it Nicky Beevens had seen coming from the meadow the previous afternoon or Alexia? "Why, that means," I burst out suddenly, "that it may have been Alexia in the meadow last night. It may have been . . ."

"Exactly," said Nugent. "And of course there might have been another reason for your father thinking you were someone else, Brent. That's pretty obvious. If he was jealous of her and had reason to believe that she liked some other man and had gone to the garden that evening to meet him . . ."

Peter had been swelling a little around the cheeks and getting very pink. He cried, "Look here, Nugent, if you mean me, she doesn't. I mean I didn't. I mean—oh, look here. I may as well make a clean breast. I—well, I think she's terribly attractive; who wouldn't? But I—I—" he faltered, and Nugent said, "You what?"

"Well, I—oh, gosh. I didn't murder Mr. Brent. And I— there's something I did get into that I tried to stop and couldn't and I didn't want to tell . . ." he faltered again, scarlet to his blond hair.

"If you mean Alexia," began Craig, "say so. . . ."

"I don't mean Alexia," said Peter. "I mean Mrs. Chivery."

"Maud!" cried Craig sitting up. "My God, you've not fallen in love with her, have you?"

"Maud—oh, shut up! That's not it. Mrs. Chivery—oh, for God's sake . . ."

188

"What do you mean?" asked Nugent. "If you've got anything to say, get it out."

"All right," said Peter swallowing hard. "But it's not easy. It—I didn't mean to. You see, well, it's the Spanish jewels."

The Spanish jewels again. And Maud's talk of investment. Peter had got stuck again, and I said crisply, "You wanted her to invest in Spanish jewels."

"*Spanish* . . ." began Craig incredulously, and Peter interrupted.

"Yes," he said defiantly, but rather miserably, too, "Spanish jewels. It was this way. I was talking—too much; you know the way one gets carried away. Anyway, I was telling about a chap I know who was in the Spanish War, and he told me about taking a truck—oh, I know it sounds utterly ridiculous, but that's what he said and what I told Mrs. Chivery about—he said he was taking a truck full of jewelry and silver that had been donated by various Loyalists from one place to another when the war was over. He was caught en route, so to speak. So he didn't know what to do with his truck load of stuff and he hid it somewhere behind an old church. He knew the exact location, and he said it would take some money for—oh, greasing palms and that kind of thing, but he insisted that sometime he was going to get the money and go back and bring out the jewelry. I don't think he really meant it; anyway the chances were all against his being able to do it, even if the stuff hasn't been found months ago. But Mrs. Chivery—well, she kept talking to me about it; said she had some money and wouldn't I get in touch with the fellow who told me about it and all that. She said her husband would be against her putting up the money and that Mr. Brent would be against it, so I wasn't to tell them. I couldn't believe that she was in earnest about it; then, when I began to think she was I—my God, I did everything I could think of to discourage it. Told her how absurd it was, the whole story. But she didn't think it was absurd at all; and I suppose things like that did happen. I mean, I remember reading stories of how the Loyalists gave up everything in the way of jewelry that they could get their hands on. I suppose some things were caught like that, in the process of delivery, so to speak, when the Spanish war ended. But as an investment it was the bunk," said Peter simply. "And I told her so. But the more I said against it the keener she was."

"Yes," said Craig, "Maud would be. But all you had to do was to refuse to take the money."

"Well, naturally I did," said Peter. "But she kept insisting. I was sorry I had ever mentioned the thing to her. And it was so—well, gosh, so completely absurd I sort of was embarrassed about it. Wished I hadn't made such a good story."

"Is that all?" said Nugent.

"Yes," said Peter. "Except I think she's still got it in her head."

"Well, all you have to do is to keep on refusing," said Craig wearily, and looked at the clock and then at Nugent. There was a wordless and rather desperate appeal in his eyes. Nugent got up. "We ought to hear from Miss Cable soon," he said. "I'm convinced that she left voluntarily. Try to be patient, Brent." His voice was kind—too kind. I thought of all the things that could have happened and then tried not to think of them as I had tried not to think so many times that day.

And I might say now that I had succeeded rather too well but not in the direction I intended. I didn't want to think of why Drue had gone, or why she stayed away without telephoning or letting us know anything of her whereabouts, but I didn't intend to let something important, a small thing but terribly important, go straight past my ears quite as if I hadn't heard it. That was carrying the ostrich act too far. Nugent went toward the door but Craig stopped him.

"Have you got the details of my father's—death, pretty well established?" he asked.

"The general set-up, yes," said Nugent. "There are two alternatives. One is that whoever killed him could have poisoned the brandy with digitalis taken from the medicine box which was then—oh, thrown away, I suppose. We've searched for it and not found it; we were in the hope of getting some fingerprints."

My hand went to my pocket. But I waited—somewhat nervously, I might add. Nugent went on crisply, "In that case, your father could have taken the poisoned brandy shortly before his interview with Miss Cable. . . ."

"Then you don't think Drue killed him!" cried Craig, his whole face suddenly alight and eager.

"I didn't say that," said Nugent, but still in a kind and quiet voice which again seemed to me too kind, as if he felt sorry for Craig, below his mask of officialdom. And that

190

meant that Nugent feared, too, for Drue. And if he feared for her, that was why he had begun to believe that she was not guilty of murder. It completed a disastrous and terrifying little circle of logic. Nugent went on, "I said there were two alternatives. The other, of course, is that Miss Cable killed him deliberately with a hypodermic syringe containing too large a dose of digitalis. But let me finish my first hypothesis. If then, your father drank the poisoned brandy and then collapsed just as Miss Cable was talking to him, she could have been—I say *could* have been—under the impression that he was having a heart attack, or he could have asked her to help him, according to her story. At which she gave him merely a medicinal amount of digitalis, and he died from the effects of the other."

"There was no poisoned brandy in the decanter," said Craig slowly. "But . . ."

"Exactly. The noise made by the falling vase, as it was probably intended to do, drew attention away from the study for a long enough time to permit the murderer to re-enter the room, pour the poisoned brandy down the drain of the little washroom adjoining the study, refill it quickly from a decanter brought from the dining room, return both decanters to their original position and leave the room again unobserved. I say that could have happened. But it still means that someone else had to pick up the fragments of the vase and the twine and conceal them in the trash barrel. That indicates a conspirator. Yet it is difficult to believe that a murderer would take anybody in the world into his confidence to that dangerous degree. And there's another thing that seems to hook up somehow and yet that obscures the issue; that's the mysterious telephone call to the police. Who called it murder before anyone else even thought of murder—except the murderer? What woman went to the telephone and called the police? If I knew that," he said slowly, "and if I knew why Drue Cable left the house without her shoes . . ."

The light and eagerness vanished from Craig's face. He looked at the clock again, and it marked only a few moments further along its inexorable course, but every moment, now, counted. All of us knew it.

But especially Craig. For Nugent went away almost immediately and after he'd gone Craig, staring at the clock again, told Peter and me the thing Claud Chivery had told him.

It was, he believed and said he believed, the motive for Claud's murder. The trouble was that he didn't dare tell the police because it might prove to be a boomerang. Claud had said "she" in talking; he had named no names, he had used only the pronoun and it was a dangerously inclusive pronoun for Claud might have meant Drue.

Craig made me shut the door before he told us.

"I don't know what it is," said Craig. "It's only what Claud told me. And the way he looked. He wouldn't tell the police and he made me promise not to; after he was murdered I would have told them but——but I don't know what the paper is that he found there. You see?"

"No, I don't," I said.

"Go on," said Peter. "Maybe we can find it. What do you mean?"

"I mean," said Craig, "that I don't know what is written on it, and I don't know who Claud suspected because of it, but I do know it was a woman. He said she."

"Oh! If it should be Drue . . ."

"Yes," said Craig bleakly. "We've got to be sure it isn't Drue before we tell the police."

He told us then, briefly. Claud Chivery had told Craig that someone had been looking up digitalis in one of his books. The book had been put back in the wrong place on the shelves and Claud, a stickler for a kind of finicky order, had seen it at once. Then (he'd told Craig) he found a paper, marking the place where the information about digitalis began.

And when Craig asked him what paper, and if he could tell who'd been looking up that particular subject, Claud had frozen up, looked scared and terribly worried, referred to the person (and without realizing it, Craig thought) as "she" and had told Craig he had to think it all over and come to a conclusion about it before telling the police or letting Craig tell them. He'd been afraid of setting them on the wrong person.

"And the way he told me, the way he looked, I was afraid, too," said Craig. "But now that Drue—where are you going, Miss Keate?"

"To my room," I said. "I'll be back presently." I didn't hurry until I was out of the room. I didn't want him or Peter to stop me. For I had to do something—anything. Night was coming on; it was already nearly dusk and there was still no word of Drue. I kept thinking of all the little wooded

192

valleys and hedges and clumps of shrubs among the low-lying hills.

I took my cape. No one was in the upstairs hall; the door to Craig's room was closed as I had closed it when I left the two men together. I crept down the stairway.

But Beevens was in the hall below.

And he had something in his hand.

I suppose it was curious, the way the kaleidoscope had already and all at once started to fall together, so the frantically whirling pieces—some big and making links like bridges, some small and unimportant but still essential—began to make a complete and coherent picture. Beevens made his contribution then for he had the famous clipping.

It was in his large hand and he gave it to me.

"I had removed it that evening, Miss, when I emptied the ash trays. The night Mr. Brent was murdered, I mean. And someone had crumpled it up and dropped it in an ash tray. I emptied them, as I always do when I remove the coffee tray. It was in the rubbish barrel and I found it and ironed it out and, well, here it is. I thought I'd better give it to you."

I didn't ask him why; perhaps because in an odd, unspoken way Beevens and I had been allies from the first. Indeed, he was the only one (except for Drue) whom I had not at one time or another suspected of murder, and I think he may have felt the same way about me. At any rate, he did trust the clipping to me to do with it as I saw fit. And I thrust it into my pocket quickly and went out the door.

Beevens didn't question, naturally; he didn't even look an inquiry as he held the door for me.

But only Beevens saw me go. On the way to the garden and the little path that started there and wound its way up and down, beside a rock wall or two, across a wooded strip, and low, rolling and dusky meadows toward the Chivery house I did glance at the clipping. It was only a few paragraphs about the arrest of some Bund members; the date line was some five weeks earlier: rather to my disappointment there was no mention of Frederic Miller. There was, in fact, no mention of any names. I looked at it quickly, hurrying toward the garden and the path, glanced at the other side which was equally short and clueless, being an account of a submarine sinking somewhere off the New England coast and part of an advertisement for stirrup pumps in case of incendiary bombs. So I thrust it into my pocket and encountered the medicine box and wished I'd given it to Craig.

As a matter of fact, however, the medicine box was one of the unimportant details in the picture; part of it, but unimportant. So nothing was changed because the little box remained in my capacious pocket. And I passed the garden where Craig had been shot (mistakenly, he'd said, by his father) and started along the winding path. It was latish by that time; still light enough to see but late enough to remind me of the dusk of the previous night and the body of Claud Chivery there in the trees. I walked faster. And realized suddenly that I was straining my eyes to watch the hedges and the clumps of shrubbery along the way, and listening with all my ears for sounds from behind me. Yet it was a relief to act; even if it meant scurrying along the uneven little path, wishing my long blue cape and my starchy white uniform wouldn't make swishing sounds in the quiet which might obscure other sounds.

Naturally, I looked behind me now and then, too. But there wasn't anything, and the police were busy then at the little lake in the hills beyond the north meadow.

Eventually I reached the Chivery cottage. I couldn't have missed it, for the path led directly to the road that came out from town (going along east of the meadow where Claud Chivery had died). I crossed the road and there was the white picket fence and gate where Claud Chivery had been photographed stepping into his car, that strange look (of premonition?) in his haggard face.

The cottage had a deserted look and it was deserted. The one general maid Maud kept lived out and didn't come to work when Maud was away. It was an odd little instance of Maud's parsimony, but I didn't know that until later.

The steps weren't swept and the shreds of vines clinging to the trellis around the little porch looked dreary and unkempt. The door, however, was unlocked. I hadn't thought of that till I got there; it seemed to me a stroke of luck.

So I opened it and went in; the hall was dreary, too, and dark and looked overfurnished with mahogany and chintz and a gleaming, heavily framed mirror that gave me back a dark and shadowy glimpse of myself. The first thing I saw, however, was the knife—a plain, bone-handled carving knife, lying on the table beside a silver card tray and a vase of withered chrysanthemums. I must admit I stopped rather short and listened, and looked at the knife.

But it was only a knife, inanimate and clean, and I didn't hear a sound, unless the dry leaves on the little porch outside scraped softly against the trellis. The cottage was breathless, undusted, unaired, with the furniture taking over the place a little inimically the way it only does in an empty house.

That perhaps as much as anything convinced me there was no one in the cottage; but I looked anyway around the first floor, treading very lightly and holding my cape close to me so it wouldn't brush against anything, pausing to listen as a cat does in strange territory, hearing nothing.

On my right hand, opening from the narrow hall was a living room, very precise, but dark with its curtains drawn and more withered flowers on a table. This led back to a small dining room so neat and yet so deserted that you couldn't imagine a meal being served on that glistening table with its silver cockatoo ornament and candlesticks; beyond this was a kitchen; from here you went to a kind of passage with narrow back stairs leading upward, a store closet or two and then (by a door which I opened very cautiously) into what was evidently Dr. Chivery's consulting room—all white enamel and glistening instrument cabinets. From here, in turn, I went on into his study, or perhaps his reception room which led again to the front hall; this made a complete circuit of the first floor of the house. Nothing had moved, nothing had breathed and all the chairs and bookshelves watched me with cold, alien eyes. Out in the tiny hall again, I glanced up the front stairs, a narrow carpeted flight broken by a landing.

There again I looked at the knife.

It was just a knife; somebody had left it there casually, I decided, in the pursuit of household duties, and forgotten it. Perhaps it had been used to open mail or to cut the strings of a package.

I did have, though, a strong aversion to touching it; after I'd seen Claud Chivery. So I listened again and, as nothing anywhere in that silent little house moved, I went back to the doctor's study.

His books were ranged neatly along bookshelves. I didn't turn on the light. It was still light enough to see, and I set myself to look for the book—a book about toxicology, Craig had said; if Chivery had a fairly large library that would cover a wide field.

As a matter of fact, it didn't; I ran hastily through the shelves, selected I believe four or five books which I thought might bear fruit, shook them upside down vigorously with the leaves open, over the big roll-top desk, and, unexpectedly, one of them did. An odd piece of fruit it proved to be, too. For a paper fluttered out, I seized it—incredulously, really not quite believing that I might actually have at last, in my hand, a tangible clue. It was a piece of thin white stationery, like that I had seen on writing tables here and there in the Brent house, and there were hurried, pencilled notes upon it.

I went quickly to a window at the west which was built into a little niche with heavy, linen draperies over it. I thrust the curtains aside and held the letter so I could catch the last of the rapidly fading daylight.

I understood the necessity for Claud's decision to keep the thing a secret. For horrible things were written lightly, in pencil, on that piece of paper.

"Toxicity of digitalis varies—each lot tested before sold as drug—symptoms vary—may be nausea, convulsion, rapid pulse—single massive dose may cause instant complete heart block—both sides of heart try to beat at once causing stop—fatal dose anywhere from—grains to—. Soluble in alcohol."

All that was scribbled hurriedly, in pencil; and below it was added a grisly, jaunty little statement: "Entire box of pills ought to be enough."

That was all. I didn't recognize the handwriting. But whoever had written it had murdered Conrad.

Claud Chivery knew that! He couldn't tell because—why because he must have thought that Maud had written it. There could be no other reason. "She" he'd said, not meaning to, when talking to Craig. Yes, he must have had some reason for believing the notes had been made by Maud. If it was not because it was her handwriting and he recognized it, it was because there was some other identifying clue in that piece of paper which led to Maud. So much was obvious. It explained his fear, his haunted eyes. It explained, if Craig was right, his murder.

But had Maud murdered him? Maud with her sweeping skirts and violet sachet?

It was just then that the cottage door opened quietly. A breath of air from outside rustled the withered chrysanthemums. Someone entered the house.

# XXI

I shrank back, swiftly as an animal, into the shadow of the heavy linen drapery, and looked to make sure my long blue cape didn't show. I was perfectly still, crushing that note against me.

I couldn't see much of the hall from the window, only a strip of carpet before the stairs and some wall and half an oil painting. But I could hear. Although I couldn't have moved if it had been Gabriel with his trumpet.

After a long moment someone spoke, softly but clearly; that surprised me, somehow, but not as much as when unexpectedly there was an answer.

So I realized there were two people in that little hall, and that they had entered together very quietly, very softly.

"You followed me," said a voice, and someone else said, "Certainly. So, this is the way of it."

"Get out of here! Go back! Go home!"

"I guessed as much. When Claud was murdered . . . Why have you come here?"

"Because I don't think the police have searched here. They wouldn't have known it was empty."

"You came to look for Drue. But she isn't here, *is she?*"

It was Nicky and Alexia. Their voices were curiously alike in quality, soft, vehement, hushed, and suddenly clearer, so I realized that they must be almost at the door of the study. Otherwise, of course, I couldn't have heard them. I shrank still further behind the curtains, at least instinct bade me do so; I was actually quite completely paralyzed and doubt if I so much as breathed.

Alexia said, "Never mind that. You've spied on me."

"My darling sister, I had to know the truth. I want some of your money, my pet. You'll have to provide for me, you know."

"You needn't try to blackmail me. I'm not afraid of you, Nicky."

"No? You're afraid of the police though, darling."

"*You wouldn't* . . ."

"Oh, wouldn't I! I want half of Conrad's money."

"*Half!*" she said scornfully.

"All right," said Nicky. "If you won't play, you can take what comes."

"I'm not afraid of you," she said again. "You tricked Conrad. He gave you money all year because you made him think you had induced Drue to go away with you."

"Why not?" said Nicky softly and with the greatest good-humor. "Conrad wanted to get rid of Drue and he did. I'm always willing to be of service."

"How exactly did you do that? I never asked; it seemed better not to know. But Drue hated you; I watched you trying to lure her away with your charm, Nicky dear; and I knew it when you failed."

Nicky's voice was less pleasant. "Oh, really? I tried to make love to her only to please you and Conrad. I wasn't serious. Yes, she turned me down; she was furious, but I didn't care. I"—a kind of complacence returned to his gentle voice—"I turned around and worked it a different way; I pretended to be her friend, sorry for her, loved her hopelessly, would do anything for her. When she left the house I took her to the train; I went in to New York with her. It worked; at least, it convinced Conrad that he had reason to be grateful to me. He could honestly tell Craig that Drue had gone away with me; and he did. That was all he wanted. Drue got in a taxi at the Grand Central station and I never saw her again till she came here. But I was of service to Conrad, and he knew it. I'll be of service to you, too, if you pay me."

There was all at once a small note of fear in Alexia's voice that hadn't been there before. "What are you going to do, Nicky?"

"I'm not going to do anything unless I have to."

"So it is blackmail. Why don't you try Craig? He's got as much money as I have."

"I already have," said Nicky almost naively. "I thought (since we're being frank) that I could invent a bit of evidence against Drue in the matter of Conrad's murder. His *murder*, Alexia; people hang for murder . . ."

"*Nicky*—" she said in a sharp whisper. Nicky went on cheerily, "I knew Drue had been with Conrad the night he was killed; I'd heard part of the row they had. I decided I could make what I'd heard sound pretty bad to the police. . . ."

"That's why you were so mysterious about not swearing to evidence against her?"

198

"Well, naturally. I didn't know yet exactly what I intended to swear to. She doesn't have any money. But I thought if Craig was still in love with her he'd pay to keep me still."

"And is he?"

"No," said Nicky ruefully. "He didn't turn a hair. Even when I hinted that I was ready now to make an honest woman of her."

Unexpectedly, Alexia laughed; there was the strangest note of pleasure and pride and, mainly, understanding. Nicky laughed, too, so for a moment they seemed to be congratulating each other's cleverness, complacently, understanding each other.

Then the little musical, wicked laughter stopped. I could imagine them, wary again, mutually on guard, watching each other like two reflections of the same face. Nicky said, "So, my dear. I've got to feather my own nest, you know. As soon as I knew Conrad was dead and that source of supply was shut off I realized I had to . . ."

"To find out who killed him, and bleed him for the rest of his life," broke in Alexia in sudden, low vehemence.

"Oh, now, dear! Only to turn an honest penny for myself. By bleeding *her*. You, darling."

"Nicky, you wouldn't dare! Your own sister."

Nicky laughed a little, but this time Alexia didn't join him. He said, "Don't be difficult. You oblige me to put the screws on, so to speak." His soft voice had an ugly undertone. "First, Conrad's own medicine, all of it, a fatal quantity was put into the brandy. Digitalis is soluble in alcohol."

"How much you know, Nicky!" There was a jeering note in her voice. "Too much, if you ask me. Be careful I don't set the police on you."

"Then later, after a vase, dear, had been pulled down a stairway and broken . . ."

Alexia interjected jeeringly again. "You really do know too much, Nicky. Did you murder him?"

". . . the brandy was changed. Poisoned brandy poured out, good brandy poured in. I figured it all out. What did you do with the medicine box? Burn it?"

Alexia was still perfectly possessed and unafraid. "It may have been planted," she said coolly. "To turn suspicion one way or another. I'm sure I wouldn't know about that, however."

"Planted?" said Nicky. "Where? Craig?"

"Perhaps," said Alexia with a little laugh.

Nicky said, "It was you, of course, in the meadow, when Chivery was killed."

"Beevens says it was you," she said, still sure of herself. "Of course, we do resemble each other."

The ugly undertone in Nicky's voice was more marked. "Listen, Alexia, you can't get away with that. You had time to get back to the house and put on that long green dress over the clothes you were wearing. My clothes! And don't tell the police I killed either. of them! That would be very foolish. I know too much about you."

"I didn't kill Conrad," said Alexia rather slowly.

Nicky gave a soft little laugh but said nothing. Alexia said, after a moment, "I had no motive."

"Oh, dear me, no," said Nicky. "Rich and attractive widow marries . . ."

"Nicky, you killed him. You had just as much motive as I had. Money."

"It won't go, Alexia. I tell you that I know things."

"But I didn't . . ."

"What of the Frederic Miller checks?" ·

There was another silence. Then Alexia said in a kind of stifled way, "All right. But if you say a word . . ."

"You took them out of his desk yourself, didn't you? So you've been in on the thing from the beginning."

"Nicky, is this a guess or do you know . . . ?"

"I know enough," said Nicky. "Part of it is guess work but extremely effective guess work. I think I know the whole story."

"You don't," said Alexia. "You can't possibly. But if you'll keep still . . ."

"I knew you'd see the light."

"You little selfish beast," said Alexia suddenly and low. "All you've ever wanted is money. Money from anyone you think you can blackmail."

"Blackmail," said Nicky. "It was blackmail, wasn't it? Never mind. It's an agreement. It's a good thing for you that you believe me and are a sensible girl. . . ."

"*Will you go?*" demanded Alexia in a voice that trembled with anger.

"Right," said Nicky.

There was another silence, then the sound of the front door opening and closing and somebody crossed the porch on tiptoe, softly. I looked out the window, but there was

200

only the hedge and the white picket fence, growing dimmer in the dusk.

So Nicky knew, or effectively pretended to know the "whole story." Whatever it was, it was so damning that Alexia would promise anything to silence him.

But if Maud had murdered Conrad, and Claud Chivery, why was Alexia willing to bargain with Nicky? And did Nicky really know as much as he pretended to know?

After a long time of utter silence in the cottage, I moved, stiffly, very cautiously, so I could see through the little crack between curtain and window casing.

Then I wished I hadn't looked. For Nicky stood in the doorway; he was looking slowly around the study, and he held the long carving knife in one hand.

Only it wasn't Nicky.

I looked closer, scrutinizing. It was Alexia in Nicky's clothes—Nicky's checked jacket, Nicky's brown slacks, Nicky's maroon scarf. It must be Alexia; Nicky had gone. All at once I understood many things. Mainly, Nugent's suggestion was right: Alexia could and obviously had worn Nicky's clothes whenever it was convenient to do so.

But there was something else—something terribly important. Oh, yes. Is Drue here? Nicky had asked.

If Drue was in that gloomy silent cottage she was upstairs, where I hadn't looked. If she was alive, why hadn't she come down, or telephoned the house or let me know somehow?

Perhaps she couldn't. Perhaps they had her locked up in some upstairs room so she couldn't telephone. Yes, I thought; it had to be that. And Nicky (no, *Alexia*) had come to the Chivery cottage. Yet she hadn't seemed to be sure of Drue's presence; she'd replied obliquely to Nicky, saying only that the police hadn't thought of the Chivery cottage. As I hadn't; as Craig hadn't, for there was no reason to think for an instant that Drue was there.

I didn't then consider why and especially how anyone could have got Drue out of the house (an able-bodied and supple young woman with a good pair of lungs), for I was watching Alexia, and afraid to watch her at the same time for fear she would feel my eyes upon her. But she didn't, for she was looking at the books I had left on the desk. No: that was wrong. She was actually looking at the telephone.

The telephone! I'd forgotten it. I could telephone, the instant Alexia started upstairs to Drue!

Well, I couldn't. I shall never forget my feelings as before I could move Alexia took one swift step to the telephone, and slashed through its wire with the knife, swiftly, as if she had wiry, feral strength in those white wrists. Then she glanced quickly around the study again and I shut my eyes to keep from attracting her gaze and when I opened them an instant later she was gone. Quietly as a cat, stalking.

There were back stairs. I remembered that. I crept out from behind the draperies and Alexia didn't come back. The big roll-top desk was beside the door which led back toward the little hall and the back stairway, and, as I passed it, a very queer little thing happened. It was an instance, I suppose, of the instinct of self-preservation, for it flashed through my mind that nobody would live like that, isolated in the country, without a revolver, and my hand went out to the desk drawer and opened it cautiously and there was actually a revolver, big and serviceable-looking, lying on top of some papers. It didn't seem at all strange; I snatched it up as if I'd known it would be there, and went on with scarcely a pause, through the little consulting room and into the tiny hall beyond.

But it was much darker than it had been. The hall was in blackness and I groped with my free hand for the stairs. Something took a kind of quivering breath out of that darkness before me just as my hand encountered hair.

Human hair.

I drew back somewhat quickly. I would have fired the revolver if I had been able to find the trigger.

Then luckily for us both, perhaps, I realized that the hair I touched was a braid. So it was Anna, and she was alive.

In fact, she was shrinking over the bannisters, away from me. Fortunately, she was simply petrified with fright, and I got my hand over her mouth before she even whimpered. I whispered sternly, "Anna, it's only me. The nurse, Miss Keate . . ."

"Oo—woo—woo—" she observed with vehemence. I held my hand harder over her teeth and was horrified to realize that she was heaving wildly up and down in an effort either to scream or sob; so I dragged her nearer and put my mouth where I thought her ear ought to be.

"*Anna, listen!* It's Nurse Keate. I'm not going to hurt you."

She heard that. A gigantic heave caught her amidship, and I thought she was going to burst or strangle and didn't care which, but she did neither.

Instead all at once she caught herself away from me, sucked in a great gulp of air while I sought desperately for her mouth again in the darkness, and then said quite clearly, but whispering, "Turn me over to the police. It's all my fault. I began it. I knew . . . Oh, Nurse, Nurse, will they put me in the electric chair, too?"

"Not if I get you first," I said between my teeth, but whispering too. "Is Miss Cable here?"

"Oh, yes, yes." I thought she was wringing her hands. "She's not hurt. She's upstairs, in a bedroom. I swear I didn't hurt her. I wouldn't have hurt her, not really. I had to keep her quiet, that's all. I was afraid. I didn't know what to do. All day; I didn't mean anything."

It wasn't the time to cut through her maunderings and get at any sense that, problematically, lay behind them. "You've got to go for the police! Quick! Out the back door!"

"Police?"

"They won't hurt you. Be quiet. Hurry."

"No, no! I lied to them! I said I didn't telephone the night Mr. Brent was killed. But I did. I knew it was murder. I was afraid something terrible would happen. And it did."

"*You* telephoned the police!"

"Yes. Yes. Oh, Nurse, I've been so wicked. I picked up the vase. I had to; I was made to do it; I didn't want to."

"Anna, you did that!"

"Yes, yes. But I didn't want to. So I hurried to the telephone. I told the police it was murder."

"For heaven's sake, Anna! What are you saying? *Who* made you pick up the broken vase? Why did you know it was murder? *Anna* . . ."

But I was too vehement. I had her by the shoulders and I clutched too hard. I only frightened her into a gibbering, quaking, sobbing jelly with about as much intelligence. I couldn't get another sensible or coherent two words out of her. And Drue was alone and Alexia somewhere in the house. So finally I shoved the revolver against Anna's neck where she could feel the cold steel—hoping it wouldn't go off but not caring very much just then. "Go out the back door," I said despairingly. "Go through the kitchen. Don't make a sound. And if you don't bring the police back here

203

as soon as you can I'll shoot you with this. I'm a good shot," I said, having held a revolver in my hand only once before in my life.

But I must have impressed her with sincerity; at any rate, something penetrated the fog of terror and self-blame around her. "I will—oh, I will—I started everything. It's all my fault. But don't shoot . . ." she quavered out of the darkness.

I had to let her go. She groped her way around me and I could hear the soft patter of her feet for a few steps; I waited, listening with all my ears.

I couldn't then explore, even in my thoughts, the incoherent, terrified flood of self-reproach I had unleashed.

I couldn't explore the conversation between Nicky and Alexia, either. Nicky's accusations, Alexia's denials and half-admissions and her final surrender to his demand were both enlightening and baffling. And there were those ugly scribbled notes about digitalis which Claud Chivery must have attributed to Maud.

But just then there was no time to grope my way through the contradictions and the half-admissions. It is queer though to remember now that I had had the key to the thing, the link in the chain actually in my hands and had not had the wit to see it. Just then my main preoccupation was Drue.

I couldn't hear anything at all from upstairs or from the front of the house, but presently I did hear the soft opening and closing of a door near by and I was reasonably sure it was Anna. Unfortunately, I wasn't at all sure she would go for the police.

There was no other sound at all anywhere. I took a harder grip on the revolver, wished I knew more of its habits, and, holding it well away from me, started up the narrow little flight of stairs; I came out into a kind of landing, barely lighted by a window. I listened there and poked my head cautiously around the corner and there was a narrow hall, going toward the front of the house, with doors opening from it.

There was no sound of Alexia anywhere and no figure moved against the faint gray light from the front windows. But I didn't know either where Drue was, so there was nothing for it but to try the bedrooms. So I advanced very cautiously across the hall and Drue was in the first bedroom I entered.

I didn't see her at first; she had heard or sensed my approach and had shrunk back behind the door. As I turned she caught a glimpse of me. *"Sarah . . ."*

Then I saw her and caught her. "Sh—sh," I reached out and closed the door softly. Her face was a white oval in the dusk; her hands gripped my arms as if she would never let me go. *"Sarah . . ."* she whispered.

"Be still. Alexia's here. Nicky was here, but I think he's gone. Drue, are you all right? Did they hurt . . . ?"

"No, no. Only I couldn't telephone! I couldn't do anything. She wouldn't let me . . ."

"She . . ."

"Anna. She's gone down now to fix us something to eat. I was listening, thinking I could reach the telephone when somebody came. A few minutes ago. I thought I heard Nicky's voice."

"You did." I was sure she was all right; and the certainty, the relief, actually surged along my nerves and muscles like an intoxication; I felt superhuman, able to do anything—only just at the moment I couldn't think of exactly what. Except get Drue out of there. And the notes about digitalis into the hands of the police. And Anna's words and Alexia's into their ears!

How, was a different matter. I wasn't really afraid of Alexia; not with Drue, to say nothing of the revolver, to back me up. Neither Drue nor myself was exactly frail and, moreover, as nurses we'd had a certain amount of training, so to speak, in self-defense. Even if Alexia had the knife, as she did, there's a way of grasping the arms and twisting them backward; at the worse there'd be only a moment of struggle.

Yes, I thought we could together manage Alexia and without recourse to the revolver, unless it became necessary. It gave me great moral support, but I wasn't sure I'd have the strength of mind actually to point it at Alexia and shoot—unless, of course, circumstances seemed to require it.

Drue was still clinging to me. "Craig . . ." she whispered. "Is he . . . ?"

"Nearly crazy," I said, listening for Alexia and trying to think and failing. "He—listen, Drue, when you left the Brent house (I mean when you were married to Craig and he was in Washington) did Nicky go with you?"

"Why—why, yes. He drove me to the station. Then he took the same train to New York; he said he had some business in town. Why?"

So that settled that, I thought rather grimly. All that I could hope was that both Drue and Craig would in the future try to develop a modicum, a bare modicum, of reason. Still the cards, as my poker-playing patient used to say, had been stacked against them; it really was true and I had to make allowances for it. I said wearily, "Tell Craig that."

"Tell Craig! But Nicky—that was nothing!"

"Sh—sh," I said quickly, certain I heard some motion outside and not intending to let Alexia catch me unprepared. Drue saw me advance the revolver steadily toward the door and froze, too, to listen.

But the door did not open and there was no further sound. After a moment I said, whispering, "Anna went for the police. At least, I sent her to get them. But I'm not sure she'll make it."

"*Anna!*" Drue shuddered. I said, "She made you come here. What did she tell you?"

"She said she knew something. Last night she came to me . . ."

"I know. The guard told us enough so we thought that must have happened."

"She was crazy with fear and with self-reproach. Really, Sarah, she was afraid of everything. She was nearly out of her mind. I tried to get her to talk and she—oh, in the end she promised to tell me what she knew if I'd help her get away from the house. She was afraid to talk there, in the house. Terrified. As if something might jump out of the walls. I couldn't do anything with her. She was hysterical. But she kept saying she knew something."

"So you came here?"

"In the night. I was going to find out the thing she knew, Sarah. She said this house was empty and no one would look for us here. I wasn't afraid, not at first. I gave her some sedative to put in some coffee for the boy on guard. . . ."

"I know that, too."

"And she brought me some of her own shoes to wear. I was afraid of waking the trooper so I took my slippers off so as to creep past him, and along the hall, and forgot to carry some shoes with me to put on once we were outside. Anna was waiting for me and she went back and got a pair of her own. You see, she was kind. I wasn't afraid of her. But then when we got here she wouldn't talk. All day I've been trying to persuade her. But she's still half-crazy with fear. Finally, when I said if she wouldn't tell me whatever it
206

was she had promised to tell me, I was going back to the Brent house, she stopped me. Obviously, she was afraid to talk, and afraid that I would tell that she knew something. She wouldn't say who she was afraid of, or why. She's in a completely hysterical state; I don't think she knows what she's doing. She got a knife from the kitchen. She wouldn't have hurt me with it, but she threatened and looked so—so determined. . . ."

I thought of the knife in the hall. Then that was why it was there, near the door and the telephone, so Anna could snatch it up and prevent Drue's leaving. And I thought, too, of that long, horrible day, with a knife in the hands of a woman who was berserk with fear.

"I don't think she would really have hurt me," whispered Drue again in a voice that denied her words. "But she threatened everything. Even suicide. I hoped that eventually we'd be found. Or that I could get away . . ."

I interrupted again, catching Drue's wrist for silence. We both listened, and I was sure that a door closed softly downstairs. The front door? Then perhaps Alexia was gone.

For a long moment there was no sound at all; gradually I became convinced that she'd gone and that, except for Drue and me, the house was empty again. In any case we had to get away. Hurriedly I whispered to Drue, "Where's your cape?"

"Over there. On the chair. Are we going?"

"Get it. We'd better try the back stairs and go out through the kitchen and back door. It's safer. I think Alexia's gone; if she's not, we can manage her."

"Alexia!"

"She's wearing clothes like Nicky's; they're so much alike. We can't talk now! I'll explain later."

She swept up her cape and put it around her shoulders.

"Now then," I said, my hand on the doorknob.

I took a long breath and opened the door quietly. Nothing happened. After a moment, my revolver well in advance, I poked my head out into the hall. It was darker, but still I could have seen a moving figure. When I was sure it was empty, I motioned to Drue to follow me. We tiptoed toward the back stairs and still no one made any sound at all anywhere, except for the tiny whisper of our clothing.

It was sensible and safer for us simply to leave and let the police wrestle with all the problems my visit to the cottage had stirred up. The police—it was just then that I realized that I didn't have the piece of paper with those betraying, perhaps convicting notes about digitalis written upon it. I hadn't even thought of it since I'd seen Alexia standing there in the doorway of the study with the knife in her hand.

I had to have it. Everything, even to Drue's life, might depend upon that scrap of paper. It was, I felt sure and Craig had agreed, the reason for Dr. Chivery's murder; he had told Craig of it, guardedly. But someone else had known it, too; had remembered it perhaps, and the fatal carelessness of the instant when it had been left, forgotten in that book. And somehow had discovered that Claud had found it, as he naturally would do if he had doubts about Conrad's death and turned to his books in order to refresh his memory about digitalis and its effects. I didn't know how Claud had given away his secret, but obviously he had done so. And what really did I know and what could I prove without those notes? How could Drue be cleared without them?

I must have dropped the paper in the little study. Again there was no time for thinking. I said, whispering, to Drue, "I've got to get something," and went quickly toward the front stairs, leaving her in the upper hall.

No one was in the hall below; it was shadowy but still it was unearthly quiet. I went down a step at a time, pausing to look and listen, and wishing the treads wouldn't creak. Halfway down I wished I'd given Drue the revolver; I'd forgotten I had it.

But I didn't go back, for it would take only a moment, I thought, to slip into the study, look behind the curtains, clutch the paper where I was sure, now, I'd dropped it, then go through the consulting room to the back stairs and call to Drue—if indeed she wasn't by that time in the kitchen.

The continued silence in the house reassured me.

At the bottom of the stairs I paused again and heard nothing. I turned into the study, my eyes intent on the strip of fast-fading gray daylight between the long linen draperies.

Somehow it was too silent in the house and in the little room; the silence had a quality of breathlessness, of hushed waiting. As if from somewhere eyes were watching me. Yet the room was undisturbed, quite as it had been and no one sat at Dr. Chivery's deserted desk, or stood there in the niche of the windows where I had stood. I reached it and pulled back the curtain. And on the floor lay a flat piece of paper.

I stooped and got the thing in my hand before I drew a breath. And it was only then that I saw that there was a letter —a note rather, only a few lines—written on one side of the

208

paper. It was so short a note that I read it instantly, there in the growing dusk, holding it so the last light fell through the window upon it. The handwriting was as black and neat as printing. "I don't like being put off like this. I know what I'm doing. I don't want anyone's advice. I have the money, and am ready to give it to you to use as you see fit. M. Chivery."

Maud. It confirmed my feeling that Dr. Chivery had connected the notes about digitalis with Maud; so he had kept it a secret; he had replaced the paper in the book on toxicology; he had told Craig something of his indecision; he had referred to Maud by the use of a feminine pronoun and Craig had thought that he might have referred to Drue. "I've got to be sure," Craig had said, "before I tell the police about it."

Who else then had known? And had killed Chivery to keep him quiet. I turned over the paper and the notes on digitalis were on the other side of it.

And all at once four things leaped out from the chaos of seemingly unrelated fact and surmise. They strung themselves together like beads on a chain. Knots on a rope might have been a more fitting simile.

But it had to be that way. For a fifth thing suddenly added itself and that was motive. A motive for Conrad's shooting Craig by mistake and in self-defense. A motive for Conrad's murder. And, because of that a motive for Dr. Chivery's murder which was the paper in my hand.

It wasn't all clear in detail. In fact it was like a blaze of light in a dark room.

And it was just then as I stood there, stunned by that sudden coherence and understanding, unable to believe it and yet unable to do anything but believe it, that someone laughed softly somewhere near me.

I whirled around. I crushed the paper in my hand; I shoved it under my cape into my pocket. Along with a medicine box and a clipping. Alexia was standing in the doorway of the consulting room, watching me quietly, her face a pale triangle in the dusk.

I had the revolver. I had only to call to Drue for help. Then I saw that Alexia had put down the knife somewhere, for her hands were empty. Nevertheless my heart was in my throat.

She said suddenly, in a low, rather lazy voice, "So it's you. Meddling again."

I wanted that letter. And Drue was safe so long as I had my eyes on Alexia. I held the revolver so she couldn't fail to see it, even in the dusk that filled the room. But I really didn't know what to do. In what must have been a kind of stupefied attempt at reason I said, "Let's talk this over quietly, Mrs. Brent."

It had the quality of a delirious understatement. I plunged on, a little berserk myself and still unable to think. "I'm glad you put the knife down. That would only make things worse . . ."

"Oh, would it?" she said, half smiling. There was a little silence. And in the silence I heard the stairway creak again.

It was not Drue. I believe it was the smile on Alexia's face that convinced me.

Someone was creeping up those stairs. And Drue was alone up there, and I had to deal somehow with Alexia . . .

*Alexia?* Suddenly in a stab of uncertainty, I wasn't sure. The pointed, smiling face was only a pale triangle among shadows. Was it Alexia or Nicky? If Nicky—why, then Nicky had never had the knife! It was Alexia who had that. So if this was Nicky standing there smiling at me, it must be Alexia creeping softly up the stairs, with the knife still in her hand.

It was not.

For all at once, clear in the little house Drue's voice floated down the stairway, through the dusk. She said on a note of question: "Craig? Oh, Peter! Peter Huber! What are you . . . ?" Her voice stopped uncertainly. Seemed to hang there in the silence and dusk.

Then suddenly she screamed.

# XXII

It was high and thin and terrible. And stopped as if choked off by hands.

The figure in the doorway sprang forward toward me just as I lifted Chivery's revolver and fired blindly in that direction. Claud Chivery being Claud Chivery, the thing wasn't loaded; it clicked emptily and I flung it full at that pale, triangular face just as Alexia reached for me. It was Alexia, not Nicky. In that split second of nearness I was sure of that. She swerved and ducked to avoid the revolver and I twisted

210

past her; she snatched at my cape and it came off my shoulders and I had reached the door to the hall.

The outside door was open and someone was running up the stairs; someone who must have entered as. I evaded Alexia, for he was only on the lower step when I saw him first. It was a man in slacks and a sweater and there were sounds in the dark little hall upstairs and I ran up the stairs after that figure leaping ahead of me into the dusk.

I think I knew that it was Craig. I think I knew that Alexia was not following me. I think I had a fleeting thought of Anna, and a desperate hope that she had gone to the police as I had told her to do. Then the figure ahead of me—Craig—vanished into the dusk above and I fumbled for the bannister still running, panting, my heart pounding in my throat. And I too came out into the upper hall.

It was so dark that I could only see motion and hear it; feet shuffling frantically, a struggle somewhere in that narrow little passage, for there was the sound of fists, a thud against a wall, a panting voice saying nothing, and then Drue's voice, "Craig . . ." she cried. "Craig—look out. . . ."

I think she said that. It was all swift, incoherent, veiled in shadows. And then I stumbled on a chair. And at the same time got a clearer view of figures, silhouetted against the gray windows at the front, struggling.

So I took up the chair. It was quite light. But sturdy.

Aside from an unexpected and sudden swirl around on the part of the interlocked and struggling figures just as I was about to strike which very nearly resulted in my braining Craig instead of the murderer, I executed my little maneuver with considerable verve. As I say, the chair was sturdy

It made quite a resounding crack. I struck again just in the interest of thoroughness but it wasn't really necessary. One of the dark figures paused, swayed a little, and just sagged down quietly on the floor and lay there.

The humiliating thing was, of course, that I took one look at the figure on the floor, one look at Craig leaning against the bannister, panting heavily, staring downward too, one look at Drue who was running toward Craig, and I put down the chair deliberately. And then sat down in it as deliberately. And leaned back my head.

However, I have never fainted in my life, with the exception of the time when I first went on duty in the operating room and that was more years ago than I care to mention. There were noises from downstairs; women's voices came shrilly and jerkily to my ears. I knew dimly that Alexia's was one of them.

But I wasn't prepared for what I saw when, suddenly aware that I had closed my eyes at something and that now a light from somewhere was beating upon my eyelids, I made a determined and curiously difficult effort and opened them again.

And I wasn't in the upstairs hall at all. I was stretched out at full length on the table in Dr. Chivery's examining room. Something cold and wet was on my forehead.

I don't know how they got me there. Drue insisted that I walked but didn't seem to know where I was going and that I relaxed, as docile as a child, upon the table which was the nearest thing to a couch in sight.

I couldn't say about that, but I do know that the sliced-off view I had through the door into Dr. Chivery's study both cleared my head and brought me to a sitting position.

For Alexia lay on the floor of the study, her legs in Nicky's slacks threshing angrily but futilely, for Anna sat like a lump on Alexia and she had the revolver I had thrown at Alexia in her hand and every time Alexia would give a violent writhe Anna would shake the revolver in her face. Anna was sobbing.

I managed to get to my feet. Just as I did so Drue came from somewhere out of my range of vision, took the revolver from Anna and said, "Get up. The police are here."

When I reached the study, just as Anna stood up and Alexia, eyes like daggers in her white face, sprang gracefully to her feet, Nugent ran across the porch and into the hall. He was followed by two state troopers. Drue said, "Upstairs. Quick."

It was then, as the men's feet pounded heavily on the stairs, that Alexia gave up. She listened, her hands clenched. Drue listened too, her face as white as her uniform. But after a long moment Alexia turned and looked at Drue. Lights were on now in the study, blazing upon us. Anna, in a corner, was sobbing again, and listening, too. Alexia didn't speak to Drue, however. Her eyes shifted finally to Anna, and she said with scorn, "Shut up. Crying won't help. I love him, too. Or," said Alexia suddenly, "I thought I did. I'm not so sure now."

I don't think Drue heard it; her face was lifted, all her

being intent upon what was going on upstairs, where Craig was. Anna heard it, though; she said, still sobbing, "You knew he killed Mr. Brent. You knew—oh, how could you help him! How could you!"

"Help him," said Alexia. "I didn't help him. I didn't know anything."

"You did, you did," cried Anna. "He told me you were helping him. He said you thought he was in love with you. He said you would do anything he told you to do."

*"What did you say?"* said Alexia in a strange kind of whispering. "What did you say?" She walked slowly, gracefully as a stalking panther, toward Anna. Anna sobbed and looked terrified but stood her ground. "Yes," she cried. "He said he'd told you to get hold of the Frederic Miller checks. He said if he had the checks Mr. Brent wouldn't dare tell the police who he was and where he'd come from. He said Mr. Brent wouldn't dare do anything because if he had the checks . . ."

"Was he Frederic Miller?" demanded Alexia, still in that strange, still voice.

"No, no. He only knew about the checks. He'd lived here —oh, for years. He belonged to the Bund; he knew that Mr. Brent liked German ideas. He knew that he had given money to the German cause. He knew—he knew . . ."

"And he said I'd do anything for him?" said Alexia.

"Yes, yes. He's always known when women liked him. He knew that you did . . ."

"Oh, he knew that I liked him, did he?" said Alexia. "That's fine. That's good. That's very good." She leaned over toward Anna. She laughed very softly and very horribly and said, "That's very good. Because now he's going to find out exactly how much I like him." She whirled around and started for the door. And I said, "Did you know that Peter Huber killed your husband?"

She stopped again. Her small, lovely face was terribly intent. She said finally, "How did you know?"

"I heard what you said just now. But I knew before that. At least I guessed."

"When?"

"When I found a piece of paper with notes about digitalis written on one side of it and a few sentences on the other side which Maud had written. Pete Huber overreached himself. He had told Maud Chivery about some Spanish jewels . . ."

Alexia smiled thinly. "There were no Spanish jewels. He told me. It amused him."

"Really. I think he meant to fleece Maud; and then changed his mind. I don't know why . . ."

"He was after more money," cried Anna from her corner. "He was going to get money from Mrs. Chivery. But then he knew that he could get more from Mrs. Brent. He said she'd give him money . . ."

"Anna," I said sharply, "was that why he killed Mr. Brent? Was it because Mrs. Brent would then be very rich, and he thought that she would give him money?"

"No, no," cried Anna. "It was because Mr. Brent found out about him. He found out that Peter was making love to Mrs. Brent. He found out that Mrs. Brent liked Peter. And he found out what Peter was—and he said he would turn him over to the police. Then Peter made Mrs. Brent get out the checks. He told Mr. Brent he had the checks, you see, and Mr. Brent was half crazy. Mr. Brent was like that. He shot Mr. Craig. He thought Mr. Craig was Peter; that was because Mr. Craig was in the garden with Mrs. Brent. Mr. Brent was going to shoot Peter, maybe kill him, maybe only wound him. He was going to get the checks back and then call the police and tell them who Peter was and that he had shot Peter in self-defense. Only he made a terrible mistake; he shot Mr. Craig instead of Peter. And then Peter knew that Mr. Brent meant what he'd said. He knew the checks—having them, I mean, in Mrs. Brent's possession where Peter knew he could get them at any time because Mrs. Brent would do anything he told her to do, she was so crazy about him . . ."

"He'll know now whether I'm in love with him or not. He'll know now," said Alexia in that deadly, soft voice, her face white and suddenly venomous and no longer beautiful. Anna went on as if she had not heard: "Peter knew that Mr. Brent would kill him or turn him over to the police. He knew that Mr. Brent was past caring about the checks—or soon would be; that's what he said. He said, 'Old Brent has gone further than I intended. He's reached the place where it's kill or be killed.' He said, 'I can't count on the checks to hold him. I've got to act.' And I said, 'No, no, Peter. No.' For you see, I knew what he meant. He was always like that," said Anna, suddenly whispering, staring into space with horror in her blank blue eyes. "He was always cruel. He always laughed and smiled and was wicked and terrible in his heart."

Even Alexia was struck with her look. Drue had turned too and was listening, and I felt her hand go out to mine. Anna said, whispering, "Yes. Always." Then my beads on a string, my knots on a rope became real knots on a rope.

I said, "Anna—" sharply again, to compel her attention. She turned her eyes rather dazedly and slowly to me. I said, "Anna, listen. He came from that German submarine, didn't he? The one that was torpedoed off the New England coast about a month ago?"

Alexia hadn't known that. I saw her stiffen. Anna nodded slowly. I said, "He hadn't lost his baggage. He didn't have any. Isn't that right?"

Again Anna nodded. I said, "Why did he come here? Why do you know so much? How could he make you keep his secret? How could he make you pick up that broken vase? How could he . . . ?"

"He was my brother," whispered Anna, twisting her hands together. "He changed his name from Haub to Huber. He came to America after I came. He worked and went to school. He learned American ways. But he was always a German at heart. And he was always like a—like a wolf. We had wolves at home, in the forests, watching and killing and"—she stopped and stared into space and whispered—"so I was afraid. I knew him. I was afraid."

Then Craig came down the stairs and into the room and Nugent followed him. Nugent closed the door behind him, so we only heard sounds of other men on the stairs and crossing the little hall; they walked heavily, as if something walked between them at the end of a chain. Like a beast.

It was, though, a man, handcuffed.

The door closed and there were footsteps across the porch and then the roar of an automobile.

That was all, really. The facts were there, inherent in what we then knew. But I listened while they wrapped the fabric of implication and circumstance around the facts. And when the time came I said my own little say and gave them a clipping, a piece of paper, and an empty medicine box. The box was really unimportant. Drue looked at it almost absently. "It was in the pocket of Craig's dressing-gown, that night," she said. "I found it and hid it."

"It was probably planted," said Nugent.

"Then it was Peter Huber that knocked me out?" said Craig.

Nugent nodded. "He was very busy just then; he had counted on your staying inside your room, in bed. It must have given him a shock to come upon you wandering around the hall. He knocked you out and dragged you in there to get rid of you. And somehow had the empty box in his pocket, perhaps intending to plant it on you all along. At any rate, he must have done so then. The medicine box, like the bloodstained gloves, was planted. They were false clues, intended to mislead us. Although the gloves had been used, all right," added Nugent, looking very grim.

They looked then at the clipping; and the paper with Maud's note to Peter Huber on one side, and the notes about digitalis he had made on the other side. It was, of course, a definite link. Not proof but a link.

"When did you begin to believe it was Huber?" asked Craig. He was leaning back in Dr. Chivery's chair. He looked better when he ought to have looked worse; part of it excitement but part of it was just general toughness, I suppose. Drue, of course, was sitting on the floor beside him, and his hand brushed her shoulder, so that may have accounted for some of it.

I replied, "Just before he came to the cottage. He must have heard Alexia and me talking; he must have guessed finally that Anna had brought Drue here, and he must have been afraid that Anna had told Drue. . . ."

Drue's hand went up quickly and I stopped to note with some satisfaction that Craig's hand closed firmly over Drue's small fingers. I went on quickly, "It was when I came back for the paper with the notes about digitalis on it. I read Maud's note then, realized (in view of what Peter had told us, trying to cover himself in case Maud told it) that she must have written it to Peter. All at once that, and the clipping and the account of the submarine on the back of it, linked themselves together. It occurred to me that it wasn't the account of the arrest of some Bund members that Conrad Brent had wanted somebody in the room to know that he knew about. It was the torpedoed submarine. And I remembered, of course, about the stories of Germans from submarines reaching our coast; like the three saboteurs, who reached Long Island. That seemed for an instant, too far fetched. But then I remembered Peter Huber speaking to

the clerk at the little haberdashery in the village. The clerk
had laughed at the recollection of how Huber had looked
when he came to his shop and bought some clothes. He got
rid of his German clothing near where he reached land,
probably stealing pants and a shirt from a cottage somewhere along the beach. Once in Balifold he made up a story
to account for his appearance, got some money from Anna"
(Anna nodded violently here) "and bought himself some
clothes. The clerk remembered the way he was dressed. That
linked up, too, you see. In the same breath it suddenly occurred to me that it was only Anna who had said that Peter
Huber was an old school friend; it was only Anna who had
given me the impression that he had often been at the house
and was an old friend of yours." I looked at Craig and, holding Drue's hand tightly, he nodded. He started to speak however, so I continued hurriedly before I could be interrupted.
"But I had also got an impression from Craig Brent that he
hadn't really known Huber long; and later Alexia said that
'none of us knew him.' So somehow, I felt that in spite of all
this talk of school friends . . ."

Craig succeeded this time in interrupting me. "I never saw
him before," he said. "He told my father that he knew a
man I had known in school. And he could have known him.
If he went to school in America . . ."

"Oh, he did," cried Anna interrupting, too. "He did. That
was why he knew so much. He spoke such good English;
nobody ever would have dreamed that he spoke German
even better. He—that was why it was all my fault, Mr. Craig.
He knew all about the family. I used to write to him, since
he was very young. I told him. That was why he came to
Balifold. He went back to Germany, you see, just before the
war began. He worked for the Bund movement here. I didn't
know that, then. He knew from me, though, how Mr. Brent
felt about Germany. He knew a man called Frederic Miller,
and he told him that Mr. Brent might donate some money.
That was before the war; that was before Mr. Brent changed
and no longer liked German ideas. This Frederic Miller, he
went back to Germany, too. But Peter knew that there had
been checks. He knew Mr. Brent wouldn't want anybody to
know what he had done. It's all my fault," she began to sob
again. "I started it. I told him about the money and the family. So when he escaped from the submarine and managed
to get on land unobserved, he remembered me and the
Brents. He came to Balifold and waited till I went to town

on my day off and found me; and he asked me all about the family. Then he asked me about friends of Mr. Craig's and I remembered a name. He really had gone to school in America, and he was so American! Are you going to arrest me? It's all my fault. But I was afraid. You see, I knew there would be trouble. I knew he wanted something. He—he asked me how Mr. Brent felt about Germany, and he said he ought to be able to get some money out of him. . . . But I tried to stop him. I met him in the meadow one night and told him I was going to the police and tell them who he was. He wouldn't let me. He had a gun. I don't think he meant to kill me; he only meant to frighten me. But I ran; in the darkness I ran into the trees and then he . . . The nurse was up above, her figure showed, moving against the light. He must have thought it was me. But he didn't mean to kill her. Or me. He didn't mean to shoot to kill. It was only to frighten me. So I wouldn't talk. And I didn't. I was afraid."

I turned to Nugent. "What was his motive then?"

"He talked a little," said Nugent. "Before he was taken away. Not much, but he will talk more. His motive was to save himself; that was the first motive. The Brents were an influential family; if he could hole in at the Brent house for awhile, and get hold of some money, he could escape without being interned. As it was, he was in danger. He met Brent at the inn, and managed to introduce himself as a friend of a friend of Craig's. Craig wasn't here then. By the time he came Huber was well established and Craig accepted him as a friend of some fellow he knew."

"Naturally," said Craig. "I didn't question it. My father seemed to be on quite good terms with him."

"They were on good terms at first. I believe that Huber thought he could still play on your father's sympathies for Germany. He must have thought so, for eventually there was a blow-up. He came out in his true colors as a German sympathizer; your father said he was no longer a German sympathizer. They had words and your father threatened to kick him out and to expose him to the police. At least, I think that happened. . . ."

"Yes," said Anna. "Oh, yes. Theh Peter asked Mrs. Brent to get hold of the checks if they had not been destroyed. They hadn't been and she did."

Alexia had been standing across the room, near the window. She said suddenly, "I was a fool. He . . . I did take the checks. But I kept them myself. I didn't quite trust him."

218

"How much exactly did you know of the murder, Mrs. Brent?" said Nugent.

"I knew nothing," said Alexia instantly. "Nothing at all." She walked slowly toward the door. "May I go now, Lieutenant?" she said. "I'm sure I have nothing to tell you and I'd like to go home. . . ."

"Certainly," said Nugent unexpectedly. "A man is waiting outside to take you. Oh, and by the way, Mrs. Brent, please give him your entire statement. Thank you." He opened the door for her and said coolly, "I'll see you later, Mrs. Brent."

He closed the door just as a uniformed trooper in the hall started forward.

But it was a week, as it happened, before Alexia was prevailed upon to turn state's evidence, and she never admitted complicity in the murders, and there was no way, then or ever, to prove what she had known. It was fairly clear though that she must have known, or guessed Peter's part in it. Certainly she had been in the meadow the night Chivery was killed. Certainly she had taken and hidden the Frederic Miller checks which Peter (telling Conrad Brent that they were actually in his own possession) held as a club over Conrad's head when Conrad discovered Peter's real identity and threatened to expose him. We never knew whether or not Peter admitted his real identity and the manner of his arrival at Balifold; but certainly Conrad guessed it from some chance allusion of Peter's or some word or look. The clipping convinced us of that. But from that time on it was, as Nugent and Craig had said, kill or be killed. For Conrad couldn't bear to let anyone know that (before the war and mistakenly) he had donated money to the Bund. And added to that was his growing suspicions that Alexia had fallen in love with Peter. Jealousy, pride, and fear, all had combined to make an overwhelming motive for murder.

I never thought, though, that he intended to kill Peter Huber. I thought that he intended to wound him, to get hold of the checks, and then to turn him over to the police. But then he shot Craig instead. And then Peter knew that he must act.

But the wind was rather taken out of my sails when I discovered that both Nugent and Craig had that day begun strongly to suspect Peter Huber. Nugent, because the Hollywood address Peter had given him was a real address but no one had heard of Peter Huber. And Craig because Alexia was in love with Peter and he had proved it, after a fashion, by asking Alexia to marry him. At first he had merely wished to protect Drue from Alexia. Alexia had the whip hand and hated Drue, and it seemed safer for Drue for him to appear to fall in with Alexia's claims upon him. He didn't think that Alexia was really in love with him; he thought that her pretension was merely pretension and that therefore there must be a motive for it. And what better motive than in covering the real state of affairs because there was danger if the real state of affairs came to light. Which summed up to Peter Huber.

When Craig couldn't get to the Chivery cottage without help, he thought of trying to trap Peter.

"Chivery had told me of the paper in his book; but not enough. I was afraid to tell the police for fear that, somehow, it implicated Drue. Then I thought that if Peter Huber was the murderer he would want that paper. I don't know how Huber knew that Chivery had it; perhaps we'll never know, but my guess is that he adroitly pumped Chivery; he'd missed the paper, of course; he knew where he must have left it; somehow he decided that Chivery had found it, as he had. So he had to get rid of Chivery; Claud was always inept and blundering; perhaps, somehow, he blundered there. At any rate, he was killed. And I knew that if I told the nurse—Miss Keate, she would come instantly to get the paper."

I must say I was taken aback. *"You . . ."* I began.

Craig had a definite expression of apology—as well he might. "I thought you'd be safe," he explained. "I detained Peter after you'd gone. I kept him until I thought you'd had plenty of time to get the paper. Then I got up and followed Peter. Sure enough, he came straight here. I was a little behind him; I was stronger, once I got started, than I thought I'd be, but still I was pretty wobbly. But Nugent . . ."

"I was watching you," said Nugent. "I hoped Miss Cable would try to get in touch with you. I thought if I kept a watchful eye on you, you might lead me to her. I only knew, then, that there was something phony about Huber. I didn't know what. But when I talked to the clerk in the haberdashery about the yellow gloves, he told me how Huber was dressed when he came in with a story of lost baggage and some money (which he took from you, Anna, I presume)"—Anna nodded, Nugent went on: "I decided there was something very phony about him; no hat and a coat and pants that didn't match. He'd stolen them somewhere as he came along, I suppose. We'll never know that probably now. There may be a lot of things we don't know. But that's the sum of the main points."

But he was wrong. Except for Alexia's activities and the extent of her knowledge, there was very little we didn't eventually know. And in the end every little piece of the picture fitted together. We were never quite sure as to how and when Chivery had given away the knowledge of the piece of paper and the things written upon it, which proved to be so fatal to him, but that was almost all we didn't know. Naturally, Peter Huber never admitted it. But the charges against him were already sufficient.

All this, of course took place some time ago. But last week there was a new chapter added to it. Craig had his first leave and came home, tanned and happy. It was a handsome wedding; there's something about an air-force uniform. Drue went away with him, stars in her eyes and an air-force emblem pinned proudly to the lapel of her blue jacket, walking down the red carpet to the Twentieth Century as if she were walking on clouds. They'll have two weeks; then Craig leaves again.

But sometime he'll be back. To a happier and better world.